WIND & FIRE

Gathering of the Storms
Volume 1

TJ MICHAELS

USA TODAY & NY TIMES BESTSELLING AUTHOR

DEDICATION

This book is, as always, dedicated to my kids. They have been super supportive from day one. This work is of special importance because it's the one I wrote when they were little. I set it aside to raise them and establish my career, and it sat on the shelf for a long, loooong time. Now, I share with you what was truly the beginning of my journey as a writer.

The world created for Gathering of the Storms is rich, full of family and love, power and deceit. Magick and mayhem. So without further ado...

Welcome to Draema!

INTRODUCTION

There is one truth: Once passion is awakened, it is as potent and lethal as any storm.

———◆———◆———

After the Breaking, many flocked from their devastated homelands to the new province of Draema to begin anew. The people who called themselves Gaian chose to walk a different path. Now, love and danger bring them together again.

———◆———◆———

As Blademaster and First Heir to Draema and its Seven Colonies, Rhia Greysomne wants nothing more than to live her life as she always has-on her own terms. But when she learns that her father, the High Counsel, has summoned a childhood friend from across the border to protect her against an unknown threat, she is more than a bit put out. And worse, a case of mistaken identity finds them facing each other with blades drawn.

Who cares that he's the one man who sets her blood on fire? So what if he's the fabled Wind Storm, Protector of the Realm of Gaia? As far as she's concerned, RuArk Miwatani is the spoiled boy she used to chase with her wooden practice blade after he'd yanked her braids as a child.

RuArk of Clan Miwatani is well aware Rhia doesn't want his concern, his presence, and least of all, his protection. Sizzling attraction wars with pride and deadly circumstances. Will it bring them together... or drive her away?

Whatever the cost, RuArk is determined to keep his word to Rhia's father, and the Ancestors who've shown him that she is indeed, his. But can he convince her that he has much more to offer than his sword?

CHAPTER ONE

"Grandfather, if you must summon me from my pleasant dreams could you at least fashion a place more interesting?" RuArk grumbled softly into the darkness.

The room was stark, dimly lit, and completely empty — no windows, no doors. RuArk leaned against a rough wall with one foot propped up behind him, arms crossed over his chest. He smiled at the image of his favorite relative — an Elder known to all their clan as the Grandfather.

RuArk's brow furrowed. The ethereal essence of the Grandfather's body shifted and shimmered. Strange. It was as if he had difficulty staying with RuArk in a place where all was typically at the Elder's command. The Dream was a place where one was not confined to the body; able to move through time and space without the inhibition of flesh and bone. There was nothing to fear, though things appeared vividly real. It was one of several places to seek wisdom and direction, or face your greatest challenges. As he gazed at the roiling image, he noted the deep frown marring the old man's ancient features.

When he finally spoke, the Grandfather's urgent words formed as ice in the pit of RuArk's stomach.

Gifts, lost to all except the Gaian since the Breaking of the world, gave protection to the wielder. Those without were vulnerable in this place. If they lost their way, their physical body remained in a state of deep sleep until they either managed to escape or someone guided them out. Unseen forces ruled this realm, and not all were friendly.

"The High Counsel of Draema sought us out in the Dream. Alone."

"Alone? Why would he do such a thing? He knows the risks better than anyone."

"He searched for your father to ask for your help," said the Grandfather. "Thank gods it was I who found him as he wandered."

"But why didn't he just come to me directly? I departed the High City not more than three days past. Negotiations were completed, and I am now on my way home."

"Not any longer. You must return to the High City. This danger is focused on his daughter."

The coldness in RuArk's gut transformed into a 'berg, though it should be no surprise to learn that *that* particular female—Rhia Greysomne—was in trouble. He hadn't seen her while he'd been in the High City this time. In fact, he hadn't seen her on any of his journeys to Draema Proper over the years. Though he hadn't sought her out, he'd made it a point to know what she was about. Surely he would have heard of any threat to her?

RuArk tensed and pushed away from the wall. "Focused on Rhia? By who?"

"The High Counsel believes one of his own is responsible. He is wise enough to accept that he needs someone outside of his own province. Now, I have told you all I can. You will have to find the rest of your answers in the *Seeking*, and quickly."

The urgent energy that rolled off the Elder's image spiked.

"What aren't you telling me, Elder?"

The Grandfather usually epitomized calm, but not today. His anger-infused growl was cut off with a thick, veil-like silence as he took an uncharacteristic moment to gather himself.

Not good.

Finally, he ground out, "There is a taint, a strange darkness in the *Other Realms*. When the Realmwalkers first noticed, it was quite subtle. Now it seems to have found a focus. It grows bolder, and nearer to the High Counsel's daughter. If you are not in the appointed place at the appointed time, the bringer of this taint will prevail."

"Prevail over what, Grandfather? Over who?"

"I cannot say. It is no longer safe here, even for our kind. But know that I have faith in you, *akicita*. As such, your Gift of Vision will not fail you."

RuArk's head tilted a hard left.

Gift of Vision? What Gift of Vision?

The ability to enter the Dream or go on a Seeking quest didn't count as a Gift considering any Gaian could do it. But the Gift of Vision? That was something different. In fact, RuArk had never manifested such a Gift, or any Gift for that matter. While some of his kin had been late bloomers in this regard, RuArk's bud had been on the tree so long, surely it had dried up and fallen off by now. He opened his mouth to ask.

With a warm smile and twinkling dark eyes that crinkled at the corners, the shifting misty presence of the Grandfather shattered before snapping whole once again.

"Go. I will get word to the High Counsel to expect your return to the High City. I will guard over Rhia as best I can until you arrive."

The Elder's shimmering image lost the battle of holding its form and winked out just as RuArk was tossed headlong out of the Dream and slammed back into his own body.

Rama Collaidh sat in his official offices. His fingertips itched to roam over the smooth desktop, to trace the rare veins of gray and silver threaded throughout the polished, white stone. At well past midnight, the window coverings were locked down tight. The dimmed iozene lamp over his workspace gave off the only light in the room. He liked the darkness. It offered a sense of comfort, sitting there surrounded by shadows.

Carefully laid plans were turned sideways and upside down in his mind as he examined them for any holes. Many of his fellow Council members considered him an ambitious, middle-aged nuisance. He could care less what his peers thought. He was in the prime of his life; wily and determined enough to achieve the impossible. *And* he had the High Counsel's ear.

Yes, his board was set and the pieces were finally moving. Just as he noted a possible strategic problem, gooseflesh plumped just under the surface of his skin from scalp to fingertips. Sweat beaded between his shoulder blades before slipping coldly down his spine. In spite of the urge to shudder, Collaidh forced his stylus to move smoothly over the viewer embedded in the top of his desk.

He didn't bother to turn toward the source of his discomfort. There was only one person, one *thing* that could make him break out in a cold sweat, that could enter his offices unseen. How long had the creature been standing there watching? Collaidh quickly dismissed the concern. His determination to have what he wanted was stronger than fear or foe.

"So, you've finally come," Collaidh muttered.

The words hung in the gloom for what seemed like eons.

"You summoned me, did you not?" The tone was flat, uncaring, and alarmingly similar to his own.

"Have you succeeded in reaching Rhia Greysomne?" Collaidh asked coldly.

Now the deep, silky voice took on a harsh edge of impatience. "Someone is protecting her, warding her while she sleeps. I cannot summon her into the Dream at all. Yet, before the warding began…"

"Get to the point, Behn. And step out where I can see you, damn it."

Collaidh forced himself to look directly into the white eyes of the thing's too-pale face. The only true color on the creature was its clothing. Even the thick, billowing tresses of his long hair were white as full moonlight. Everything about him was unnatural. Yet for all that, how did he manage to be so bloody handsome?

Once he was fully into what little light there was, Behn smiled.

The grin chilled the blood. Collaidh's lip curled at the sight of gleaming, elongated incisors — longer than any normal man's. And slightly yellowed.

Must be from endless cycles of feeding.

The thought, both disgusting and terrifying, turned Collaidh's stomach.

Yes, Behn spoke with sophisticated diction, but he was *far* from civilized. And only a fool would forget it.

"When asleep," Behn said, "a person without the Gifts is vulnerable once inside the Dream. Strangely, Rhia does not have this vulnerability. The most I could do was deliver the most fantastic nightmares. I believe I was slowly wearing her down, though I could not directly manipulate her."

"You think she's Gifted? That's impossible!" Collaidh shot to his feet, slammed his palm against the sturdy desk hard enough to sting. "Her father is the High Counsel. The man is Draeman, through and through."

"Yes, but Rhia is half-Gaian, is she not? Perhaps the mother has passed on a Gift?" Behn insisted calmly.

Collaidh frowned. *Hell.* He hadn't thought of that. Hadn't anticipated any of these delays. But he had to keep the upper hand. Behn had proven to be keenly intelligent, single-minded and ruthlessly ambitious—a creature that would take advantage of any perceived weakness. No one could ever know he'd enlisted the aid of a creature that shouldn't exist—one that had rediscovered how to manipulate magick long lost...

But then, who would believe it? After all, this was Draema Province. Science ruled all.

With a smile that felt venomous even to himself, Collaidh pushed the thoughts away, deciding to force his point with his unwelcome, but much needed visitor.

"Look, the only people with Gifts are Gaian. Rhia's mother was, and remains, the only Gaian woman to marry outside her province for too many cycles to count. The woman is long dead, and certainly not around to teach her daughter about Gaia, Gifts, or anything else. And we all know the High Counsel hasn't tried in the least to teach Rhia about her mother's people since the girl was eight years old. Perhaps you're simply not capable of getting the job done."

"Careful, old man."

Behn's feral growl sent Collaidh's heart into a stutter, but he was unwilling to give any ground. Collaidh ground his back teeth. This was his show to run, damn it. No way would he allow Behn to take control. He painted his face with a calm façade and refused to look away from those piercing, ice-white eyes that seemed to bore right through his forehead.

"I said forget the High Counsel, Behn. We need that woman. We need Rhia, period." Settling back again into the plush cushions of his chair, Collaidh turned and unlocked a small drawer. "Perhaps this will help," he said as he held out a small amber vial filled with a milky looking fluid.

Collaidh steeled himself as perfectly manicured, long, semi-translucent fingers reached toward him. Little blue veins made various patterns underneath the smooth white skin. It made Collaidh's skin crawl when the lukewarm fingers touched his palm to retrieve the vial.

"What is this?" Behn asked.

"Don't worry about what it is. I called in a favor from a friend in the Society of Physicians. It won't harm her. Since the Dream business is no longer an option, you'll need to be more direct. This will make Rhia a bit more cooperative."

"Fine. I will deliver it to someone who can get

close to her. It must be done discretely if we are to avoid suspicion."

"I agree. You can't be seen here," Collaidh sniffed.

"If there is one thing I am good at, it is concealing myself from friends and enemies alike. And if I choose to be seen, I will simply be mistaken for my brother, would I not?"

The sneer in Behn's voice was unmistakable. Collaidh grimaced at the bitterness in those words. Was it justified? Definitely. But he couldn't afford to be moved by it? Not now. Not ever.

"Perhaps," Collaidh responded, but didn't think it possible that Behn would ever be mistaken for his brother, Bryan—a man who looked fully human, while it was obvious that Behn was... not. "But don't take any chances. I don't want anyone to become aware of your presence here. Besides, those teeth and eyes of yours would give you away for sure. You'd be shot on sight. What good would you be to me then? Unfortunately, we need each other so let's make the best of it, shall we?"

"You promised to give Rhia to me. You will keep your promise, old man."

"Yes, yes, yes," Collaidh said, waving his hand dismissively. "I said you could have her once she's served my purpose. Now leave me alone. I have work to do."

Collaidh turned his back and ignored the wave of cool anger emanating from behind him. He didn't hear Behn leave, but was vastly relieved when the little hairs on the back of his neck finally stopped dancing.

Sara rose and donned a warm, fluffy robe. She crossed the dark room to turn up the delicate-looking iozene sconces mounted on the walls. As she reached out her hand to adjust the brightness, her skin went cold. She was no longer alone. *He* was here. She expected no greeting and received none. He didn't care for niceties, only obedience.

"You will put this in the First Heir's teapot this morning. Do you understand?"

"I understand." Sara replied softly, her head tilted down in a genuinely terrified posture. "But her companion brings her breakfast in the mornings. How am I supposed to do this?" she asked with a shaky whisper.

"You will find a way, Sara."

She nodded quickly as he gave instruction and pressed a small glass vial into the center of her sweaty palm.

"Do you want to know what it is, sweet Sara?"

"N-No, sir. No, I don't." Sara clutched the vial firmly against her breast. Knowing too much simply wasn't a good thing with this man. He moved closer, his long, dark coat swished against her bare ankles as he shifted behind her. His breath was both warm and cool against the nape of her neck. Darkness radiated from him.

She shivered uncontrollably.

"Good girl, Sara. Very good indeed." He crooned against her skin as his fingers skimmed lightly over her shoulders. Her mind said she should run screaming from this creature, but her body wanted him — wanted to feel the thick mass of snow-white hair slide over her body. To feel sharp canines scrape against her shoulder as he took her roughly. Her sex warmed and softened in need of the thick erection pressed against her backside. Ashamed, Sara closed her eyes against her physical reaction to such an unnatural man. When she opened them again, she was back in bed.

A wave of relief swept over her. It was a dream. It always seemed so real. Even the sensitive buds of her nipples puckered at the false memory of his breath wafting over her skin. She rose, wrapped her robe closely about her body, and went through the motions she could have sworn she'd already done. Slipping her hand into the warm pocket, Sara went still when her fingers wrapped around a small glass vial.

"How in blazes does he do that?" She almost wished she had the courage to ask him. Almost.

She washed up quickly. Dressed in her Houseman's uniform and slipped the vial into her trouser pocket. As she rushed to the kitchens, Sara pushed away guilt for what she was about to do. Failure equaled pain—lots and lots of brilliantly delivered pain—courtesy of a much too-handsome devil.

He was supposed to exist only in dreams. Unfortunately for her, he didn't seem inclined to stay there.

CHAPTER TWO

By the time Rhia made it to the dining hall, she looked and felt like every description of hell she'd ever read about in the old story books. In addition to the sweat and dirt stains that covered her tunic, her leggings sported a long, jagged rip. The fabric flapped annoyingly as she walked, baring a good amount of bruised thigh. She'd almost had her leg sliced open in the middle of teaching the final knife-fighting session of the day. Good thing she hadn't been instructing laser whips instead. Geesh.

She pushed the thoughts away and focused on what awaited her upstairs in her rooms—a blasted bath, and she couldn't wait to sink into the warm... ewww!

She sniffed and then sniffed again. Was that rank smell her, or the filleted protein on her plate? Not wanting to offend, Rhia ate quickly at a table closest to the wide double doors and headed up to her apartments.

The twitchy burn in her legs made her hiss out loud as she climbed the tower stairs. Wiped out, and absolutely tired of being so damn tired, she forced herself to trudge on. Why did her place have to be on the only floor that couldn't be accessed by a lift?

Finally, at the top of the tower stairs, she reached for the key around her neck. Her hand brushed the sharp corner of a note she'd completely forgotten about. Removing the crumpled piece of paper from her breast pocket, Rhia immediately recognized her father's bold, flowing script. Even bolder words had her bristling before she was halfway through the short missive.

To: Rhia Greysomne, First Heir to the Seven Colonies of Draema Province

Consider this a formal reprimand from the Office of the High Counsel. I don't have time to run all over the City looking for you as you take on more and more responsibilities. I had to send a Houseman to find you to deliver this note. I'm sure he's just catching up with you and it's probably well past dinner time as you're reading it.

"Damn it, how does he always know?" she wondered aloud.

You are hereby relieved of all duties except for the diplomatic responsibilities of the First Heir. In addition, you may teach one, and only one, combat or blade class. All of your other duties related to the Society of War have been assigned to other officers. Further, you are to leave at first light for Harbor Station to inspect the two new airships built for the coastal patrols. You will also inspect the troops stationed there under your brother's command. Joan Rouillard and Brita Shae will accompany you. To make the journey shorter, I've assigned you a hover driver. He'll take you to the train, where you'll board for Harbor Station. And no, you may not take the outmoded form of transportation you prefer—that damned horse of yours.

It was bad enough he was making her take the train to the harbors, but she wouldn't be allowed to even transport herself to the station? Not that she knew how to operate one of the hover things anyway, but that wasn't the point. And Moonlight was *not* outmoded, damn it!

With an annoyed huff, she finished reading.

I advise you to find time to enjoy yourself while you are at Harbor Station, young lady. You will come to my offices before you leave to pick up a message for your brother. When you return to the High City, your life will change considerably.

Regards,

Grey Greysomne, High Counsel of Draema Province
Commander in Chief, Society of War

Her father had sent a note to tell her off. This was a new experience. Grey Greysomne usually delivered any displeasure directly to her face. But a note? Geez, how impersonal could you get? And what did he mean her life would 'change considerably' when she returned from Harbor Station? And why did she need to go inspect a ship or troops? Her younger brother was the Harbormaster for a reason. That man knew all there was to know about the blasted vessels. What a total waste of time. But as one of the highest-ranking officers of the Society of War, she had her orders and would obey them. Of course, she wouldn't admit to being secretly pleased with the opportunity to visit her brother and his family. Perhaps she'd rest better there.

Rhia cringed as she recalled the weeks of nightmares so terrifying, so *wrong*, that she'd jerked herself awake with a scream on her lips. There'd been several nights where she'd awoken with sweat-soaked bed linens stuck to her body as she sat huddled in the center of the bed. She was sure her skin had tried to crawl away and hide a time or two, as well.

But last night everything had changed. Sleep had been peaceful and strangely calm with the presence of an old man. Her dream had been simple — the man seemed to enjoy nothing more than keeping her company, and the nasties had stayed away. It would be nice to drift off and not wonder what was in store. Maybe some rest and a change of scenery would do just that. Perhaps Harbor Station was the ticket.

Rhia read the note again, stuffed it back into her pocket, and fumbled with her key tag. The flat, square fob gleamed dully in the bluish light of the iozene lamps set into the walls. Holding the tag to the center of the panel next to the door, a familiar click indicated the release of the lock.

One step into her private domain, Rhia felt the cares of the day melt away. This space was uniquely hers. It was strategically unsound to have walls an enemy could hide behind, so there were none in this space. Instead, it was large, airy, and tastefully arranged so she could see from one end of the suite to the other without obstruction.

The sleeping area was dominated by a huge, curtained bed, but it was the floor that defined the space. It was covered with soft, gray, hand-knotted carpets. Where the carpets ended, so did her sleeping area. A large mosaic of tiny gray and white tiles in the shape of the sigil of the House of Greysomne covered the dining area floor. It was centered by a large table; its base of polished marble was topped with a thick, smoky glass pane. Off to the left was the mantel covered with awards and weapons, over a wide, and thankfully blazing, iozene fireplace.

A few steps past her large, four-post bed, a chilly

wind sent the silky bed curtains billowing. The midwinter breeze flowed through the glass doors that led to her private balcony. Only... she was sure those doors were closed and locked this morning. Brita would have been the last person out of these rooms, and she would never have left them unsecured.

Shivering from the whoosh of cool air, Rhia dropped her blade and belt down on top of the dining table with a loud clunk as she passed. She pressed the little switches that controlled the wall of thick, beveled panes and waited impatiently as the glass slid silently along the tracks.

The moment the balcony doors closed, her trouble meter tipped off the scale. Turning ever so slowly, she peered into the darkness. Sharp senses tried to see and hear everything at once as her eyes adjusted.

The open curtains let in the glow of a half-moon, whose light was obscured by a passing cloud. Looking past the mantle, Rhia peered toward the bathroom entrance. The sheer curtains that gave her privacy were pulled open as usual.

However, what was *un*usual was the shadowed figure standing there. A black cloak swirled around a body as it took a step forward, and the "it" was revealed as a man.

"Hello, Rhia."

Bryan Collaidh? Aw hell. She hadn't seen him since she'd made First Blade, cycles ago. The haunted look on his face, and the dark shadows under his eyes, made it obvious those cycles had not been kind. His pale skin stood out in stark contrast against lackluster, shoulder-length black hair. Didn't he know greasy hair was out of style in Draema? And what was with the all-black garb?

The creep hadn't left the province under the best of circumstances. As far as she was concerned, he was still unwelcome in the High City, and certainly unwelcome in her personal space.

"What the hell are you doing here?" she asked, not bothering to hide the contempt in her voice.

The lines of his mouth hinted at the cruelty she knew he was capable of. A malevolent black gaze followed her steps. Deep set, and round as old-fashioned playing stones, his eyes seemed too large for his face. He looked like an overgrown guppy, complete with thin, pouting lips. An image popped into her head of this unwanted guest, complete with gills and fins. His lips glub-glub-glubbed as bubbles floated up towards the surface of the river she wanted to drown him in.

Her amusement faded quickly as she considered the situation. It took a bold man to break into her apartments with no fear. Why would he take such a risk? The answer was obvious—he still didn't have any goddamn common sense.

Rhia watched him closely as she walked across the room. The glowing fireplace halfway between them cast his smooth, black clothing with an eerie, orange tint.

"I asked what you're doing here, Bryan." At the mantle now, she stretched her hands toward the warming flames, appearing completely at ease.

"I've come to visit you, old friend," he drawled, moving slowly toward her. He attempted to smile, but it must have made his face hurt. The skin appeared to freeze just around his mouth in the middle of the feeble attempt.

"Old friend? What are you, nuts? I haven't seen

you since the day you decided to use my face as a punching bag."

"I'm a changed man, Rhia. Cycles of surviving on the borders can do that to a person." He ground out the words as his gaze seemed to focus on something far, far away. Some called the borders "Hell's Eastern Seventh Level." Judging from the menace rolling off of her nemesis, like dust clouds of choking malintent, the name must be pretty accurate.

She took a deep breath, then another. Blast it, she'd always been calm when meeting a foe. But she'd never faced a known enemy whose very presence dragged one of the worst moments of her life out of the locked dungeon of her mind.

Her typical pre-fight calm was nowhere to be found. No, she was torqued the hell off. And this wasn't going to end nicely.

She almost smiled.

Biding her time, Rhia leaned against the smooth mantle with one arm draped casually atop the ledge. Her fingertips brushed the hilt of the specially commissioned blade her father had given her on her sixteenth birthday. For a few seconds she considered pulling the razor sharp work of art down off its mounting, but changed her mind. The blade was too special to dirty on the likes of Bryan Collaidh. Too bad she didn't have a laser pistol handy. At least those left wounds that didn't bleed much. Rhia was sharp enough to know that this little conversation was going to end in a fight, and the less blood on her tile, the better. Getting blood out of crystal grout was no easy feat.

Then she noticed that Bryan wasn't moving. Simply stood there, wasting her time.

"Look, Bryan, I'm tired. I had a long day, and I really don't feel like being bothered. I was so busy this evening I was two hours late to dinner. Now I'm two hours late for bed. Can't you just go away? Perhaps we can talk in the morning." Knowing she didn't mean a word of that last part. After all, there was nothing to say.

"You have grown into a beautiful woman, Rhia. And I think I'd rather talk now. Besides, I've returned to Draema Proper for one purpose. To claim you."

Laughter bubbled up and out of her throat before she could stop it. She just couldn't help it. Claim her? Ridiculous! Her smile was genuine, but her thoughts took another turn, and her insides turned with it. What if he was serious? A serious lunatic, that is. He wanted her? Why? He certainly didn't love her. She didn't think he even *liked* her.

Sigh.

Okay, he had about an inch on her in height, and maybe twenty pounds in weight. The calculations only took a moment. She could take him down fast, then call in a favor to a couple of the soldiers who roomed on the floors below. The advantage of living in her father's Citadel – it only took seconds to get someone up here to help drag the body away.

But Bryan still hadn't moved. Not even to blink. Perhaps a reminder that she outranked him would push him over the edge so they could get this over with.

She rolled her eyes and said sleepily, "Get out, you idiot. Otherwise, as the highest ranking officer in the Society of War, I'll personally have you assigned to the iozene mines with all the other miscreants."

Then she waited for him to lose it like he had

long ago, when he'd taken a closed fist to her face. Her offense? A rank promotion ahead of him. Angry and full of jealousy, he used his failure as an excuse to abuse her. In his mind, the anger had been all her fault. Personal responsibility? *Puh.* Those two words weren't in his vocabulary.

Hands raised in surrender, he headed toward the door. Halfway there, he changed direction.

Damn it.

He looked back and forth, between her and the katana lying on the table. The metal under the black leather, which crisscrossed elegantly over the handle, gleamed dully in the moonlight. Bryan picked it up, testing the weight of it in his hand.

Calculation flared in those cold, black eyes as he took a single step, pivoted and threw the weapon clear across the room. It bounced off a wall near the front door with a loud clang. She had no doubts now—the man was definitely nuts.

From rage to cool civility in a blink, he crooned, "I hear you've made Blademaster well before the usual ten cycles. But it doesn't matter whether you're a Blademaster or not, we're going to reinstate our former engagement."

Bullshit.

One hand on her hip, she took an angry step forward. "My father didn't approve of you back then, and he certainly won't approve now. Besides, if you were on the up-and-up, you wouldn't have broken in and waited for me in the dark. What the hell do you really want?"

"Give me a minute. I'm sure you'll figure it out." He lunged.

Rhia was ready, and ducked past him so fast he

found himself facing the fireplace with nothing but air where she had been seconds before. A clean kick to his kidneys from behind slammed him chest-first into the mantle. The wind whooshed from his lungs. After a few wheezing breaths, he faced her with eyes drawn tight in an angry frown. And a bit of... shock?

"Surprise, asshole."

He hadn't expected her to be able to defend herself without a weapon. Well, good. But she'd rather have a blade between them. Rhia ran for her steel.

Bryan dove, taking her feet out from under her. She went down hard, skinning her cheek on the smooth, hard mosaic under the dining table. But stinging cheeks were a relief. If she'd landed a few more inches to the left, her jaw would have made solid contact with the glass and marble of the table.

She rolled over with a groan and was happy to be in absolute pain rather than knocked out cold.

Then he was on her, trying to capture her hands as they connected with his eyes, cheeks, and lips. Rage, thick and palpable filled the bit of air between them.

"I'll have what I want whether you agree or not, Rhia." *Pant.* "Once I fuck you." *Snarl.* "I'll present evidence to the Council."

What the hell?

"Your *honor*," he sneered as if she had none, "will require you to declare me your mate. Our houses will be joined, one way or another. Good thing you were altered at the Age of Consent. Without a hymen, at least it won't hurt. Much."

Whoa. How did he know when she'd been altered? And what the hell else did he know? The records of every member of the Society of War, especially hers as First Heir, were classified. No one knew her secret other than her father, and her friends, Brita and Joan.

Her mind screeched to a halt. The law was clear. As female First Heir, she'd had her hymen painlessly removed at the Age of Consent as required. But afterward, Rhia didn't have the Draeman privilege of screwing around.

While mates, lovers and Sensuan were carefully recorded for all members of the Society of War, for Rhia the rules were a bit different. She had two choices — she could take an assigned lover for a time, whose identity and time of service were carefully determined and recorded...

Or, she could take a mate. Period.

Her mate's identity would remain secret for a time until she declared the union to the Council, or proof of consummation was given. Vows could be taken in the presence of her father and a witness, or she could elope. This was to keep the First Heir's mate from being assassinated before he could actually say, "I do."

No one, especially Bryan Collaidh, should know that her records were clean – no assigned lover, no mate. If he managed to prove he'd had sex with her, she was screwed. And not in a good way. No recourse. No way out.

Except to get free. Right now.

Rhia jerked her hand loose. A fist connected with the side of Bryan's head, sending it sideways with a wicked snap. The jeweled dagger always strapped to her thigh was almost in her hand when the bastard dropped his full weight down on top of her. She just couldn't get a full breath. Her head spun. Wriggling black spots swam around her field of vision.

Ugh, she was going to throw up.

A backhand to the jaw didn't help. She hadn't seen the blow coming and now both her hands were above her head, held securely in his grip. His free hand brutally squeezed and twisted a tender breast. And he had an erection. *Ewww.*

She swallowed hard as more bile surged and her dinner bubbled threateningly at the base of her throat. Frustrated and angry, Rhia let out an ear-piercing scream when Bryan pushed his hand roughly underneath her tunic searching for the top of her leggings.

When the skin of a clammy hand touched the flesh of her belly, she went completely still.

"That's more like it, bitch," Bryan growled, yanking on her already ripped and torn clothing to expose her underwear. "I knew you would see things my way, Rhia. You always were a mewling little puke. It's your fault I ended up on the borders all those cycles. Your fault! If you hadn't run to your father blaming me for our little misunderstanding, I would have surpassed your rank by now. You deserved a beating then, and you deserve one now."

Wasn't there an old proverb in the ancient books that said pride goes before destruction? Obviously, the man wasn't much of a history reader.

In his haste to dip into her goodies, he released her hands to get a better grip on her bottoms. Her elbow crashed into the middle of his throat. Suddenly *he* was the one having trouble breathing.

Now wasn't that just too bad?

Knee to the groin preceded a full-contact left hook. He rolled completely away, eyes watering as he gasped through his bruised windpipe. It seemed he couldn't decide whether to hold his throat and gag, hold his balls and moan, or soothe his swelling eye.

On her feet, she yanked up her leggings and retrieved her blade from the carpet near the door. The corner of her mouth lifted at the exact moment Bryan realized the only way out was through her securely locked balcony windows or the front door. The first option was a no go. But a four story fall wasn't high enough to knock any sense into his hard head anyway. And unfortunately, Rhia and her blade stood in front of option number two.

There was a third option—part him from the family jewels he'd tried to force on her moments ago.

"You wouldn't kill a man in cold blood. You don't have it in you." But the quaver in his voice said he didn't believe his own words. He knew she'd do it. Knew she'd shred him. Sweat dripped from his brow and trailed down his clammy, pale skin like wax down a spent candle.

Neither of them heard the door open.

CHAPTER THREE

His party had shown none of their discomfort or concern in their expressions at the suddenly pressing journey back to Draema Proper. In fact, if not for the chilling mounds of snow piled along the roads and the biting winds, it would have been a good time under clear, and amazingly vivid, blue skies.

They'd moved quickly through the buffer zone that separated Draema Seine from the capital of the province, Draema Proper. In the distance, the High City had been a welcome sight, rising from the heart of these lands. Built in the middle of its seven colonies, this was the most advanced area in the world. The dawning sunlight had reflected various shades of pink and purple off both the inner and outer walls; all of which were built with the famous, silvery-white Draeman stone.

Sleek looking buildings and tree-lined walks led into vast, city squares. The High City boasted a mix of rolling hills, and neatly-groomed pastures alongside well-kept roads. Some were laid with cobblestone, while others were covered by a smooth, dark, magnetized substance that allowed the passage of small conveyances called 'hovers'. Horses were still used here for sport, but inner-to-outer city travel typically meant a ride in one of the neat little vehicles, or a spot on the magtrain. RuArk preferred the wild, open spaces of his own province, but didn't hesitate to admit this place held wonder for those who appreciated such things.

Though he'd brought more than thirty warriors on this journey, only RuArk and a single fireteam of six warriors had passed through the city gates this morning. There were very few of his people in this place, yet he'd been immediately recognized. The advantage of being the son of the ruler of one of the neighboring provinces was being waved through the towering gates quickly. Well, that, and the reputation of being a ruthless bastard that took down enemies hard and fast with no promise to ask questions later didn't hurt either.

Through a second set of lower walls that surrounded the Citadel, the High Counsel's right-hand, Mannon, had greeted them and rushed them into a meeting. From this morning's arrival, until leaving the High Counsel's chambers moments ago, they'd worked through one planning session after another until everything was in place.

Though so tired his muscles weighed down his bones as he dragged himself toward the guest apartments, RuArk could not ignore the flash and tensing of excitement that tapped at his gut. As if something long dead was coming awake inside him, stretching and unfurling itself in anticipation of seeing where this new turn in life would lead.

And Rhia was smack in the middle of this, this... whatever it was.

As instructed, he'd gone to the *Seeking* place

immediately after his encounter with the Grandfather in the Dream, and had indeed seen a sliver of what was to come. In spite of the intrigue and danger to the woman, what would occur between them would be hot as the midsummer sun. RuArk knew from the *Seeking*. Felt it as he replayed that vision over and over in his mind. Damn near ached for it now that he knew Rhia was somewhere near. Strange, he still hadn't seen the flesh and blood star of his *Seeking* vision, but he would soon enough.

RuArk steered his First Commander, Sharyn, toward a wide archway that opened into a large, starlit atrium. The space was filled with lush, green trees, shrubs and a little stone bench where one could sit and enjoy the sun or moon overhead. At the rear of the atrium, two sets of mirroring staircases took off up the tower walls to a landing where tall arches led to wide hallways. The stairs continued up the walls, winding their way to another landing, and yet another.

Finally, they were at the top. There were no hallways or arches here—only two doors separated by a ten-meter wide, colorful mural of the Draeman countryside painted directly onto the gleaming white walls.

He'd just pressed the key against the wall lock of the rooms he would share with Sharyn when a panic-inducing yell rang through the tower. He looked toward the sound and cursed.

Sharyn's gasp of surprise, followed by her quiet chuckle made him grimace. He hadn't meant to say that out loud, especially in the presence of a lady. The High Counsel put him in this part of the Citadel to keep an eye on Rhia. He'd hoped the job could wait until she returned from the made-up errand they'd created for her at Harbor Station.

"Apparently not," RuArk muttered and moved quickly towards the source of the noise. Through her slightly open door, two voices were clearly heard, both of them yelling. Not wanting to be mistaken for an intruder, he opened the door carefully, just enough to peek inside. The scene that met him was wrong on too many levels to list.

A greasy looking fellow had Rhia flat on her back on the thick carpets, trying to rip her trousers off. She was obviously not cooperating. The man's fist connected with her jaw. The blow should have knocked her out, but Rhia was moving and moving quickly. Her next breath saw her up off the floor and brandishing the wicked, long blade of a katana made in the old style.

Her intent was clear—skin the greaser.

Rhia's hair was dark, fire streaked and tangled all over her head. But the blood. There was so much blood. It was on her face, streaming down her neck from her eyes, nose and mouth, enough to soak the collar of her top.

RuArk kept his expression neutral, but he really wanted nothing more than to rip the greaser in half. Hell, he might not love Rhia yet, but it was only a matter of time considering the Ancestors clearly meant for him to have her. The moment he'd accepted the *Seeking*, she'd been given into his care. And this man dared to threaten her? Not bloody likely.

His first thought was to kick the door in the rest of the way, stride across the room and grab the idiot by his scrawny neck. But he'd be a fool to simply stroll into the room and surprise a woman with a sharp blade in her hands and hellfire in her eyes.

In spite of the obvious injuries, her fighting form was perfect; her handling of the blade smooth and experienced. She held no fear and knew she was in a position to deliver a killing blow. And he couldn't blame her one bit. In truth, it was Rhia's ability to handle her *visitor* that helped keep RuArk's anger in check.

RuArk anticipated her move, knew the exact moment she'd decided to slice open the man's chest. What was she thinking? The scandal it would cause—a man in her rooms this time of night, and a dead man at that. Not to mention all the blood and guts that would have to be cleaned up.

And it would ruin his investigation.

One step through the door, RuArk called out quietly. "Excuse me. Is there a problem here?"

Rhia glanced away from the groveling swine on the floor and looked into eyes full of such a wondrous mix of gray and silver, they reminded her of the waters off Draema's southern coast.

RuArk Miwatani—the bane of her childhood existence. A bane she hadn't seen in so long she was surprised she recognized him. It was the eyes. Stormy sea, silver-as-fog, captivating eyes. Simply unforgettable. Ever. She had to look up a bit to meet his gaze, but once she caught it, Rhia was stuck right there.

Blazes, he was breath-stopping. Gone were the boyish good looks and mischievous expression. In their place was an angular jaw, high cheekbones and the confidence of a grown man.

A long, thick, black-as-sin braid was pulled

forward over his shoulder to brush against the middle of his stomach. His skin, though quite a bit fairer than her own, was such a warm bronze that even now, at the end of midwinter, he appeared to have spent a good deal of time under the glorious sunshine. He wore an unadorned, dark gray, fine gauged tunic, with dyed-to-match trousers. The outline of thick, roped muscle was visible beneath the supple material.

He closed in on her with a step so light she still didn't hear his footfalls even though she was watching him walk into her space.

And how the hell was she noticing this in the middle of a life or death struggle?

And what the hell was *he doing here*?

As far as she was concerned, he was yet another man in her space without her damn permission. Enough gawking. Back to business.

Rhia returned her attention to the weasel groaning on the floor and raised her katana for the final blow. But before she could take a step, RuArk grabbed Bryan by the collar of his finely appointed cloak, and the back of his finely appointed trousers, hauled him out the door, and tossed him down the closest staircase.

While Bryan tumbled, Rhia's attention remained on RuArk.

She looked him dead in the eye—or tried to, given his typical tree-like Gaian height—and proceeded to tear his head off with her tongue.

"Look, asshole. I know you warrior types are used to throwing the muscle around, but this is Draema. Here, people don't interfere unless they're asked to interfere. If I'd needed help I would have..."

Rhia snapped her mouth shut mid-sentence. The most beautiful woman she'd ever seen stood directly behind the most ruggedly handsome man she'd ever known. Bone straight, thick, and black-as-midnight hair was partially covered with a length of translucent silk that could only be described as sensual. Actually, her entire outfit seemed to be one big wispy scarf. Her skin reminded Rhia of the summer fruits that, according to the histories, used to grow in the now non-existent southern locales so long ago.

"Peaches," Rhia whispered, though she truly hadn't meant to say that out loud.

Rhia knew her hair was a tangled mess. Her face was swelling and surely beginning to display various colors in addition to being covered with drying sweat and blood. She wasn't sure why she cared that this man might compare her raggedy, torn appearance to this exotic woman. Nope, she shouldn't give a bloody goddamn... but she did.

And if this female had stood here the whole time, then she'd seen Rhia act a complete fool. She flew past 'caring' and skidded to a halt at 'mortified'.

"Blasted hell," she muttered.

Maybe the blows Bryan had landed on her face had shaken her brain loose because there was no way she should notice how ridiculously delicious RuArk's lips looked with that bit of a smile spread over them. Gah.

"What do you want, RuArk? Aren't you a little far from home?" she snapped, forcing a blizzard of coolness into her words.

"You screamed. Loudly." He took a careful step toward her. His words may have been just as frosty as hers, but the look he gave was equal parts 'smoking hot' and 'royally pissed'. "I can't resist taking care of such a beautiful lady, especially if she's in distress."

RuArk's tone slid over Rhia's frazzled nerves like warm, honey syrup while his expression took on a mysterious quality. Could he see through her funky-assed mood straight into her head? Had he uncovered all the secret thoughts swirling around in there, all thoughts of him?

"Anything else I can do to assist you?" he asked. He was bossy as ever, entirely too close, and looking at her as if he knew something she didn't. Icy anger began to melt. Fast.

Rhia shivered, but not from fear nor an adrenaline crash.

It was... Anticipation? But of what? And who? Not RuArk, for sure.

After all, she'd known this man forever. Though he'd been a boneheaded, spoiled, king's son, she'd carried a torch for this particular pain-in-the-ass for years. Memories she'd pushed to the very fringe of her mind peeked their heads up and over the ragged edge of her consciousness.

She remembered RuArk putting straw in her hair.

RuArk besting her at wooden blade practice.

RuArk pulling stupid pranks on her, and getting her in trouble with both their fathers.

Sigh.

RuArk holding her hand at her mother's funeral, wiping the tears from her cheeks and telling her it would be okay.

RuArk wrapping her in his cloak while she huddled in misery as they left the burial grounds so far away in Gaia province.

RuArk singing to her—quite badly at the top of his lungs—on her tenth birthday after talking his father into bringing him on an unscheduled visit, just to give her a birthday present he'd made with his own hands.

RuArk telling her he was going away to train for his role as Protector of the Realm of Gaia.

RuArk, staying away for years. Fucking *years*. Even when she'd been aware that he'd come to the High City on official business, he'd never once sought her out.

But it didn't matter now. The last time she'd seen him, Rhia had made a couple of trips to her own personal hell and back. She'd become her own woman—a woman who would never need saving by anyone. Ever.

And that included the gorgeous man towering over her.

"You should visit the Physicians, Rhia. It's getting late. I will escort you, if you wish," he said.

So he was trying to save her, *and* tell her what to do? *Not.* Her out-of-whackness dissolved, replaced by a wash of hot anger. And a bit of unexplainable fear. Rather than dealing with the latter, she squashed her emotions into the toes of her blood-spattered boots and straightened her already-ramrod spine.

"I'm fine and I can see to myself. So fuck. Off. RuArk."

She nudged him out with the tip of her katana, and practically punched a hole in the wall lock panel. The door slammed shut. So what if her behavior was irrational. Who cared? Besides, nobody asked the big guy to appear out of nowhere anyway. And she certainly hadn't asked him to toss that pig, Bryan Collaidh, down the stairs when she would have rather given him a few choice cuts.

Did it matter she'd been a shrew to a man who'd

always set her pulse racing and put her senses on edge? Or that she'd bled all over the place in front of an exotic looking woman in a daringly sexy outfit, all after learning via a stupid note from her father that she'd been stripped of everything that made her who she was?

Rhia stomped around her apartments, hurling every curse word she'd ever heard her soldiers use, then switched over to a couple of different languages just to draw it out a bit longer. She soon found that growling and cursing weren't enough. She yelled her frustration to the top of her lungs.

"She was so grateful for your help. Really, it was quite clear by the way she slammed the door in your face."

RuArk turned to scold a not-so-amused Sharyn, but snapped his mouth shut at Rhia cursing loud enough to be heard through the thick door. Sharyn scowled, but didn't say another word, choosing instead to disappear into their suite across the landing and head to her own bedroom.

As for RuArk, it had been a long time since he'd had a reason to see the humor in anything but a good fight, yet here he was smiling, then laughing outright. The sound rumbled up through his chest in a deep, full timbre. And all because of the fate the Ancestors handed him — a fate named Rhia Greysomne.

His own rooms secured, he slipped his blades beneath his pillow and burrowed into the thick, down bedding. Keen senses detected no danger as he relaxed and closed his eyes to meditate.

He'd received word that the rest of his men had slipped quietly into the City and settled into the non-descript, seldom used guest quarters on the far side of town. At dawn, Rhia would depart for Harbor Station on the errand they'd made up for her, and RuArk would visit the High Counsel to finalize the details of their plans.

After her behavior tonight, he almost wished the High Counsel was going to be the one breaking the news to the hellcat next door. Almost.

He and Rhia's first meeting after so many seasons had been far from expected. He'd expected happiness, and light, and fun. Then again, he had enjoyed tossing the greasy fellow down the steps. In the end, it didn't matter whether Rhia liked that he was here for her or not. He had a job to do—keep her safe and make her his.

As he drifted off, the *Seeking* quest he'd taken after his visit from the Grandfather flashed to the forefront of his mind.

Carried on the arms of the Wind, RuArk looked down upon the land with admiration. The beautiful, rolling hills were covered by a spectacular white, snowy blanket that sparkled like diamonds and luminescent pearls. The bright, full moon reflected off the frozen meadows. And there were so many stars. They filled the pre-dawn sky, twinkling their greeting to the Wind as It passed, carrying its companion.

Off in the distance, RuArk spotted a faint glimmer on the ground. The light appeared to be a small campfire, out in the middle of the ice-covered lands. What would anyone be doing way out here in midwinter? They circled around as RuArk searched for any signs of life. The place was deserted.

"What's going on here?" RuArk asked in a whisper.

The Wind gave no answer, but instead settled directly over the small flames, whipping them up into a firestorm. It flared wildly in spite of the snow covering the ground. The energy from the fire joined itself to that of the Wind, and the Wind became a great storm also. Side by side, the firestorm and the windstorm grew together, reaching up into the starlit sky until it seemed brightened by a second sun.

Then RuArk felt it, just as the Grandfather said. A taint. A subtle hint of foul aura just out of reach, focused on the flame. It faltered until it ceased to give as much energy to its union with the Wind. As the flame wavered, the windstorm and the firestorm were both diminished. The mighty forces of nature became nothing more than a slight breeze and a small campfire once more.

Here, just as in the Dream, he didn't experience true physical sensation, but only a fool would ignore the trickle of apprehension slipping up his arms. He turned to the North, but saw nothing. To the South, East and West, all was silent. But he knew something, someone, was out there. Perhaps multiple someones.

After endless moments, he spotted a woman alone in the night, gliding along the snow-covered meadows. The sleek outline of her body was shrouded in shadow. She moved with easy grace. Careful yet confident, she possessed an inner strength that made her appear more hunter than prey. Who was this woman, now almost as near as his own skin?

Looking more closely, RuArk almost tumbled out of the Seeking and back into his physical body in surprise. The glow from her amber eyes pierced his soul — Rhia Greysomne, daughter of the High Counsel of Draema Province.

Oh, he remembered Rhia, stubborn and headstrong as a young girl. He was now being set on the path back to her as a woman. There was danger, yes, but he sensed that she needed something more than protection. But what could she need more than her own life?

It had been endless seasons since he'd seen her, yet even after all this time, and in this place, his body reacted strongly to her presence. Gods, her essence was exquisite; her aura strong and clean. She was not the source of the foulness on the air. But whoever, or whatever it was, seemed to follow her, long for her, covet her from a distance. Strange.

RuArk reached out, but she didn't respond. Didn't seem to sense him at all.

Flashes of him and Rhia in a loving embrace danced before his eyes. They were smiling. Touching. Arms twined around one another as he loved her fiercely. Then they were sharing stolen moments, a quiet word.

RuArk rolled over in his bed and let the memory of the *Seeking* continue to wash through him and fill his mind even as sleep claimed him. After accepting what had been shown to him, he remembered being returned to his physical body. And there he'd sat until gooseflesh had risen on his bare arms and legs. In fact, he'd watched the sunrise through the opening of the *Seeking* place and breathed in the lingering scent of sweet, warm female until it had completely faded away.

And now, the woman of his *Seeking* was just across the landing. Just out of reach. A woman he'd thought of often, but hadn't pursued. Had longed for, but believed to be out of reach. RuArk had no idea how things would develop, but it wasn't his job to worry about it. All he needed to do was find and stay on the path that had obviously been chosen for him.

Rhia was his, and he would protect her from whatever danger lurked.

And RuArk couldn't wait to begin his new job.

CHAPTER FOUR

Back from Harbor Station, Rhia woke refreshed, but not relieved. The nightmares hadn't returned, but the calming presence of the sweet old man that had replaced the horrors had been usurped by a towering gray-eyed god that beckoned her with a shameless grin and the crook of a finger.

RuArk Miwatani.

Her dreams now bordered on sensually insane. In them, RuArk had stroked and touched her in places no hands had ever been but her own. Just imagining what true, downright dirty sex might be like with him, sent the blood rushing beneath her skin, made her breasts swell and her nipples strain against her underclothes.

Too bad hot-n-wild sex came with a mate. RuArk had never expressed any interest in her like that, plus Rhia had no prospects and sure as hell wasn't looking for any.

Yes, her childhood-friend-now-dream-lover had saved her very real backside by not allowing her to kill that frog-eyed idiot, Bryan. But that was no reason to start dreaming about him, right?

She rolled over and untangled herself from the

bed covers. Thanks to a quick trip to the Society of Physicians before heading out of town to Harbor Station, all of the bruises and swelling in her arms, back, and face from her little confrontation with Bryan Collaidh were practically healed in spite of the spectacular spectrum of colors on her skin.

She'd known RuArk forever and hadn't seen him for just as long, and all that time she'd remained happily free of hunky-Gaian-warrior-please-touch-me dreams. Yet the very night he'd gotten rid of her unwanted guest, the man had started waltzing into her head at night, and brought with him a ridiculous longing that shadowed her no matter what she was doing. Asleep or awake, all she could think about was him.

And it was starting to piss her off.

"Come in," she called out at the light chime of the door. Her companion, Brita, and her best friend, Joan, bustled in with breakfast. Well, Brita bustled and Joan shuffled. True to his word, her father had given all of Rhia's training classes to other officers, with the exception of the one Joan was to assist her with this morning. How the High Counsel ever talked Joan into getting out of bed this early was beyond Rhia.

Joan waved sleepily and passed Rhia's bed as she followed Brita to the dining table. In obvious need of caffeine and food, the woman pounced as soon as Brita sat the covered tray down. She quickly poured herself a cup of black coffee and inhaled the reviving aroma.

"Joan, I don't think I'll ever understand the whole coffee thing," Rhia said around a big yawn. "Don't get me wrong, I like a pot of black bean water as much as the next person, but I don't need it to become conscious in the mornings. You should get more sleep."

Joan stuck her tongue out at Rhia, who grinned earnestly after her friend had taken a couple of fortifying sips and began to show signs of life. Those signs included piling her plate with grainbread slathered with calmonut butter and taking small bites between big gulps of coffee. Each mouthful was accompanied by a grimace. Rhia couldn't blame Joan. After all, the stuff did taste like woodboard covered with adhesive paste.

Brita pulled all of the heavy drapes back from the windows. Bright sunshine flooded every inch of the large suite. Such brilliant light and clear blue skies were rare for this time of year, but certainly most welcome.

Rhia climbed out of bed and padded naked to the bathing alcove. A quick look in the mirror had her shaking her head. The purple and blue splotches below her eye had faded to a faint outline of sickly yellow brown. It still looked like hell, but at least it wasn't painful anymore.

She tied up her hair, climbed into the tub—thankfully it was always filled and ready—and began to wash briskly. This was probably her favorite room in this whole building. Draeman were brilliant, really. The pool's water was continuously cycled through a filtration system and kept at a set temp so she could bathe anytime. And because the water was constantly cleaned, she didn't have to sit in a tub of gunk and pretend she was getting clean.

"Brita, there's something I've been thinking about since I started dreaming of that old Gaian man I told you about," Rhia called from the bath, leaving out the fact that RuArk had taken the old man's place. "Gaian don't typically make their homes here. Other than Mannon, the Sensuan females who came with my mother a long time ago, and myself, sort of, I don't think there are any Gaian people in the entire province. What could have possibly brought my mother to a place where she was practically the only one of her kind?"

"Your mother came here because she fell in love with your father. He traveled to their lands more often than he needed to when he was younger. We all knew he was working on more than trade agreements," Brita said as she popped in, turned on the iozene fireplace and popped out again. "He loved her deeply. Everyone loved her. She was such a marvelous woman, strong and honorable. You're a lot like her, you know."

Rhia listened quietly. The deep, desolate pit of her soul that used to overflow with her mother's love was now filled with her own ambition. She'd accomplished everything she'd ever set out to do yet, there had been no satisfaction in it lately. She needed... what?

An image of RuArk filled her mind. It was quickly squashed into the carpet of her mind and stomped on ruthlessly. She couldn't have him, so it made no sense to allow herself to dwell on the man.

Brita swooped into the bath just as Rhia climbed from the water. With sure solid strokes, Brita dried her charge from neck to knees. The smirk on the older woman's face when she glanced at Rhia's tightly-drawn nipples conveyed her thoughts. Rhia scowled. Brita snorted, unmoved by the sour expression. No surprise there. The woman had never been moved by expression, stubbornness, obstinance, or anything else typical of a headstrong young lady.

"Rhia, why do you put yourself through this

torture?" Brita asked, handing Rhia her clothes for the day. "You've done a pretty good job of hiding it until now, but admit it, girlie. You're horny. I don't understand what you're waiting for."

Not bothering to answer as she dressed, Rhia yanked her shirt over her head. She flinched as the soft fabric scraped over tender flesh through her underwear. Damn it. Maybe her monthly time was coming up or something. No way her skin should be this sensitive.

"There are plenty of men in Draema. You've got seven colonies of male flesh to choose from in this blasted province. Maybe if you stopped carrying that big knife around…"

"It's not a knife, Brita. It's a katana."

"Whatever, young lady. You knew that once you hit the Age of Consent all those hormones would kick into overdrive. It's been that way since the Breaking of the World."

"Yep. That synthetic food you all eat is the problem. All those growth accelerators, hormones and god knows what else," Joan snorted with laughter from the other room.

The woman was a total advocate for returning to eating 'real' food rather than the bioengineered stuff developed to keep people from totally starving after the Breaking. Problem was, very few people knew how to make real food anymore.

In fact, Rhia didn't personally know anyone with the skills except Joan and she'd learned from an old Gaian Sensuan who'd passed on some years ago. That left the history books as the only means of knowledge when the Houseman became inspired enough to try one of the old recipes, for which they rarely had the correct ingredients. Yuck.

"So you'd rather us eat bull balls soup, Joan? Really?"

"The dish was called Rocky Mountain Oysters, Rhia. It wasn't a soup, and we couldn't make it if we wanted to, considering buffalo don't exist this far south anymore." Her chuckle was followed by a very sisterly sounding, "Smart ass."

Brita cast Joan her "hush up" glare and picked up where she'd left off. "Anyway, I don't understand why you don't just get the paperwork done for an assigned lover or at least a Sensuan. If you had sense enough to get that pesky virginity taken care of at the Age of Consent, why not take the next step?"

"You know we Draeman folk are highly sexual people," Joan chimed in. "Having an assigned partner is wonderful. Having one you love is even better. But, oh girl, a Sensuan is past amazing. You don't even have to take off your clothes. They just work their, well, whatever it is they do and my goodness." Her best friend fanned herself and whispered, "Whooo!"

Sex without having sex? Now that was a hell of a feat. But Rhia had never been interested in half-way or "sort of" doing anything.

"There's more to it than the sex for me. You both know that, Joan. I won't be stuck with a man that cares more for my title than for me as a woman." Like that Bryan Collaidh asshat. "And I certainly don't want one I can kick to pieces whenever he pisses me off."

"First off, kicking your man for any reason is dysfunctional as hell. And yeah, you say that's what you want, but you're so used to running things, could you really handle a man that you can't push around?" Joan asked as she abandoned a small square of grainbread for a handful of dried winterberries she fished out of her pocket.

Rhia curled a lip in a sneer. Joan simply crossed her arms over her chest. One side of her mouth lifted in a challenging you-know-I'm-right grin. Rather than answer the question, Rhia's mind wandered. How did Joan stay in such good shape? The woman hated sparring, loved her bed and often skipped the typical Draeman diet of vitamin and protein rich synthetic fare. Instead, she gorged on calorie loaded, old-fashioned food whenever she could spend enough time in her kitchen to make it. In spite of her unconventional diet, Joan sported compact, firm muscle.

Shorter than Rhia by at least a head, Joan was a gorgeous woman. Skin as silken as deep cocoa. Cropped, natural platinum curls contrasted with her skin and gleamed in the bright sunlight streaming in from the balcony windows. Dark brown eyes were set under thick lashes and manicured brows of the same striking blond hue. A pert little nose, full hips, lips and, even Rhia could admit, a nice set of breasts, finished off what was a very nice package. In a word, her best friend was a knockout. So why didn't Joan have a mate herself?

"I'm so short on time, if I didn't love my duties as First Heir and Blademaster I swear I'd..."

"You'd go nuts is what. And being horny isn't helping," Joan said matter-of-factly.

"Then I guess it's a good thing I work off most of my stress while I'm teaching."

"Teaching? You mean thrashing the soldiers? I'd hate to be a student in one of your combat classes, Rhia."

"Speaking of classes, we have one to teach, so

let's go."

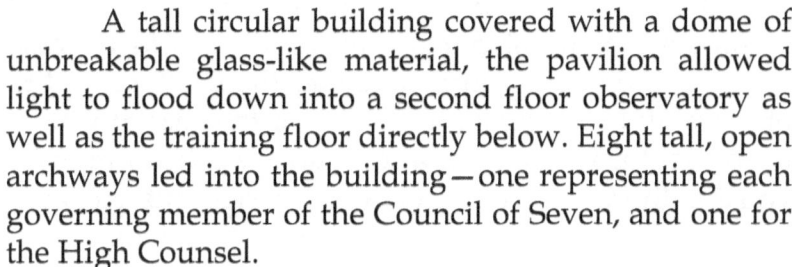

A tall circular building covered with a dome of unbreakable glass-like material, the pavilion allowed light to flood down into a second floor observatory as well as the training floor directly below. Eight tall, open archways led into the building—one representing each governing member of the Council of Seven, and one for the High Counsel.

As they passed beneath the arch of the House of Greysomne, Rhia smoothed down the edges of her sparring uniform. While the charcoal gray of the fabric attested both her house and her rank of Blademaster, the cut had another purpose.

Her clothing was more than pieces of cloth fused together to cover her body, it was a teaching tool. The cropped top dipped just enough to reveal the valley between her breasts, but fell several inches short of her waist to show her tummy. The leggings were pliable and stretchy so she could move through the exercise forms more easily. And the whole thing looked painted on.

Distractions could get a soldier killed, and there was nothing Rhia loved more than teaching, even if it meant she needed to occasionally use underhanded combat techniques. If she could make her students better fighters, it was worth every minute spent laser scrubbing congealed blood off the tiles of the training floor or sending them off to the Society of Physicians to be stitched up.

Joan moved off to the edge of the group while

Rhia stepped into the middle of the room. All talking ceased and every eye turned to her.

"Whether you're returning to your own province or accepting an assignment in Draema, before you are given a classification and released, you'll accompany some of our seasoned soldiers to Draema Porto. There you'll join the crew of the DP Tactical I to observe and participate in patrols of the coastal waters to the south. I only have a few more weeks to prepare you for those exercises, so expect a rigorous workout every time you step into this building. Understood?"

The reply was a unified and hearty "Yes, sir!"

"Good. While I was away, our Society's most skilled commanders have led you through the forms with the blades. Today we'll wrap up your blade training with a few changes I'm sure you'll appreciate." Not bothering to hide a sly grin, Rhia gestured to the specially delivered muck on the floor.

The utter silence told her that the students were surprised. Excellent.

"Joan, send the first soldier into the circle," Rhia called clearly before placing her sparring mask over her head, and then drawing her blade.

Joan quickly chose a short, stocky Midjey man from the northeastern hills. He was so hairy and thick-necked he looked more like a dwarf from the ancient fairy tales. There were very few full blood Midjey anymore since their people, like so many others, integrated into other societies for survival's sake after the Breaking. The Midjey were amazing stonecutters who, in spite of their thick fingers, could create the most intricately carved stone pieces with such detail the rock seemed almost alive. Carving alone made them experts with heavy weaponry since wielding a hammer with skill could down an opponent.

As the man approached, each step made a crunching sound in the gravel, sand and dirt until the mud sucked at the ankles of his boots.

The Midjey crouched, made his first thrust and saw too late that Rhia had already moved. Overextending as he raised his much thicker blade to meet hers, he slipped in the mud and landed flat on his back with a thud and a very loud '*uummph.*' Eyes as wide as saucers and grumbling under his breath, he dared not move a muscle with Rhia's exquisitely sharp katana pressed against his neck.

"You can't expect an enemy to be a gentleman by always allowing you to strike first. If that's the case, you may as well have him over for tea." It was the nastiest analogy she could think of given how much she hated tea. She smiled as she helped the stocky, and now very dirty, Midjey to his feet as the rest of the class chuckled quietly. The back of his tunic plastered in mud, he bowed politely and left the circle with a grin and a bit of a limp. The man was a good sport. After all, she was right about the tea.

Rhia instructed from the middle of the large demonstration circle. Soldiers surrounded her, all ranked First Blade or higher. They all belonged to the Society of War under the jurisdiction of the High Counsel, her father. After the anarchy that followed the Breaking, this Society was the first organization to arise out of the madness. Men and women, like these, had freely shed their blood to defend Draema and her allies against encroachers for as long as anyone could remember. It was the oldest and most respected guild in the Province. And today, these seasoned fearless soldiers belonged to her.

This is going to be fun.

"Joan, send another," Rhia shouted over her shoulder with an evil grin as she deftly tossed her three-foot razor sharp blade back and forth from hand to hand.

CHAPTER FIVE

RuArk watched Rhia from the back of the throng of soldiers. All of them were fully dressed in combat gear and bristled with various weapons.

From kinderschool to their twelfth season, every Draeman boy and girl, no matter which colony they lived, learned a few of the old arts with a wealth of what RuArk considered the "new". The old arts were sword fighting, horsemanship, bow and wrestling. But Draema's specialties were target practice with laser pistols, energy staffs and hand cannons. In fact, huge pulse cannons were mounted atop the outer walls in strategic spots, facing away from Draema and out toward her neighboring lands. After all, this province still had enemies. Lucky for them, Gaia was not one of them.

Taller than everyone here, RuArk hunched his shoulders and sank as deeply into his cloak as he could. His task was to observe anyone who seemed suspicious, as he'd done all over the High City every day that Rhia had been down in Harbor Station inspecting airships. As a result, he and his warriors had uncovered quite a bit of useful information, which would have been impossible to glean if the High

Counsel hadn't sent her on that little trip.

The High Counsel had spread a rumor that RuArk had returned so soon after his last visit, in order to arrange another trade agreement for Gaian coffee and chocolate in exchange for prime horses bred in the far western part of Draema. It was a plausible cover, but he was still careful with his movements. The last thing he wanted was for the pawns in this little conspiracy to get wind of his real goals and spook the mastermind he hadn't yet identified. Or worse, cause them all to panic and do something stupid, like attempt to kill Rhia off-schedule.

The ring leader could be just about anyone with the ability to get close, like the pale haired female in the circle right now. No, scratch that. While her enthusiasm was unmistakable, her forms weren't smooth enough, which spoke of inexperience.

Women fighting wasn't something RuArk saw often. Gaian women recognized the power of their femininity, and had no desire to be soldiers. Other than Sharyn, no women served under him. Yet, as he followed Rhia with his eyes, he realized there was something quite sexy about this battle-skilled woman — the way she moved, the way she owned her space.

The flex of her body and strength of each delivered blow sent the blood rushing south until his stones tucked in tight to his body. Gods, his cock had terrible timing. And how was it, he already had a soft spot for the Blademaster he watched beat the hell out of her students?

Speaking of students, that's all he saw here. No one was skilled enough to be an assassination mastermind, so it was time to leave and explore other options.

"You there. Into the circle."

RuArk raised a dark brow in response to the summons and groaned inwardly as he watched Rhia's Second, a woman named Joan Rouillard, pin him with a glare. He'd watched the short, dark-skinned woman shuffle around the pavilion all morning with sleepies in her eyes. And now those sleepy eyes were firmly on him.

He smiled like a rogue and said silkily, "I am only observing this morning."

"I don't give a damn."

Really? That smile had always worked with women, yet this one snorted at him.

"If you just wanted to watch you should have stayed up there," Joan snapped, pointing over his head with her blade to the glass enclosed observatory on the upper floor. So much for charm. Guess it didn't work on a woman who was tired, shivering with cold, and obviously not in a very giving mood.

And now Rhia began to make her way over to no doubt investigate the delay.

Not good.

She removed her guard mask and tucked it under her free arm. She was still a short distance away when her eyes widened. Strange how she could scrunch up her face and still raise one side of her mouth in such a vicious sneer. But the expression lasted mere moments, and just as quickly, her features smoothed into a serene mask. But those fiery eyes conveyed a wealth of meaning.

Inner strength was evident in the set of her chin and proud natural stance. Intelligence and satisfaction reflected in her golden eyes. He took her all in at once. Skin so smooth it was perfection. Deep brown hair was thick and wavy with fiery red and auburn strands that gleamed against the darker strands and danced with color. Today it was pulled back from her face in a thick braid tied with a dainty little gray ribbon at the end.

His fingers itched to pull the ribbon loose and play in that mane of beautiful hair to see if it was a soft as it appeared. If he buried his nose in it, would he catch the same scent that had teased him when he'd seen her while *Seeking*?

Thoughts halted when the woman's sword arm snapped out with a very nasty blade at the end of it. That blade whipped to a stop at his chest, directly above a male nipple.

"Is there a problem here?" Rhia asked with wide-eyed innocence, owning the same words he'd used when he'd interrupted her fight with the black haired greaser in her apartments. The point of her blade sank into soft silk. Good thing he'd dressed as a Draeman this morning, leaving off his typical leather garb. At least the shirt could be stitched, though his nipple didn't appreciate the nearness of the steel.

Joan stood stock still, her head tilted to the side with a half-grin on her face that said "You're going to get it now" before turning to Rhia to seal his fate.

"I told him he was up next, and he refuses."

Thanks, Joan.

"Is that right?" Rhia taunted, with a chilling grin that complimented the whip of the midwinter breeze outside. "No soldier is to refuse when called, practice or not. Hey, you look kind of familiar." Brows rose in mock delight. "Ah, I know. You're a noob! Are you sure you should be in this class?"

She knew exactly who he was, but hadn't revealed it. Why? It was a stupid question. This was her game, her domain where she could goad him while surrounded by people loyal to her. And by the look on their faces, they might just run him through and save Rhia the trouble.

If she wants to play, then I am certainly up for it.

Thank the Ancestors for the discipline that kept him from grinning right back. Bowing only slightly — moving more than a hair would cause a bigger hole in his shirt, he said, "I apologize, Blademaster."

Damned woman. He couldn't believe how badly this was going. But this was, after all, Rhia Greysomne, and if she was anything like the hellion of her youth, it was about to get worse. Made him wonder what it would be like to hold all that fire in his arms. To be the one to bring that heat flowing out of her as she lay beneath him. Or on top of him. Or up against a wall. Or on the floor...

"Care to say what's on your mind, newbie?" she snarled quietly, her lips drawn tight around her teeth.

Yes, this woman he definitely knew. One side of his mouth lifted. Wrong move. She'd been somewhat aggravated before, but his pleased expression obviously wasn't appreciated. Temper pricked, she took a step closer.

The nick in his skin stung and he thanked the Ancestors that Rhia had such incredible control of that blade. He was grateful he'd chosen dark clothing this morning. At least it wouldn't show the blood.

Whether she knew it or not, she'd already drawn first blood, severely limiting his options of how to get out of this mess with his honor intact. He didn't like humiliating a commander in front of her men but...

Nothing to be done for it, he sighed to himself. The Grandfather always said, "Once you've stepped in a pile of shit, you're going to smell whether you keep the other foot clean or not."

May as well sink both feet.

"I believed you were Blademaster here, yet you've blooded me for no reason. Perhaps I was mistaken of your station given your manners." RuArk looked down at her, crossed him arms over his chest and awaited her response.

Joan's mouth dropped so wide open she could have caught several fish if she'd dunked her head through the melting ice on the river. *Perhaps that would wake her up.* The woman also backed up a couple of paces and must have known what was coming. RuArk had to admit he had a pretty good idea himself.

"You know who I am." Definitely not a question. "How dare you speak to me like that." Rhia's words sounded much too calm and did not match the fire flashing in those amber cat eyes of hers. The sword point sank a little deeper into RuArk's left pectoral. The little nick was a thing of the past. It was now a wide but controlled cut, oozing blood down the front of his tunic. Most men would be squirming by now from the pain or the sight of the blood. RuArk was hardly bothered at all, and it only seemed to annoy her more.

Rather than answering her question, he simply arched a brow in challenge. The result—sudden silence. No movement. No sound. RuArk wondered if anyone still breathed.

Rhia withdrew her blade from his chest with a snap then stepped so close he could feel the heat radiating from her body. She tried to stand toe to toe with him, but even at her unusual height, her head only reached his chin. Realizing she couldn't stare him down, she rose up on her toes.

Each breath he took was filled with her to the point he almost moaned at the natural scent of her body. He wondered what soap she'd used that morning. His gaze dropped to the path that a bead of sweat made as it snaked down her neck and disappeared between her breasts. That stubborn chin of hers was set just below a pair of lush lips made for kissing. And she was just close enough that if he dipped his head, he could seal her lips with his.

Even pissed off she was a lovely sight. Gods, he was a goner. In danger of losing his balls, but a goner, just the same.

But this staring contest wasn't going anywhere.

So he said, "Rhia, I do think your father was remiss in not spanking your ass when you were a child."

"Pffft! Step into my circle, sir," she hissed through clenched teeth. She turned her back on him, walked away, then paused to bend over and stick out her backside. RuArk's mask of indifference slipped—the woman wiggled her butt at him! An obvious gesture of how she felt about his thoughts on her lack of discipline. Stiff with anger, she stalked to the middle of the circle where she waited. Her belly button peeked out at him from under that cropped top. Blasted woman.

RuArk stripped, drawing all eyes to the thickly muscled machine that was his body. Belt, scabbard and Draeman-styled trousers all came off, leaving only a leather breech to accompany his boots as he stood to his full height. If anyone wondered about his Gaian heritage, he was sure there were no doubts now.

Rhia's grumbling was just loud enough for RuArk to catch a few choice words as he moved closer to the center of the circle where she waited.

"Spanking? Hah! ... kick your ass ... peel your hide ... bloody blasted man." And on it went until they stood facing each other, poised and ready to move through the forms.

Practically naked in the frigid morning air, he wanted nothing to hinder his movement, and went to meet Rhia with his blade and nothing else. This woman didn't hold the rank of Blademaster for nothing. While he was a Gaian warrior and doubted Rhia could beat him, he had no intention of going to the Society of Physicians for stitching after this.

CHAPTER SIX

Rhia watched him approach on silent feet, his movements relaxed and confident. Soft-soled boots made no sound in the sticky muck and gravel on the floor.

He moves like a damn cat.

His leather breech left very little to the imagination and her eyes zoomed in on his legs. She didn't know another man in all of Draema with thighs like these. Blazes, they were huge, flexed with every step, and showed off the smooth taut skin stretched over each cut of muscle.

Draeman men were muscular and fit, but they were nowhere near as tall, thickly built, and certainly not as darkly handsome. Putting it plainly, they were nothing like this man. Squashing a ridiculous *zing* of lust down into her boots, she abruptly turned away with a pretense of examining some minute piece of lint on her shirt, angry at the heat creeping up her neck. She was supposed to have some self-control, not stand there gawking at the man because of his incredible physique, though his handsome features were on display with all that beautiful hair pulled back and away.

Rhia knew he was anything but new to a fight. The night he'd picked up and tossed a squealing Bryan while barely drawing a breath made it clear enough. Not to mention the fact that he was raised to be a fighter, just as she had. From the moment he was born, he'd been groomed to be Protector of the Realm. His stance screamed pride—pride in his warrior's body, and even more pride in his heritage and ability to do his job.

Damn. He's going to kick my ass. But she just couldn't seem to stop pushing. She'd walked in here feeling brazenly wicked, and it was just his luck to bring out the total witch in her. And if the witch wanted to come out, Rhia would let her play.

'Cheeky bastard,' she fumed. *'And he's not beautiful, either, damn it!'*

Sure, whatever.

For several moments they just stood and eyeballed each other.

"Well?" Rhia taunted, and with that, it began. She came with a fast move called Strike of the Mantis, her blade angled down like the claw of that long extinct insect, bringing it around swiftly. Not many practiced this style anymore, and not many could counter it either. When he did so perfectly, she switched to Sweeping Dragon. He countered with Blocking Sway and Clipping Wings.

Neither gave any ground.

———◆———◆———

The woman had considerable skill with a blade, but RuArk wasn't actually trying to beat her. He simply wanted to take measure of how she moved and what style she liked to fight. Her strength and speed was admirable. He knew a lot of men who would have been hard pressed to keep up with her, but none of them were hardened Gaian warriors. Rhia was good, but he knew he was faster and stronger with the advantage of reach and height. He'd let her have her fun, but enough was enough.

He stepped forward and attacked, putting all his strength behind each drive. He was overpowering her and knew the blows sent painful vibrations up her arm. Soon her wrist would go numb and she would be unable to grasp her blade. All he needed to do was wait her out.

But Rhia kept herself under control and fought on with everything she had. Just when he was sure she would give in, she swung a well-aimed foot and kicked him in the knee. He couldn't believe it. It seemed that when the woman couldn't win, she would cheat.

He shouldn't be surprised. His own father, King of Gaia, had taught her to fight dirty against bullies back in kinderschool.

And he'd been caught off guard at her underhanded tactic just long enough to allow his sword to be sent spinning across the floor. In an act of honor, or perhaps foolishness, she threw her sword aside to face him in hand-to-hand combat. He took two steps toward her when she grabbed him by his long braid, and fell backward bringing him with her. At the last instant she added an unexpected kick that sent him flying over her head to land sprawled on his back on the muddy floor. Where had she learned that? It was a dumb question.

"My father, you know, the one who didn't spank

my ass enough? Well, he always taught me that the only fair fight is a *won* fight," she said. On her feet, she moved back out of reach, ignoring the roaring cheer of her students.

He was up quickly and didn't bother to hide the admiration in his expression. RuArk knew he wasn't an easy man to face in a fight, and an even harder man to throw. Whether it was blades, on foot, on horseback or hand-to-hand, he was a formidable opponent. And this woman managed to hurl him across the floor.

Then she was on him, all fists and feet. With quick hands and moves that were second nature, he blocked her attempts.

This time he anticipated what she was doing when her foot flashed out. The kick landed, but not in the intended spot. And though she'd put all her weight into the blow, she bounced right off to land with a splat in the mud.

Suddenly, Joan shouted, "Stand down, all of you!"

It took RuArk a split second to look around. Every last soldier in the pavilion now had a blade drawn. One word from Rhia and they'd have been more than happy to take her place in the circle and promptly slice him to ribbons. None of them seemed to care that this was supposed to be a practice session.

He could handle several grown men, but there would be some broken bones and lots of bleeding. When Joan moved forward, RuArk grew concerned. He didn't know if he could handle these two women without hurting them. And if he hurt Rhia he could forget the soldiers obeying any order to stand down.

In a sneaky move of his own, he grabbed Rhia, spun her around and pinned her arms to her sides with her back plastered against his chest. Joan grabbed Rhia around the middle, struggling to pull her out of RuArk's arms. He let go. He didn't let his guard down even if both women were now sprawled in the mud. Instead, he stepped back, crouched down in a stance prepared for the next attack.

As he blocked a jab to the ribs, Rhia used his raised arm to slip underneath and then attach from behind. She reached under one of his arms, wrapped him in an unbreakable hold and pulled him off balance down to his knees. She applied pressure to the artery that allowed blood to flow to his brain. With this hold, it didn't matter how much larger or faster he was.

His field of vision began to blacken about the edges, and he knew he had only a few more seconds before he passed out on the floor. He would wake up in less than a minute, but he'd have a hell of a headache and a gloating woman on his hands.

RuArk reached back, grabbed her beneath her arms and lifted her over his head. He rose from the floor holding her suspended above the hard, muddy floor and shook her like a rag. It took considerable strength given Rhia was no stick doll, not to mention her attempts to knee him in the head. He slammed her back against his chest again and stood with a very unhappy and dizzy female wrapped firmly about the shoulders. When Rhia started struggling again—gods, the woman was strong—he tightened his hold a bit more knowing she'd either give up or pass out. And with Rhia, it would surely be the latter.

Joan screamed in her friend's ear, "Rhia, cut it out! Stop struggling!" She then turned on RuArk, too short to get directly in his face, but yelled loud enough to make his ears ring.

"You let her go!"

RuArk didn't reply, but continued to apply the required pressure. Sweat rolled down Rhia's face and if her shallow breathing was any indication, her lungs were having a hard time of it. But she refused to give up. They were a filthy mass of tangled hair, muddy arms and legs and neither ready to give any ground.

"Rhia! Stop it, now!" Joan tried to pull Rhia loose without actually touching RuArk.

This was ridiculous. He stood in a room full of armed soldiers, muddy as a dog, his arms around the First Heir. The woman he would spend his life with happened to be trying to kill him in the middle of a cold, semi-exposed training area when he was supposed to be looking for traitors. It was just too much. RuArk couldn't help it. He fell backward to the floor, took a very dirty Rhia with him and started laughing. A deep, booming sound that resonated through the pavilion.

"I. Refuse. To. Lose." Rhia hissed and thrust a well-aimed elbow into RuArk's stomach. Her grimace said what he already knew — all she managed to do was hurt herself. Then she tried to reach up to pull his hair, screaming to the rafters. Good gracious, this was madness. He laughed hard enough to shake his whole body, along with the woman on top of him.

Thankfully, only soldiers and Council members were allowed on the ground floor of this building. RuArk was sure that was the only thing that kept all the heads that peeked into the doorways from becoming a large number of bodies that filled up the room.

Fucking hell.

Grey Greysomne entered the pavilion with

several of the Council of Seven trailing after him. He was surprised they hadn't come sooner with all the cheers and yells that carried through the open archways.

"Rhia, there's no dishonor in losing fairly. Now cut it out," Joan hissed as she knelt in the muck next to her friend. Lowering her voice to an urgent whisper, she said, "The whole Council of Seven is watching. And your father."

Her father?

Blasted hell.

Rhia stopped struggling. Joan stopped yanking on Rhia. Both women were mortified. The asshole underneath her continued to grin.

It took Rhia a few moments to realize that her arms had been released and she was now lying on top of the man as if she belonged there. In spite of the cold winds rushing through the open archways, her body was sweaty and hot. Her face was on fire. Not that anyone could see her flushed skin through the plaster of dirt.

With all the dignity she could muster, she rolled off RuArk's chest, stood and turned to face her students, the Council members... and the High Counsel himself.

Grey Greysomne stood in the sparring circle not more than five feet from where the three of them had been sprawled. Joan nervously attempted to dust off her tunic and breeches, but only managed to rub the dirt in deeper. Rhia's formerly gray cropped tunic looked slept in, the knees of her matching leggings torn, stained and caked with mud. She tried to smooth her matted hair away from her face. And RuArk's deep, rumbling laughter still filled the pavilion.

The High Counsel's lips pressed into a grim line, his eyebrows drawn into a deep scowl. But the man looked more perplexed than upset as he calmly took in the scene without saying a word. The other Councilor's chins had dropped to their sanctimoniously fat chests as they surveyed the grimy mess with wide eyes. With the exception of her father and Councilor Collaidh, these were the most indulgent people in all of Draema. Rhia almost rolled her eyes at their gasps as they held their plump little fingers to their breasts in utter horror. So what, the First Heir and her assistant instructor had been rolling around on the floor, kicking and screaming like crazy people.

The High Counsel approached with ease. "Rhia?" That was all he needed to say.

She stood there, working her mouth, but nothing came out.

"This is new," RuArk whispered into her ear.

"What?" she hissed back.

"You, speechless."

"Rhia, you know what I want to know." The High Counsel crossed his arms over his still well-built chest and waited for her answer.

"Yes, father. Well, I... uh... see we were... and Joan, but then he wouldn't, and I... Oh blasted hell."

"The Blademaster was demonstrating how to fight without a blade, sir. I did learn some new techniques. It was most enlightening," RuArk cut in.

And what the hell was going on here anyway? RuArk yet again acted as if he were new here, but they'd known each other since she was born. And her father wasn't disputing RuArk's words? This was just... weird.

Chancing a peek his way, the current bane of her existence rewarded her with a blinding smile and as graceful a bow as he could muster without slipping in the mud. His gray eyes sparkled with mischief as he winked.

Rhia eyes went wide. That was a 'you owe me one, woman' wink if she'd ever seen one.

With a nod, the High Counsel said, "Rhia, meet me in my office. One hour."

"Yes, sir." After a smart nod of acceptance, she turned to the assembly. "Second blades, right here tomorrow morning as scheduled. Everyone, clear out. I don't want to hear a sound as you do it. Dismissed."

She and Joan moved stiffly toward the closest archway. Feet slid and flapped as they went. Their eyes fell on RuArk as they passed with scowls cold enough to rival the chilly morning air.

As she moved further away from him, Rhia grumbled, "I don't know if I'm angrier with that man or myself. My father saw me rolling in the mud, brawling like a common street fighter. Oh, but I'll get even with that, that... Grrrr. Just wait."

With an exasperated sigh, Joan replied. "It isn't his fault you lost your wits, girlfriend. And it's not his fault you lost the fight either."

"Of course it's his fault," Rhia said out of the side of her mouth. "That's my story and I'm sticking to it."

CHAPTER SEVEN

Sara set the tray on the dining table in the High Counsel's offices. Bowing and wringing her hands nervously, she asked, "Is there anything else, sir?"

She couldn't look into his eyes, not after what she'd done. Perhaps she could still get out of here before Rhia's body was discovered. The tea would be found laced with whatever she'd put in it. She would have to flee and quickly. Terror swamped her. Where was she supposed to go? The High City had always been her home.

"Sara?"

The High Counsel watched her from the same hand-carved wood and polished stone-inlaid desk that had been gifted to him from the Gaian people as a wedding gift so many seasons ago.

"Yes, sir," she stammered as her gaze snapped up to meet his. She hadn't been listening to what was being said. Too busy thinking about how she'd slipped into Rhia's room not long ago. As a Houseman assigned to the Citadel, it was her job to anticipate the needs of the household... and to know that the First Heir always returned to her tower apartment to snack and change clothes after the early morning class.

And Sara had... No, she wouldn't think about it. The man who came to her in the dark would take care of it. He would take care of everything.

"Is something wrong, Sara? Do I need to send a Physician to you?"

"No, sir. I'm fine, sir, really. Um, sorry, sir."

"You may leave now, Sara."

RuArk watched as she flew out the door. The woman's eyes were haunted, held more than a little fear and something else that he couldn't quite pin down. Intuition had long been his friend and it told him to put a watch on that one.

The High Counsel motioned RuArk toward the food-laden table. "I'll join you in a moment. I have a few things to take care of." He returned his gaze to the stack of papers in front of him and after a moment or two of charged silence, he said, "So, I see that you and Rhia have become reacquainted."

"If that's what you wish to call it," RuArk chuckled as he sat. Recalling Rhia's ferocity in the circle, his fingers touched a tender spot just below his jawline where her elbow had caught him. A couple of self-applied stitches had closed the cut on his chest. And the swelling beneath his right eye was easing up thanks to a quickly applied med patch that all of his warriors were required to carry at all times. You never knew when you'd find yourself in a battle... like this morning.

"I intended to be in the pavilion only long enough to observe the behavior of the soldiers. It stands to reason that whoever is behind this plot has unrestricted access to your daughter."

"I hate all this mystery, RuArk," Grey said.

"Have your men uncovered anything more? I agreed to send Rhia to Harbor Station to give us a few weeks to poke around without her interference. The woman is everywhere, teaching one combat class or another, seeing this ambassador or that diplomat. We don't want her to start suspecting things when she notices you are everywhere she happens to be. Especially since you've been to the High City many times over the years on business and she hasn't seen you on any of those visits. At all. She hasn't mentioned it, but you can be sure she certainly noticed."

Well, that had been on purpose. His decision to avoid anything and anyone that might distract him from becoming the unquestioned Protector of his people had seemed a sound choice at the time. Now, given the current circumstances, he wasn't so sure.

RuArk inclined his head in agreement. "I was a fool to believe I could get out of the pavilion without her noticing me. That is her territory, after all."

Grey Greysomne laughed and almost choked on his coffee. "RuArk, who wouldn't notice a six-and-a-half-foot brawny warrior with hair down his back, worn in the traditional Gaian style? We Draeman are considered a bit hipper than that. And a breech over your dangly bits? I don't even want to think about where you ended up having to scrub the mud from."

RuArk enjoyed the moment with his father's old friend, but the humor was short lived.

"I tossed a man out of her apartments the night we returned to the High City."

Grey rose so quickly, papers scattered to the floor as he strode to the dining table to join RuArk.

"Who the hell dared to enter her apartments?" he thundered.

"Whoever he was, Rhia hurt him badly. Grey, he was trying to take her against her will, forcing her right there on her floor. She brought him under control quickly. When I got to them, he was bleeding nicely and about two moments from being able to never have children."

RuArk gave the High Counsel all the details, from the lank dark hair, bulging eyes and pasty white skin, down to the size of the man's boots. He left out the part about the unexplainable anger and possessiveness that made him grind his back teeth when he'd seen Rhia on the floor with blood on her clothes and welts on her face. The *Seeking* had shown him that she was his and it had taken all his self-control not to let Rhia finish the job.

"Sounds like Bryan Collaidh, Council Rama Collaidh's son. That bastard left the High City cycles ago for something along the same lines. Son of a bitch."

"Rhia was ready to kill him and would have succeeded if not for some unwelcome intervention from me, hence our disagreement in the pavilion this morning. She was trying to repay me for interfering. But if this Bryan person is involved, we will know soon enough."

"He's always wanted Rhia. They were engaged when they were very young."

"Engaged?" Gut did an unexpected freefall as he experienced a jealous pang that made no sense. Rhia hadn't been his way back then. If he was honest, she wasn't his now. Not quite yet.

"Yes. It was during the years you were away training for your role as Protector." A flicker of grief passed over the High Counsel's face. "It ended badly, RuArk. Rhia spent some time under the care of the

Physicians. I knew the man was back in the High City recently, but didn't think he'd be stupid enough to even contact Rhia. She hates him, and he knows it. Well, this certainly puts some urgency into our plans."

"Urgency? You mean other than your daughter's attempt to skewer me?" RuArk chuckled, trying to bring a bit of levity into the situation. It was obvious Grey felt bad about what happened to Rhia all those years ago, but RuArk seriously doubted it was the man's fault. After all, even when Rhia was little, when she got it into her head that she wanted something, she went after it with steam to spare... even if that something was bad for her. It's part of what made her such a formidable fighter. She was no holds barred about everything. Always had been.

"We must definitely end this plot against her before she kills me."

"She is splendid isn't she?" The High Counsel's grin was wide though his eyes reflected a weary sadness. "She's just like her mother," he sighed. The smile faltered all together. "Looks like her. Fights like her, too. I wish I would have sent her to spend time with her mother's family across the borders more often but by the time I got my head on straight, I was too late. Rhia's only aunt is long gone now." The silence afterward said more than words ever could. Grey Greysomne had been a devoted husband, and now felt guilty for not being a better father.

The depth of the man's love had made such an impression on a young RuArk, that even now he recalled the wonder at the two adults who'd smiled wistfully at each other all the time.

"Rhia's a strong and honorable woman, but so much more vulnerable than anyone realizes. She's spent so much time fighting men that she hasn't had time to enjoy being loved by one. And I certainly don't count," Grey said quietly. Pouring two more crystal mugs of rich Gaian coffee, he handed one to RuArk.

"It will be a challenge." One RuArk looked forward to. "And her one hour has come and gone yet she's not here."

"Don't worry. If Rhia is anything, she's a keeper of her word. She may be late, but don't doubt she'll be here. So," he said, lifting his mug to RuArk in a toast. "To you and Rhia, and whether you realize it or not, the saving of this mighty province and its seven colonies."

Slowly uncovering the trays full of dishes, RuArk watched the High Counsel close his eyes and inhale deeply. It was times like this that he really appreciated his culture. RuArk was honored that the High Counsel had gone out of his way to have the cooks prepare Gaian food. He would never understand why the Draeman preferred their artificial, bland, tasteless, plastic-like fare to real food.

Thankfully, instead of grainbread with calmonut butter, there was hot vegetable stew, and fresh crusty bread seasoned with what smelled like sage and slathered with butter. And, as always, a pot of hot, dark Gaian coffee. RuArk spooned himself a bowl of the savory fare. It smelled heavenly. He wondered if Rhia could cook, but seriously doubted it. After all, this place had a whole Society of Housemen for those kinds of things.

Forcing a chunk of what looked like poultry past his lips, RuArk chewed quickly and took a swallow of coffee to wash it down. After a few bites, RuArk took a deep breath and did his best to swallow. It smelled wonderful, but that was as far as the pleasure went. Perhaps the main cooks were off today?

The High Counsel put his spoon down. "So what are you thinking?"

"I think we should have the private ceremony. But just you, Rhia and me. No Council members since we don't know where loyalties lie."

"I'd like to have my man, Mannon, come in as a witness. He's the last Gaian serving in this house. And it would mean a lot to me if we did it the old way. I remember your customs well. I'll speak the words and it will be done."

Silence reigned for the rest of the meal, but RuArk's mind traveled a mile a minute. This task had more to it than he'd thought. Not only was he gaining a mate, but a mate who wanted nothing more than to stick him in the gut and end him over a matter of pride. Even if Rhia weren't a half-Gaian woman who knew nothing about what would be expected of her, she'd still be a hand full. He grinned into his mug.

Ancestors, I must be insane.

Breakfast done, RuArk followed the High Counsel to a lounging area where several plump chairs formed a semi-circle in front of a blazing glass-protected fireplace. Neither man chose to sit.

RuArk's recalled the reaction of his body as he'd held Rhia locked in his arms. His arousal had been unexpected, swift and so strong he had to fight himself to maintain control of his cock while he physically fought with Rhia. He'd never experienced such a thing, especially in the middle of a fight. He'd slowly squeezed the breath from her body in hopes she would surrender just so he could let her go.

With a sheepish grin, RuArk asked, "Do you

think she remembers all the, uh, *events* from when we were kids?"

"Oh, she remembers, all right. I could see it in her eyes while you were rolling around in the mud together. It took every ounce of my self-control to act like I didn't know you when I walked into that pavilion and saw all your arms and legs tangled up together in that muck. It almost killed me not to laugh outright.

"Luckily, your man, Marth sent a young boy to me with a message that I'd better get to the training pavilion right way because 'the Lady Rhia was going to skewer a very tall man'. I knew it had to be you. Even when you accompanied your father on visits as a boy, Rhia was always after your skin."

"Well, it might have had to do with my tendency to sneak up on her and yank her braids. Gods, she ran like the wind trying to catch me. There were a few times I almost didn't get away."

"Remember when she tried to run you through with her wooden practice sword? Ha! That was classic. How old were you two back then? Eight, maybe ten cycles old?"

"She was seven or eight. To my shame, I was almost thirteen. I was too old to taunt her, but I couldn't seem to help myself," RuArk said with a smile.

"Rhia chased you into my pigeon cote and wouldn't let you come down. In the end your father and I had to come fetch you because we were the only ones who could get past her."

"I'd really rather forget that one. I missed the evening meal and father made me stand and apologize to her while covered with pigeon feathers and enough bird shit to mat my hair to my scalp. A lot of finger pointing that evening. Gods, I hope she's forgotten that."

"Well, if she hasn't," the High Counsel said with a salute, "may your gods help you."

Help him indeed. Rhia had grown up, but after what he'd seen today, RuArk didn't think she'd changed all that much. She was still the most beautiful female he'd ever known. Even when she was a child, there had been an unmistakable beauty just underneath those sinfully dark, red streaked pigtails and skinny legs. As a woman, she was breathtakingly lovely with silken skin over firm, sleek muscle. Her dual heritage was evident in the blend of her features. She was also stubborn, sharp tongued, ill tempered, ill mannered. And he wanted her. Badly. Gods help him indeed.

Rhia walked into the High Counsel's offices, nodded at his secretary and moved quickly down the hall to a set of double doors.

"Sara, what are you doing here?"

Visibly startled, Sara jumped and turned so quickly she almost fell backwards against the door. The blood drained from her face and she appeared to be shaking like a leaf.

"Sara, I asked what you're doing." Rhia asked crisply, both impatient and suspicious. The girl looked like she'd just seen a ghost.

"I, uh, I'm just surprised to see you, is all."

"Why? I live here... and so do you." Sara was a member of the Society of Houseman and assigned to the citadel. They'd been running into each other in hallways for ten years. So, why the surprise?

Strange.

Swallowing convulsively, Sara answered, "I delivered the breakfast trays, Blademaster. I was, uh, waiting quietly for a sign that your father was ready for me to take them away. I didn't want to disturb the High Counsel and his guest."

Stammering like she'd sustained a brain injury, Sara managed to babble and execute an awkward bow. Rhia furrowed her brow and watched the woman practically run down the long hallway, constantly looking back over her shoulder as she went. Well, she didn't have time to worry about Sara right now.

Her father just had to be angry with her and she needed to wrap her mind around what she would say to smooth over the debacle in the training pavilion. Pushing the door open to her father's private study without knocking, Rhia strode inside.

"Father, I can explain what hap…" Skidding to a halt, her mouth snapped shut, fists planted on her hips. Cheeks heated as she demanded, "What the hell are *you* doing here?"

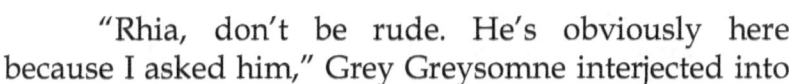

"Rhia, don't be rude. He's obviously here because I asked him," Grey Greysomne interjected into the sudden tense silence.

"Sorry, father."

She didn't *look* sorry as she quietly closed the door behind her and came fully into the room to stand directly in front of the two men. Squaring her shoulders, she extended a hand in greeting.

"Hey RuArk."

Two simple words, yet they slid over his soul like a soothing balm of the sweetest healing oil. RuArk couldn't think of a single thing to say so he simply looked his fill instead.

The cropped tunic and leggings she'd worn into the circle at dawn allowed subtle peeks at her cute little belly button and creamy skin, but this new outfit hugged her body like an old familiar lover. Her curves were covered in a sleek one-piece affair made of shimmering fabric that caressed her ankles, slid up and over sleek, muscled calves to her thighs where a curved, jeweled dagger was strapped to one of them.

The outline of strong abdominal muscles made his fingers itch to explore the little ridges and valleys underneath her lush breasts. Even the curve of her collarbone was visible through the material.

His body tightened as he took in the lush firm lines of her body. Suddenly RuArk didn't like the idea of Rhia walking around in this outfit where any and everyone could get a good look at her. He didn't give a damn that it was normal wear in Draema.

A smile played at the corners of his mouth as Rhia began to fidget under his close scrutiny.

"Our previous meeting was a bit out of the ordinary," she pressed, hand still extended. He stepped possessively close, accepted her offered hand and turned it over to plant a gentle kiss at the pulse on her wrist. That pulse quickened the moment his lips made contact with warm skin. He heard the breath catch softly in her throat and saw her stomach muscles subtly tighten and flutter. And then she seemed to squash it all down. Fast.

He still hadn't spoken.

Rhia turned to the High Counsel, brows

furrowed in agitation. Palms out in front of him in man's universal "don't look at me" gesture, her father shook his head and leaned lazily against the fireplace to watch what would surely end up to be a nice display of emotional fireworks.

He swore he wouldn't bring it up, but the words slipped out anyway.

"I remember you flying through the sparring field firmly attached to the back of a horse, your hair full of straw and waving a wooden sword."

"Yeah, and I thought I'd never, ever lay eyes on you again." She had the decency to blush before turning away. "Aw hell, that didn't come out quite right."

CHAPTER EIGHT

As a Draeman woman, boldness was in her genes, especially when it came to the opposite sex. Earlier, she'd been busy trying to pummel this man into the ground, but now Rhia eyeballed him as subtly — *not* — as he had her. Her gaze roamed up one side and down the other, starting with his strong, angled jaw line. Deep gray eyes were tilted up at the sides just like hers. Wide chest tapered down to a trim waist and his huge thighs were set apart in a casual, yet solid stance.

He was bronze, big and beautiful, with a hint of a reddish tone to his skin. Dressed in what she knew was traditional Gaian clothing, broad shoulders filled out his leather tunic. Leather hadn't been used in Draema in ages, but she found herself wanting to smooth her fingers over the supple-looking material. Instead, her eyes dropped down to the 'V' where his top was unlaced at the neck to expose the striations on the slabs of chest muscle. No visible hair, just smooth, taut skin. How had she missed this earlier in the training pavilion?

His long, slightly damp mane hung loose down to the middle of his back. Glossy, midnight black and thick, it was bone straight without a hint of wave.

Considerably longer than her own, Rhia's fingers itched to play in it. She hadn't seen a man with hair this long and soft-looking since the king of Gaia visited when she was little.

Must be a Gaian thing.

She cocked her head to the side.

I think I like Gaian things.

She bit her lip when the words almost slipped out of her mouth.

What words described such a fine specimen of a man? It didn't matter because she'd never get to do more than look at him. She had her duties to her people, and they didn't include this or any other Gaian. After all, even if she wanted to be mated to RuArk, it would mean leaving her home. Not happening. And she wasn't silly enough to think that a man like RuArk Miwatani would leave Gaia for her.

In the end, duty was all she knew, what she was good at.

For once in, well, ever, she wished her life was more than fucking duty… for a moment, anyway.

"Rhia?"

"Yes, father?" Still looking up at RuArk, her throat worked convulsively as she met his stormy gray gaze. She watched him watch her through a mask of unreadable lines. Then those stormy grays softened to a glowing silver, like the sun reflecting off the soft mists that caressed the valley after an early spring rain. This barely visible transformation from hard ass warrior to simple man, well it… moved her.

"Rhia?" the High Counsel called again.

Her father's voice seemed off in the distance as her mind was trying to catch up with the dancing in her blood. She wondered at his size, his height. There wasn't one soldier in the High City she couldn't stand toe to toe with. It was an uncommon experience to stand in front of a man whose chest was level with her mouth. She licked her lips at the thought of what that chest might feel like if she pressed her face against it.

Boy, he sure has grown up to be beautiful.

"Rhia, RuArk is here because I sent for him."

Well, she'd figured that part out all ready.

"To be your mate."

Stunned her out of her sensual daze, she turned shocked, unbelieving eyes on the man who'd sired her.

"What?"

"You heard me. It's past time you chose someone anyway."

"But I *didn't* choose," she countered, fists finding their way to her hips as one sandaled foot tapped out her annoyance.

The High Counsel waved away her protest. "What difference does it make? He's an honorable man and I believe he meets your, uh, special criteria seeing he came out of that little wrestling match of yours in one piece."

Rhia's entire body felt as if it were on fire as she blushed clear down to her toes. "Did you really just bring that up, dad? Seriously?" RuArk glanced back and forth between her and her father, clearly wondering what he was missing in the conversation. Well, she sure as hell wasn't going to clue him in on the 'requirement' her father had just mentioned. No way in hell.

Oh, this subject had to be changed and fast. Rhia pushed down her rising angst and tried to keep her voice from rising. She'd never been much of a screamer, but this situation might just call for it.

Gesturing toward the giant next to her, she said, "Father, I don't even know this man." It wasn't quite true, but so what.

"You've known him forever; you just haven't seen him in a while. Besides, that doesn't matter. You need RuArk."

"Need? Father, I don't *need* anyone. You of all people, should know that."

Suddenly her father looked old. Tired. With a sigh, he slowly pushed away from the mantle and crossed the short distance to stand in front of her. His expression was somber, strained.

"Rhia, I can't keep this from you any longer."

Tilting her head, she quirked a brow as her gut began to free fall. What the hell was going on here? Spine stiffened with a chill, unsure of what he was talking about, but positive it couldn't be good.

"There's a plot against our family, against you in particular. RuArk is here to look into the matter and protect you."

"Father, I've been in danger every day of my life. My job is dangerous. Just being First Heir is a risk. There've been rumors of plots to overthrow our family since the inception of this province. Has it ever happened? No," she countered.

"Rhia, this time is different."

"Father, if this so-called plot is real, you know I won't run. I'd rather fight and —"

"And what," he flared. "Die? You'd rather die than lay down your damn pride?"

Her *damn pride* was all that kept her going. It was the reason she worked as hard as she did. Stung, but unmoved by the rebuke, the soldier inside of her squared her shoulders, not even close to giving in to her father's suggestion.

"Look, Rhia, we can talk about this as much as you like, but in the end you're going to join with RuArk. As for not needing anyone, you probably owe this man more than you care to admit seeing he rid you of some unwelcome company a few evenings ago."

Blasted hell.

"Tattletale," she ground out of the side of her mouth. Eyes sparkling with mischief, RuArk grinned shamelessly and executed an elegant bow. She wanted to kick him in the shin.

Grey turned to RuArk. "So, when would you like to leave for Draema Neine? The sooner the better, I think."

"Let's leave that decision for later. We will finish the tasks here first, then leave for our new home." RuArk glanced at Rhia and she felt her disgruntled expression grow into a confused one. Again he let his gaze rove over her body and she felt her face change colors as yet another blush stole across her cheeks.

Forcing herself to focus on something other than the way this man made her stomach wiggle, she asked, "What tasks? What new home?" she demanded, not missing the fact that the younger man was telling the High Counsel how things were going to go down.

The two men continued talking about plans that were obviously already laid. When had all this occurred and where had she been to miss it? Neither invited her to sit when they reclined comfortably in the plush chairs in front of the fireplace to enjoy the warmth that blazed within the old relic. Again, Rhia's fist slammed into the favored spot on her hip and a foot tap, tap, tapped.

Her father didn't even bother turning to look at

her when he asked, "Oh, I'm sorry Rhia, did you say something?"

The skin on her forehead felt tight as furrowed brows created a fierce scowl on her ever-heating face. But she wasn't embarrassed. No. Now, she was pissed.

Muscles tense, she took a deep breath and forced her voice to lose the edge that she felt creeping into it. "I asked what. New. Home?"

"I'm giving RuArk the township of Province Springs in Draema Neine."

Her mouth fell open as he continued speaking with his hand-picked son-in-law to-be. Thin patience had become microscopic patience. All the earlier attraction for RuArk that had danced along her nerve endings dissipated like so much smoke.

"You know RuArk, I failed to mention the colony of Neine has three townships. Yours is right on the Coalrado River with a natural harbor large enough to sail several ships right up to the piers. Do you fish? The estate is massive with low walls marking its perimeter and a deep freshwater lake sits about a half mile inside. The backside of your villa looks down on it. Beautiful view when the sun is setting."

"What of the fortifications?" RuArk asked seriously as the two of them continued to completely ignore her. Damn it, if she turned one more shade of red, she'd explode.

"There are three walls of protection. The province outer wall separates Draema from the Borderlands. It's forty feet of solid stone, gated, and guarded by the toughest soldiers Draema can provide. There's a two-mile buffer zone between the outer wall and the walls of Province Springs itself. Great trails for riding.

"Hovers don't work way out there since none of the roads are magnetized that far from the High City, not that you're interested in that kind of thing anyway. The buffer zone also has several roads to Draema Seine to the west, and Draema Salone to the south. Did I mention Draema Neine is a hub for the Society of Horse Breeders? We don't use horses much here in this part of the province, but you'll find prime horseflesh in Neine."

Rhia was appalled. Her father was actually bribing the man! No wonder RuArk had already agreed to leave Gaia. When she was finally addressed she was so angry the inside of her jaw ached furiously from clenching her teeth.

"So, Rhia, what do you think? I think you should mate right away, unless RuArk chooses some other date."

Teeth still clenched, she ground out, "Shouldn't I have a say in any of this? About who I spend my life with? And you're giving him Province Springs in exchange for me? Father, that's the most antiquated thing I've ever heard you say. We haven't observed that dowry bullshit in Draema since long before the world broke over seven hundred cycles ago."

"Well, the Gaian *do* observe that dowry bullshit and we'll honor them by observing their customs in this matter. It's been awhile since we've spoken of your mother, but don't forget she was Gaian, through and through. If not for RuArk's father, I never would have met such a lovely lady. Besides, your new lifemate must also give something for you, and all I've asked for is his protection."

It was true. They hadn't talked about her mother in a very long time. Rhia was eight when she'd died.

She missed her so much that even after all this time, it was still a painful business to even think about. Her father would bring her up now to manipulate this farce of a mating? Obviously so.

Blasted men.

The High Counsel pressed his advantage. "As for choices, I allowed you to *choose* whether to make that little trip to the Physicians or not. You should have received a partner or Sensuan at the Age of Consent. Now, you're past the Age of Consent *and* the *mandatory* Age for Joining. Leaving you alone about it was my way of allowing you to make the choice when you were ready, even though I was breaking the law. But I can't leave things this way, Rhia. Not anymore."

Gods, she hoped RuArk didn't know what the High Counsel was talking about. She felt like her flame streaked hair was ablaze.

"Rhia, you know I love you more than anything in this world. This will be good for you and all of Draema. Trust me."

This couldn't be happening. It felt as if she was being thrown off a pier, arms wind-milling wildly as she teetered on the edge of a dock. And gods knew she couldn't swim. "B-But who will take care of all my students? Who will see to my responsibilities?" It was all she knew. All she'd had for too many years to count.

Grey Greysomne faced her with love and pride shining in his eyes. For the first time in a very long while, he hugged her tightly to him. When he stepped away, the loving father had disappeared as quickly as the warmth from his arms had. The High Counsel bore the stern expression of a ruler bent on his duty.

"As First Heir, your first responsibility is to obey the High Counsel. Your second is to provide the next

First Heir. That's something you can't quite do by yourself, no matter how good you are at being a soldier."

Then the High Counsel and Commander-In-Chief of the Society of War played his last hand.

"This is a direct order, Rhia."

Damn it, she couldn't disobey now. There was only one person who outranked her in the Society of War, and that was Grey Greysomne himself. Swallowing her frustration Rhia lifted her chin, squared her shoulders, and gave him the words he wanted to hear. After all, if there was one thing she understood, it was duty.

Fuck.

With a deep breath and a steady timbre in her voice, she said, "Yes, sir."

CHAPTER NINE

Her words were calm and solid, but there was no missing the fire in her eyes. The woman was angry, but better angry than dead. And if the sultry heat in her gaze when she'd looked him over was any indication, given time his little warrior might just come to desire him.

Grey quickly stepped over to a small table and snatched up a carafe of wine and filled an exquisite crystal glass. He held it out to RuArk. With a dip of his head, RuArk accepted.

"And now for the words," the High Counsel insisted. As if summoned on cue, which he was, Mannon stepped into the room and witnessed the short ceremony.

After following the High Counsel through the exchange of vows, RuArk drank half the contents in the goblet as a symbol of joining his life to Rhia's, and then he passed the wine to her. Rhia held her calm resolve and appeared to release her anger in a soft huff and drank deeply. She never took her beautiful eyes off of him, not even when Mannon produced the declaration for the official records. All three signed with Mannon as the witness to the joining.

He marveled inwardly at the tightening of his chest—it was pride, plain and simple. This was an accomplished woman standing before him. Strong. Smart. Funny in her own stubborn way. Hardheaded, but honorable. Add to that the intense attraction he felt for her and he couldn't have been happier.

Happy was one thing. But time would tell whether he was being wise. After all, he may be accepting of this union, but Rhia didn't appear to be all that awed by the prospect. None the less, she was, as of this moment, officially his.

"It's a done deal," the High Counsel crowed and practically yanked Rhia into RuArk's arms. "Now, if you two will excuse me, I'll have Mannon make arrangements for the delivery of the deed to the Province Springs estate, as well as having this document entered into Rhia's files so the union cannot be challenged, though we won't announce anything yet. You two talk for a while. In private. We'll have dinner in the hall tonight. Mannon, let's go. And Rhia, please try to be on time."

The slight hum in his soul suddenly burst into a deep almost tangible rhythm, as if he were tuning himself to Rhia's unique song. Along with this awakening of sorts came the need, the desire to be closer. Instinctively reaching for his Source, he started when he felt Rhia's flare in response.

Ah, there it is. She recognizes me, my spirit. RuArk watched her honey brown eyes widen, then darken as she took him in. Hmm. The puzzled expression that crossed her lovely face was a bit of a surprise, though a pleasant one. For once in all his wondering since he'd learned Rhia hadn't truly been taught about her mother's people, RuArk was selfishly glad she'd not shared or touched her Source with another. And it would be his pleasure to teach her that there was more to it than what she'd just experienced.

"Rhia? Did you hear me? Be on time."

"I am *always* on time," she snapped back.

"Riiiight," her father called over his shoulder. The word rang with a certain *'of course you are'* quality. Humming softly and almost dancing across the thickly carpeted floor, the High Counsel tapped the wall lock and sailed out the door with Mannon on his heels.

As soon as they were alone, Rhia rounded on him. "You told my father what happened that night in my apartments?"

RuArk grinned. The little fireball challenged him even now. Well, the beauty certainly had heart, doing what most grown warriors wouldn't dare. His head tilted and he regarded her without a word. She obviously couldn't have cared less about his answer anyway and plowed right on ahead with her left toe tapping away on the carpet once again.

"Did you also tell him I had Bryan under control and you butted in where you weren't *needed*?"

"I told him you had things well in hand prior to my arrival, yes." RuArk moved into her space. He was so close, the heat radiating from her wonderfully lush body brought her unique scent to his nostrils. Mmm, it was so enticing, like fresh cinnamon swirled into the sweet red wine they'd just drank. Fingers flexed as he resisted the urge to slide them up and down her bare arms.

"I love the way you smell."

Her hips jerked, as if her first instinct was to back up a step, but her feet rooted themselves to the spot anyway. Skin flushed and her scent burned brighter, filling the bit of space between them. She turned away when her mouth worked, but nothing came out.

Speechless twice in one day? It had to be a record.

Unable to resist the urge to touch her a second longer, he took her gently by an arm and eased her back around to face him once more. The backs of his fingers teased her jawline and softly stroked her cheek. It felt like... like luring a wild cat or a raptor bird. But not into a trap. No, never that. More like getting the fiercest natural hunters to trust, to accept, and perhaps gentled to his touch without worrying about losing his hand.

Finally, she said, "RuArk, look, I'm sorry. I don't know about this. I need some time to get used to you, get to know you again. The RuArk I knew cycles ago has been gone for so long, I don't know you anymore."

"But you will like this RuArk so much better than the boy you knew. I promise you that, Rhia."

RuArk's thumb traced the path her tongue had just taken across her bottom lip. What was happening to him? His resolve to accept his destiny with this woman didn't waver, but his legendary self-control marched resolutely South until it hung by a thread, looped around his cock. The last thing he needed to do was kiss the little firebrand, but for all the world he couldn't help it.

His arms closed around her and she had just enough time to look surprised before he kissed her breathless.

Yes, she'd shared a few kisses in her lifetime, but there'd been no passion, no hunger. Just a meeting of lips. The end.

So why did RuArk's touch ignite her like a flame put to raw, unfiltered iozene?

Strong but gentle fingers seemed to burn through her jumpsuit as he deepened the kiss. She moaned into his mouth as he leaned her backward. When she felt the probe of his tongue, it seemed natural to open for him.

He tasted of wine and coffee laced with sweet, dark chocolate. Blazes, she never knew lips could feel this good, be this hot or deliciously wicked. God, she could kiss him forever.

Though unsure she was doing it right, Rhia let instinct take over, moving her mouth beneath his. For a few moments, she forgot that she'd been forced into a joining, that she had no desire to change her life and go haring off to Draema Neine, or run from whatever threat had been discovered.

For a few moments, she was simply a woman absolutely turned on by a man, and took from the enthralling kiss as much as she gave.

Thinking became completely out of the question when RuArk groaned in the back of his throat. The vibrations traveled from his lips to hers, and straight down her spine, leaving a tingling trail down her back. She trembled as his hands smoothed over the lines of her hips, leaving nothing but gooseflesh and quivering muscle behind.

Would sex light her up as much as the simple act of meeting his mouth with her own? She hoped so.

RuArk pulled back long enough to ask, "Your

permission to touch you here?" Swift intakes accompanied the tap of his firm hands against her left ass cheek.

"Absolutely yes." Arms wrapped around her now, there was no doubt to how much he enjoyed having her close when his engorged sex pressed flush against her belly. The thick ridge seared through her jumpsuit, reached for her, alive and throbbing. Rhia melted. The slow burn in her gut was fanned to a living flame so hot it burned away what little wits she had left. Did that little moan come out of her throat? More importantly, did she really care?

RuArk released her mouth to nibble along the soft flesh of her neck. She started when he nipped the spot just below her ear that she hadn't even known was sensitive. His lips were so warm and soft. She was done for.

"RuArk," she breathed raggedly, tilting her head to give him better access to another sweet spot at the hollow where her shoulder and neck muscles met. He nipped her again. She hissed through her teeth, it felt so good.

"You're mine, Rhia," he whispered, as soft as a butterfly's wing against her ear. "And I," he nipped the tight tendons of her neck again, "am all yours."

Her head fell back as if the muscles were made of wet paper. She couldn't help it. Goodness, it was all she could do to form words when all she really wanted to do was pour herself all over this man. This man who had waltzed into her life, then into her dreams with such boldness she was taken aback, set off center until she teetered on the edge of herself.

A self she'd worked too fucking hard to define to lose now.

Gee, way to douse yourself with cold water, Rhia.

Perhaps some conversation would help her get her wits back.

"So…" He rubbed his cheek against hers, then kissed a path down her jaw. Okay, that felt good.

All right, let's try that talking thing again.

"So, uh, where have you been all these years?" She knew the answer, but wanted to hear him tell it. Needed to rein it in a bit.

"I've been looking after my people, protecting them, as is my duty. For the last several years I visited Draema Proper to renew the yearly contracts with your father. I wanted to visit with you, but you were always somewhere else."

Yep, she knew that because she'd been careful to find herself in field training each and every time. Why? Because he was, and had always been the only man who could move her this way. She also knew she couldn't have him, so what was the point of trying to maintain a friendship with him over the years? No, she'd had things to do, rank to earn and a status to secure. Now, as he kissed a moist, breath-stealing trail along her throat, not a single reason that came to mind for avoiding him made any sense.

And he was moving that lovely mouth over hers again.

After a few moments, she broke away. Rhia didn't remember grabbing big handfuls of his clothing, but she was certainly scrunching it good as she gulped mouthfuls of air like she'd run a six-minute mile. She'd grown up learning plenty about the mechanics of sex. She'd even hoped to have a strong attraction to whoever her potential mate might be. But this? This was beyond strong attraction. It was tumultuous and potent as cherry brandy. She stood there like a newly foaled colt, wide-eyed and wobbly kneed, thankful when RuArk's hands lightly stroked the muscles on either side of her spine. Not to bring her to passion, but to soothe and relax as they stood in silence for a moment.

Once her wits settled in her head, they brought along some unwelcome company—embarrassment. Here stood a man who'd been bribed to marry her and she'd practically dissolved under his touch. Damn, she'd never known herself to be the easy type. And she wasn't going to start now. Mate or not, he was going to have to work to win her affection. Wasn't he?

"I, uh, I need to take care... Of, uh... My duties," she said lamely, turning her face up to see a self-satisfied grin planted on the face of a very pleased RuArk. He'd knocked her socks off and he knew it. His ardor had come down a notch, his expression neutral, but she knew a gloat when she saw one. Her temper snapped into place like a newly strung bowstring.

"Do you have to be so blasted arrogant?"

"Of course. I am a Gaian male and it is my duty to pleasure you. I'm *supposed* to be good at it."

"I'm supposed to be good at it," she mocked, then tensed. Something moved in her periphery and she was instantly primed to protect herself. She turned and met the eyes of the woman who'd been at RuArk's side the night Bryan had been tossed down the tower stairs.

Absolutely still in a shrouded corner of the room, she stood in a skimpy outfit similar to the one she'd worn the night. Rhia made out the woman's weapon, a bow, barely visible in the shadows. What the hell was she doing in here?

All the fluttering in her womb vanished, replaced by an icy chill to match her new disposition. She pushed against RuArk's arms, but she may as well have tried to move a ton of Draeman stone. She finally gave up and settled for glaring up at him while he continued to stroke lazy circles down the middle of her back as if nothing was wrong.

"Why are you suddenly angry, Rhia?" RuArk asked.

"That's why I'm angry," she said, pointing to the shadows where the woman stood. "I had no intention of sharing intimate moments in front of an audience, RuArk." Especially a moment that sapped her will and weakened her knees. And she'd abandoned herself to it like a feline in heat. Not that she'd ever seen a feline in heat, but that was beside the point.

"You could have refused," he said in a soft, but matter-of-fact tone, bending forward to nuzzle her hair just behind her ear. The base of her spine started to tingle and she pushed away from him again. This time RuArk loosened his hold, but didn't give any ground. She craned her neck and scowled up at him.

"It didn't cross my mind to refuse your kiss, blast it!" she hissed.

RuArk flashed a self-assured, warrior's smile and said, "I know."

Rhia rolled her eyes. He was right, but he didn't have to *act* so right about it.

"Arrogant bastard. Keep your bloody kisses." She swung around on her heel and stalked away, a confused jumble of anger, desire and just plain '*grrrr*'. Just as she reached the door, she turned on her heel.

"My father thinks I need you. I'm woman enough to admit my body wants you, but I certainly don't *need* you. I suggest you get to understanding the difference, warrior."

He shook his head at her as one side of his sexy mouth lifted in a smirk.

Rhia rolled her eyes and slammed the door as she left him in her father's office. Now all she had to do was figure out why the hell she was so jealously upset, and whether she was mad at him... or herself.

CHAPTER TEN

Back in her apartments, Rhia peeled off her jumpsuit and exchanged it for a pair of black trousers, a white synthsilk shirt, black riding boots and a light cloak. A quick stop at the dining table to sniff a creamy bowl of typical, tasteless Draeman soup had her wincing. It smelled like paint. She glanced at the pot of lukewarm tea sitting next to it and curled her lip.

"Blasted tea," she grumbled. Sara knew she hated the stuff. Why in hell had she started putting it on the tray for Brita to bring it to her rather than her regular coffee? Yuck. With a slam, the lid was replaced and Rhia settled for a piece of fruit and headed to the stables.

Groomed and fitted with light reins and no bit, Moonlight was led quietly to the rear of the Citadel. Rhia rode out of the grounds, out of the High City and into the buffer zone that separated this colony from its neighbors, Draema Seine to the East and Draema Salone to the South.

Hovers were the preferred mode of transportation in Draema Proper. The lightweight, floating vehicles ran smoothly and quietly on magnetized roads. While they were wonderfully efficient for travel inside the huge City, Rhia was a nature girl. She loved the feel of her horse as it stretched out beneath her, strong and alive, as they flew through the parks and along the trails. She much preferred the rays of the sun on her face than the warmth filtered through the sunshield of a hover any day.

Once out on the trails, she inhaled deeply, taking in the natural elements around her. The trails smelled of rich earth and fresh green grass, and were lined with bright green stalks and blooming honeysuckle. The land was alive with vines and plants, all budding in anticipation of full Spring.

Pondering her morning, it all seemed surreal in a cackle-inducing kind of way.

In just a few hours she'd had a fight with a big Gaian warrior and lost, followed by an order to mate with that same warrior. Then came a kiss that turned her brains to mush, and a dusky beauty who'd watched it all. Her physical reaction to RuArk bordered on insane. Fireworks had gone off in her brain, heat gathered in her womb. Maybe she wasn't normal? Maybe her lack of intimacy, cycle after cycle contributed to her horny state? No, her abstinence had been by choice. If she had to do it all over again, she couldn't think of anything she'd have done differently.

So preoccupied with trying to figure it out, the hours passed, yet the groomed rolling hills and endless meadows with sprigs of budding colorful flowers went unnoticed. So did the gathering clouds.

She flinched when the first fat raindrop splashed coldly on the tip of her nose several miles from home. Though it was early afternoon, the cloud-darkened sky made it feel more like evening.

By the time Rhia found herself standing in front of a typical white stone two-story cottage in a neat row of homes a couple of rings from the citadel, she was miserably cold and wet.

A robed Joan opened the door, took one look and left Rhia dripping puddles on the covered porch.

"Lose the shoes and all those wet clothes, Rhia. You look like a drowned rat."

"You've never seen a rat, drowned or otherwise," Rhia mumbled, removing her soggy boots. She placed them in a large basket next to the front door along with her light cloak and every stitch of clothing. Teeth chattering, she stepped over the threshold and closed the door behind her.

Joan held out a thick robe of soft spun crème wool and a matching towel. The fabric felt like silk, was as thick as old-fashioned looped wool, but not the least bit scratchy.

"Ree, what are you doing riding out in this rain? Go over to the couch and dry your hair in front of the fireplace. I'll fix you some tea."

Joan chuckled at the expression on Rhia's scrunched up face.

"I'm kidding. I know you hate the stuff. How about some coffee?"

Rhia donned the robe quickly and made her way to the impressive and equally familiar living area. Everything in Joan's house was white and immaculately clean. Thick, plush carpets in which Rhia loved to wiggle her toes, complimented the comfortable couch with its huge overstuffed cushions that sat in front of the iozene fireplace. Even the glass table in front of the couch had a sparkling white stone-looking base with silver slivers running through it. Rhia sat and inhaled her favorite scents which wafted from Joan's kitchen—cinnamon, apples and, thankfully, coffee.

Joan called out. "What's going on? You look a bit out of sorts and you smell like wet Moonlight."

Damn it. Just beginning to relax, Joan's question caused Rhia to stiffen up all over again.

"Well, with that answer, or lack of, I think you need something a bit stronger than coffee. I've just mulled some wine. I'll serve it up and let's cut to the chase."

Joan poured two mugs of wine and joined Rhia in the living room. The wafting scent of honey and spices always reminded her of the Christentide holidays. After moments of sitting without either of them talking, Joan ran out of patience. Never one to beat around the bush, her best friend leaned forward, sat her mug on the table in front of the sofa, and turned an impatient glare on an already irritated Rhia.

"Alright woman, what happened in the meeting with your father? And who was that gorgeous hunk you challenged this morning? He looked awfully familiar, but I couldn't place him, especially given the wildness of the, uh, situation."

Joan the diplomat. Bleh.

After a fortifying gulp of warm red, Rhia scooted down into the plush cushions of the couch.

"He's RuArk Miwatani," she said with a clearly disgruntled sigh.

"RuArk Miwa…? Wait, he hasn't been around in forever. I remember you used to chase him around with your practice sword when we were kids. The last time we saw him, he was going off to train to fulfill his duties as Protector of the Realm of Gaia. That was him in the circle this morning? *That* hunk of male perfection is RuArk Miwatani?"

"Yep. That's the one," Rhia spoke into her cup, obviously none too happy.

Joan crowed. "Oh, Rhia, he's totally gorgeous. What's he doing here? And acting like he's new in the High Counsel's service when he's known your father all his life."

'He's in the High Counsel's service, all right,' Rhia thought, taking another large swallow of hot, spicy wine.

"So, what did your father want to talk to you about? Are you in trouble for that spectacle in the training pavilion this morning?"

"No, I'm not in trouble. I'm mated."

"What the fu...? Mated? For rolling in the mud? To that fine as hell warrior? Maybe I need to go roll in the mud. They haven't cleaned it all up yet have they?"

"I'm serious, Joan."

"So am I," she squealed, scooting just out of reach as Rhia tried to pinch her.

"My father called me to his study to tell me RuArk is here because he sent for him. To mate with me on a totally permanent basis."

Joan, in the middle of pouring herself a second mug of mulled wine, promptly sat the kettle down with a loud thunk on the thick glass of the living room table.

"Well, he certainly meets your criteria of you not wanting a man you can pound into the floor, eh?"

"Is that all anyone has to say about the man? That he meets my criteria?" Rhia, wine forgotten, was now on her feet, pacing, as Joan's robe flapped around her knees.

"So, what's the problem?" Joan asked.

"I haven't seen him in, what, ten or fifteen

cycles? He was never really mean to me, but it doesn't change the fact that he did tease me back then." And she'd carried such a torch... No, no, scratch that. "What if he's become a total asshole? Besides, I just don't feel like myself where he's concerned." He was overwhelming. And he would expect her to surrender to him. But 'surrender' just wasn't something she knew how to do.

"You can't possibly be upset because you've caught the most gorgeous man on this side of the border who happens to be an old family friend *and* the son of a king? Not to mention he's a warlord."

"I just don't see why RuArk's profession is important in all of this. What does it have to do with me having to uproot and leave behind everything I know?"

"Everything you know? You're going to Gaia?"

"No, Draema Neine."

"Rhia, you aren't making any sense. You're staying in your own province and he is leaving his. For you. But you're upset? Not to mention this man is worthy of joining with the First Heir. Even I know they call him the Wind Storm. None of his enemies have ever been able to catch or track him. And he's never lost a battle. Ever. Why do you think we keep petitioning the Gaian to allow our soldiers to train under him? We don't do much warring with our neighbors, but Gaia has to keep the Borderlands in order, plus those wild assed, unsettled provinces to the North. Tough job, that."

Rhia sat wide-eyed and tongue-tied. She'd been so out of sorts about the mating business and her insane desire for her bodyguard-husband, she hadn't taken the time to think about *who* he really was. He wasn't *just* the boy she knew. Not anymore. As much as she'd ignored her Gaian heritage over the years, even she was familiar with the stories around the Wind Storm of Gaia.

It was well known that Gaia had the best trained assassins. Skilled soldiers from other provinces petitioned Gaia yearly for a spot as one of the Wind Storm's soldiers. It was almost unheard of for an outsider to be accepted among those giants, but many tried anyway.

Wind Storm? Yep, she knew all about him. What she hadn't known was that RuArk, *her* RuArk, was the man behind the myth.

She had a living legend in her father's house and hadn't even realized it. She knew of his exploits, all of his battles. Everything. She'd battled, kissed, married and then told off the Wind Storm? Blasted fucking hell.

"I made a complete fool of myself today. What am I going to do? And stop gaping at me!" She knew Joan was shocked to hear such a confession from her. Rhia didn't usually care what anyone thought about anything she did. But for some reason, she cared about what RuArk thought of her.

"You tried your best to beat him Rhia. You should be glad you didn't succeed."

"I'm not talking about that."

"Well, what the blasted hell are you talking about then? For goodness sake, Rhia, he's not a Noman from the storybooks. What's wrong with you?"

"I've told him off, challenged him to a blade contest, and... Oh hell, when I see this guy my heart leaps into my throat and I just lose it and I don't know why. My father says he's a good man and thinks I need him to protect me." She was very careful *not* to say what RuArk was supposed to be protecting her from. "But I was given no choice in the matter, none at all. And what if he's not being straight with me? After all, Bryan Collaidh had been a perfect gentleman when I first met him and…"

"Will you forget about that Bryan idiot? He has nothing to do with this. I'm so tired of hearing about him and all the other assholes every time a potential mate stumbles across your path. This is what you'll do, woman. The next time you see RuArk, be receptive. Give him a chance, Ree. Your father's not stupid. And neither are you. Do you honestly think that just because you haven't seen RuArk in a long time that it's changed who he is at his core? More importantly, would your father bring him here if that was the case? It won't hurt to trust him unless he gives you a reason not to."

There was no arguing with Joan's reasoning, though she really wanted to. So instead Rhia sat, sipped, and then sipped some more.

After gathering up their cups, Joan tapped her shoulder in a show of camaraderie. "Hey, it's getting late. Grab your wet stuff and I'll walk you home. I would suggest we take my shiny new conveyance, but the thing is more of a pain to get out of the drive than to simply walk such a short distance. You can borrow some of my clothes to get back to the Citadel."

"You know your clothes don't fit me. They're cut too short, but fit too large."

"Well, you can go naked. I'm sure RuArk wouldn't mind if…"

"Oh, shut it, smart ass."

"You know I love you, Ree."

"Yeah, yeah, just give me the blasted clothes. And bring something for yourself. We're having dinner with my father tonight. You can meet, or rather *re*-meet RuArk."

"Re-meet? You know that's not a word, Rhia."

"Oh, hush already." Yet there was no suppressing the wiggle in her belly at the thought of seeing that man again.

Sigh.

Marth stilled in his chosen corner of the huge stables to watch and listen as the two women turned Rhia's horse over to the groomsmen.

Other than the young boy who'd delivered his message about RuArk and Rhia fighting this morning, Marth had allowed no one to see him since the day they'd arrived. But tonight he would reveal himself and Joan Rouillard was the reason. At home in Gaia, he'd never seen anyone like her. She was so beautifully dark, her skin as smooth as chocolate silk. Her short, curly hair was as light as summer sunlight, beyond blonde and contrasted brilliantly against her dark skin.

He'd trailed Rhia daily, and since the two women were together often, he'd become pretty familiar with Joan as well. He couldn't help but compare them and Joan caught his eye every time. Rhia was tall and femininely muscular, but Joan, who was obviously fit, had everything in abundance. Her breasts were full, her hips wide. Marth was a big man and Joan was the kind of woman he could wrap his arms around without fear of breaking anything. The only parts that appeared dainty were her small waist and little feet. Perhaps he'd get a chance to span his hands across that waist and nibble on those feet.

"Joan, it's almost o-seventeen hundred. We only have an hour to get ready for dinner."

Joan slowed, then stopped altogether in the stable's gigantic double doors, looking back toward the stalls as Rhia stepped out into the still-pouring rain.

"Joan, can't you move a little faster?"

Marth smiled in the shadows when Joan didn't answer, but looked back in the direction of his hiding spot, trying to see into the shadows. Rhia stood in the doorway and peered past Joan's shoulder trying to see what her friend was looking at, but he knew all she saw was the back of Moonlight's rump as the groomsman led the huge mount away.

"I thought I saw something," Joan said. "I'll be right along. Just give me a minute."

Rhia called over her shoulder as she turned and disappeared into the gloom. "Sure. I'll have a bath ready for you when you get to my place. Hurry up and get out of this weather."

Joan stood just inside the stable doors, watching Rhia move her quickly along the tiled walk leading up to the wide stone steps of the High Counsel's residence. When the woman turned back around, her eyes widened as Marth moved slowly across the large building, headed right for her.

"Hello, my name is Joan. I'm a friend of Rhia's. You came with RuArk from Gaia, didn't you?"

"Yes."

"Are you joining us for dinner in the hall?" she asked, her voice deepening with a sensuous quality that made the base of Marth's spine tingle. Being this close to Joan wreaked havoc on his senses. He didn't see any point in playing games with her or trying to hide his attraction.

"No," he spoke gently, appearing to lean casually against a hitching post, but he was all predator. He let her see it in his eyes as they traveled slowly from her cropped, platinum curls down to her small booted feet. She dipped her head at his assessment and gave him something else to adore—a deep dimple on her right cheek.

"You don't say much, do you?"

"No," his grin widened.

"Well, nice to meet you. Perhaps you'll change your mind about dinner," she said, offering her hand for a friendly shake.

He took her extended fingers, stepped deliberately too close and raised it to his lips. Turning the palm up, he planted an intimate kiss on the inside of her wrist. Her dark brown eyes clashed with his flaming green ones. Knowing she was as much a warrior as he was, he held back a grin when she demurely lowered her lashes. She moved away and off into the rain muttering under her breath.

"If all Gaian are like you, perhaps I need to get me one."

Marth would ensure her words became truth. He was a warrior. And when a warrior saw something he wanted, he would have it.

CHAPTER ELEVEN

RuArk stood on the landing near the top of the tower atrium, brooding as he pondered the woman he'd been sent to protect. In spite of Rhia's noble status and outrageous behavior, she had yet to whine, cry or connive her way out of facing the consequences of her actions in the pavilion this morning. Nor had she balked when he and her father said the words that made her his forever. RuArk was reluctantly impressed, which made his mood all the more sour, though for the life of him, he had no idea why.

He prided himself on his patience and iron control, but Rhia stretched both to their limits. The woman had gone off riding alone, not an hour after her father told her of a plot against her life. RuArk had never put his hand to a woman, but by the time Marth reported her safe return just before their scheduled dinner, he'd been ready to lay her over his knee. Stiff-necked. Stubborn. Luscious and so—yes, a Draeman word was more than appropriate just now—*fucking* beautiful.

The one woman who turned his common sense inside out, didn't want anything to do with him. Oh, she may have taken the vows, may even find his touch hard to resist, but that didn't mean her heart was in it. Interesting. Wooing a woman wasn't an activity he typically engaged in, yet found himself strangely exhilarated by the thought of the chase.

Eyes raised in quiet supplication, RuArk whispered a prayer to the Ancestors. "You have gotten me into joining with this woman. I expect you to guide me through it. Or at least help me to stay sane."

His gaze shifted to Rhia's door at the barely-there sound of a soft *schnick* followed by metal gliding on well-oiled guides.

Finally. What did a woman do that made getting dressed take so long?

Rhia and her best friend stepped out onto the landing. RuArk continued to lean against the wall as if he hadn't a care, yet his head had taken off into the atmosphere at the sight of her. His body tightened until his skin felt snug from neck to knees. Thankful for a long dress tunic he forced his hands not to adjust the quickly filling cock in his leathers. It was times like these when he wished men weren't such visual creatures. And why in all the hells was this the only woman who got to him, who made him want to jump her and throttle her all at once? He raised his eyes again to the stars that shone through the glass ceiling above. With a snort and a subtle shake of his head, he hoped like hell his prayer had been heard.

"Good evening," Rhia said politely. If he didn't know better, he'd swear she tried not to smile. Definitely stubborn.

"It is indeed."

The two women moved toward the stairs with such feminine grace he could almost forget Rhia's attempt to gut him like a fish, followed by the two of them mercilessly wailing on him with fists and feet.

He'd fully expected them to waltz into dinner wearing combat gear, boots and trousers. Or at the very least, one of those much-too-revealing one piece outfits Rhia had sported earlier.

Tonight she'd exchanged her soldier's garb for a silky-looking skirt. The matching short jacket was embroidered over the left breast with her family's sigil. The fit and flow of the fine material screamed sensuality as it clung to her hips, then fell in a silvery-gray swish around her knees as she walked. The high wedged shoes made his fingers want to trace the straps around her ankles and then travel part way up her muscled calf to play with the bare skin there.

The ensemble was finished off by a single strand of creamy white gems clasped around her throat to match her earrings.

Her hair was twisted up into an elegant style with wisps of red-streaked curls floating against her ears and nape. Perhaps he could play in it later.

He stepped to her, unsure what to do with his hands.

"Woman, you are simply beautiful. And your hair…" His words trailed off.

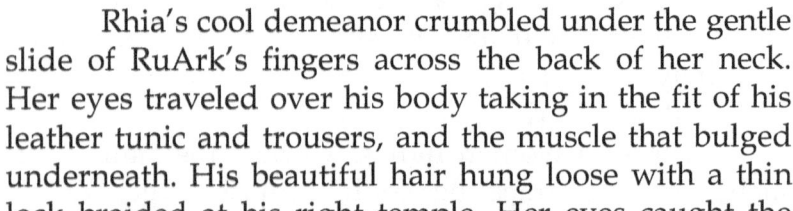

Rhia's cool demeanor crumbled under the gentle slide of RuArk's fingers across the back of her neck. Her eyes traveled over his body taking in the fit of his leather tunic and trousers, and the muscle that bulged underneath. His beautiful hair hung loose with a thin lock braided at his right temple. Her eyes caught the unusual ornament tied there—a small feather. A coup feather to be exact, taken with reverence from an animal extinct for at least a thousand cycles. Tiny red, black, yellow and white beads were woven down the shaft and it was tied to the braid with a thin leather thong.

Rhia might not know much about her mother's people in particular, but she knew her ancient history when it came to wars and battles. The Elders of many of the ancient races gave these ornaments to warriors who had shown great prowess in battle. Nothing like this was preserved in Draema. Even the Society of Antiquities, who kept the most complete museums, had only a few pieces of rare collectibles salvaged from the ruins after the Breaking.

The Gaian must hold their culture closer than anyone really knows, she thought.

She reached up to touch his raven locks, but pulled her hand back. What in blazes was she doing? She was First Heir and Blademaster. She couldn't be seen groping men in the hallways, even if she and RuArk were ma-, mar-, marri-... damn she couldn't even *think* the word.

Pretending to have her head together, she decided to keep up the pretense hoping it would eventually become reality.

She took a deep, steadying breath. Big mistake. His scent swirled around her like tendrils of smoke that made her want to inhale him. No candy-smelling man here. He was clean and musky. Almost spicy. Definitely all male. His hands still played at the base of her skull. The slight, rough texture of his fingers moved across her neck, tangling in the curls with a *brush, brush, brush* as he rubbed back and forth. The sensations combined on her skin and sent a buzz straight to her brain.

Blazes, her senses were on overload, but she stuffed them deep down inside and painted on a calm, confident expression. The shifting angle of RuArk's head and the barely noticeable stiffening of his spine told her he'd noticed her withdrawal, though she hadn't physically moved a muscle.

She took a step back at the intensity of his gaze. He closed the distance and enfolded her in his arms, his intentions clear as he lowered his head.

Oh blazes, he was kissing her again. Stole her thoughts, her very breath, swept her up in a torrent of want just as quickly and effectively as when he'd kissed her the first time early this morning. And she was honest enough with herself to admit she liked it. He held her tight against his chest and plundered her mouth with teeth and tongue until she kissed him back with such fervor there was no way they would make it to dinner.

Rhia lost herself in the taste and feel of him, sliding her hands down the lean lines of his body, taking in his masculine scent. Sweet grass and sage. She'd always liked sage. A growl sounded in his chest when Rhia leaned into him, reluctant yet honest in his wanting. She moved her mouth slowly, yet hungrily beneath his—needing, demanding more without words. His response to her touch was a welcome surprise. Good to know she wasn't the only one knee deep in the unexpected.

RuArk's eyes darkened from their gray hue to a deep molten silver. Lips slightly parted, he looked absolutely dreamy. He stroked her cheek and spoke, his voice a deep growl.

"I can envision going to bed and waking with wearing this same expression, your body wrapped around mine. Long legs draped over my longer ones."

Her body heated instantly.

Whoa. Who would have known that sexy talk would flip her switch like this?

His firm flesh beneath her fingers was such an aphrodisiac, Rhia had to force herself to separate mind from body just to regain a bit of control. She couldn't recall feeling such frantic craving for a man. Ever. Her mind splintered as his kisses became endless, sweet, erotic nips as he slowly, very slowly, released her.

Rhia jumped at Joan's quiet 'uh-hem'. Her body language solidified into the upright Blademaster again when she noticed two others standing with her best friend.

Turning to their audience, Rhia said sweetly, "Please, excuse us for a moment?" Grabbing RuArk by an elbow, she tried to lead him away from the others and back into her apartment. He crossed his arms over his chest again, his legs firmly apart.

"Will you come on?" she ground out, her lips tight, and the set of her jaw even tighter when RuArk didn't budge. With effort, she swallowed the sigh she wanted to release with all the dramatic ability she possessed. "I need to speak with you a moment. Please."

He leaned forward and whispered in her ear, "All you had to do was ask in the first place." His voice was even, though one side of his mouth lifted in amusement as he pulled away.

The wall lock clicked and the door slid open. The second it closed again, Rhia found herself backed up to the nearest wall.

When he released her, her lip sheen was non-existent and her breathing, erratic and deep. Each pull of air into her lungs sent a zing down to her sex that caused the traitorous organ to dance around in her underwear like it wanted to get out. Hell, she guessed it did want to get out after waiting so long for a man that actually got under her skin. But now wasn't the time for this nonsense. Even if it was filled with lots of 'feel good'.

Besides, she was supposed to be mad at RuArk. How dare he and her father decide her life for her. They had no right to force her into a marriage by playing on her honor.

They couldn't make her... Damn. It wasn't working. Her temper simply wasn't cooperating. It was too interested in how gently he touched her. He was careful not to push too far, too fast, one hand playing around her waist and the other teasing the skin just beneath her jaw.

So much for being pissed off. In fact, she was getting annoyed with her 'mad' for not showing up when it was supposed to. Mad was all she could think of to help stiffen her spine, to resist the ultimate loss— of herself.

Easing past him and away from the wall, she stalked further into the room, then stopped dead in her tracks. What the hell was she doing? Moving closer to a bed in the same room with RuArk was *so* not smart. She was sure she looked crazy backtracking, but who the hell cared when one's sanity was at stake?

"Do you have to kiss me like that? Twice in one day you've practically eaten me in front of that scarf wearing woman, and now in front of my best friend and some guy I've never even met."

———◆———◆———

Still standing near the door, RuArk leaned against the wall — he seemed to be doing that a lot lately where Rhia was concerned — and said nothing as the bright intuitive light in his mind flared on. His feisty, blade wielding beauty was embarrassed by her reaction to his touch. He filed that knowledge away and pressed his advantage.

Moving slowly and purposefully closer, he let his intentions flare in his eyes, let his gaze take on a dangerous glint as the lines of his face tightened with determination. At this moment, he was the Wind Storm. Predator. Hunter. And though he still couldn't believe it, *mate*.

When he was almost within touching distance she raised her hands, palms out, and braced her feet firmly apart as if to ward him off.

Pffft. As if.

He snorted, then laughed outright at her annoyed frown.

"You are my mate, Rhia. Thankfully, I am drawn to you. I am not totally out of control, but it is a close thing. Keep my hands to myself? I have no wish or will to do so." His fingers slipped up and over the soft skin of her arms. "As a warrior, it is a difficult thing to admit to any woman, even my own."

"Well, I want you to stop touching me until I get used to this marriage business." And then he heard the words drift across his subconscious, *'Because I lose it every time you touch me.'*

He took a moment to process what she'd

unknowingly let slip, then said, "I would gladly grant whatever you request..."

The triumph left her eyes, though she smiled anyway, probably because she'd won.

"... Except for what you just asked of me."

Rhia's brows snapped together and the grin was wiped away by a clearly frustrated sigh.

"You're just being difficult. Nothing new, that," she grumbled.

"What? Would you rather I dislike you? Not be attracted to you? Be disgusted by you? Woman, does that even make any sense?"

Of course it didn't make sense, but he knew she certainly wasn't going to admit it.

"We're late for dinner and the last thing I want is my father to walk up on me being eaten by a Gaian warrior in the hallway."

Gods, the visual her words created was absolutely sinful.

"Eaten by a Gaian warrior? I can't find a single thing wrong with that particular thought." He knew his expression was beyond wicked as he stepped toward her again. "Would you care to...?"

"Oh, hush. You know that's not what I meant."

"Are you sure?"

"Okay, time to go. And definitely time to change the subject," she snapped as she walked to the door, opened it, turned and said with as sweet a voice as he'd ever heard her use. "Can we go to dinner now? Please?"

"Was that so difficult to say?"

"You have no idea."

Oh, but he did.

Back out on the landing, he was glad to see his

companions speaking comfortably with Joan. "Rhia, please meet Linc and Sharyn, my First Commanders."

Rhia stuck her hand out in greeting and flashed a genuine smile to Linc. But when she turned to Sharyn, she extended the same greeting she'd given Linc, but her body language was altogether different. If Rhia's voice got any cooler or her back any stiffer she'd break into pieces.

RuArk wondered what that was about for as long as it took Rhia to start down the stairs. The lovely view of her backside knocked away the concern and his eyeballs tracked every movement, even as his heart began to engage.

Joan hoped that Rhia's unspoken jealousy about Sharyn's role in RuArk's company would fade now that the two women had been formally been introduced. The other woman's rank as First Commander would certainly explain why she was always with him, day or night. Unfortunately, the wispy thing she called clothes looked exactly as Rhia had described as she'd sat on Joan's couch soaked to the bone. While Rhia was prone to wear skimpy outfits too, even Joan had to admit that Sharyn's clothes were blatantly sensual.

Tonight the woman's shimmering jewel green sarand or saland or whatever it was called, floated about her body like the mists at the bottom of a waterfall. The rich color set off both her deep golden skin and jet black hair. Her bedroom eyes were deep brown and angled up at the corners like an exotic cat's.

Just like Rhia's.

Turning her attention away from the other woman, Joan concentrated fully on Linc. He was just as vibrant as when she'd met him in the stables not more than a standard hour ago. Yet, he seemed... different somehow. He'd been all business then, not even telling her his name. Now he had a ready smile and his unusual hazel-green eyes sparkled when he was into mischief or teasing RuArk. But his easy humor in no way made her think he was a fool. Fools were *not* First Commanders. Period.

Linc made his way to her side and took her hand through his arm as they walked toward the large hall for the evening meal. Joan waited for her cheeks to heat with blushes, for his nearness to send her wits into the ether, and was a bit perplexed when none of that happened. No breathlessness. No *zing*. Nothing. Perhaps she'd imagined her reaction to him earlier.

Joan smiled up at Linc, disappointed that her heart didn't race. Strange. It had practically galloped out of her chest when they'd met the first time. "So, you decided to join us for dinner after all?" she asked.

"Of course. I wouldn't miss it for the world."

"I'm glad. When we spoke earlier I didn't get your name."

"When we spoke earlier?" Linc said, bemused.

Joan tilted her head and smiled, puzzled. Perhaps he had a short memory or something? She knew it couldn't be a case of mistaken identity because there couldn't possibly be another man on the planet like this one.

"We're just meeting for the first time, I'm sure," Linc continued. "I would not forget skin such as yours. It reminds me of the fragrant beans we grow at home."

"Beans?" Joan scoffed, tilting her head again. She knew one of her platinum brows had shot up a good inch. She could hear Rhia giggle at the comparison. Joan thought about kicking Rhia in the backside for laughing as Linc explained.

"We grow coffee and cocoa beans in the fertile foothills of my province. You have tasted Gaian chocolate perhaps?"

"No, I don't believe I have."

"The fragrance is one of a kind." His voice was smooth and seductive. She looked up and gasped at the heat in his eyes, now a smoldering emerald green.

"And it makes the most delicious chocolate. Dark, rich and creamy. It melts in your mouth, in fact." He leaned in closer. "It will melt all over your fingers if you hold it in the palm of your hand." Towering over her, he breathed deeply, inhaling the fragrance of Joan's hair. "I can almost taste it," he whispered for her ears alone. Joan's mouth dropped open.

His words conjured such wicked pictures in her mind, she blushed to the roots of her curly blond hair. Surely her cheeks were some shade of purple. Draeman women were in no way demure about their sexuality, but goodness, his talk was far more erotic than anything she'd heard lately.

But still, no butterflies or squirrely stomach. Realizing she must have mistaken her attraction to this man when she'd seen him earlier, she quickly changed the subject to one of her favorite topics—horses. As she chatted, Linc's gaze locked on something just over her left shoulder and stilled. Expression distant, as if he listened to something no one else could hear, looked for something no one else could see. Then his brows drew taut and his expression cleared. The strange look was there for only a few seconds, and if she hadn't been watching him so closely Joan would have sworn she'd imagined it.

They almost ran into Rhia's back when she came to a screeching halt and then turned to face them.

"Rhia, what is it," RuArk asked softly.

"I-I'm not sure," she said "That was just weird."

"What?" they all asked at once.

"I'm sure it was nothing. Let's get into the hall. I'm starving."

"Rhia?" RuArk pressed.

Expression thoughtful, she said, "It was the strangest thing I've ever felt, like someone had brushed close by, only it was in my head like an echo or a shadow. Not like the prickly feeling I get when there's danger. Now that I think about it, I felt something similar when we were, uh..." She paused. "When we met earlier in my father's office."

Joan knew that what she'd left out was the whole kissing part of that particular meeting in the High Counsel's office. Perhaps her good friend had simply been zapped senseless by the man's sexuality.

"Don't worry about it. Right now there's simply too much going on in my life right now to worry about a few chills, RuArk."

RuArk obviously wasn't moved by Rhia's attempt to brush off whatever she'd just experienced. Joan bit back a smile when her friend attempted to change the subject.

"Do you know that when you're pissed, your speech switches back and forth between Draeman common and that old fashioned dialect I remember your father speaking when I was a child?" Rhia asked.

RuArk glared at her.

Okay, so he wasn't being distracted.

"I'm fine, RuArk. Seriously."

Joan glanced toward the others in their party. Sharyn wore what Rhia had described in confidence as the woman's serious-as-usual expression, and it clearly said that she didn't believe Rhia for a second. Too bad. Joan knew that Rhia didn't care in the slightest.

"We're going to be late. Let's get moving," Rhia said.

Ignoring the questioning looks of those around her, Rhia turned her attention to the hallway. The carpeted runner muffled their footsteps as they approached the dining hall. The noise of the gathering reached her ears long before they ever reached the wide-open double doors. The reason for the gathering stung, but was quickly washed away by the buzz of excitement pouring out of the room.

The positive vibe was strong, all because people had come to see this powerful man who walked calmly next to her. Part of her wanted to preen because he was technically hers. The other part of her that didn't appreciate the circumstances still wanted to kick him in the balls.

CHAPTER TWELVE

Their party of five entered together and were greeted by escorts who smiled and chatted as they led them to the gigantic table at the front of the room.

Tonight, the chandeliers and sconces were turned up high until the iozene gas-filled orbs cast a shimmer on everything, making it all brighter than usual so the splashes of color stood out in vast relief. Red and burgundy runners graced the tables. Potted evergreen trees with their light green spiky needles were strategically placed around the room, and their complimenting displays of greenery on each table sported little cream colored cones.

Now that they had the ability to bioengineer almost anything, they could make the most luxurious-looking objects and not feel guilty about it since the costs were minimal. The high table was an example of that. Made to look like the texture of wood, the top of it was a lovely shade of light brownish-pink that reminded her of the shells down near the southern shores at Harbor Station. Polished to a lustrous sheen she almost hated to eat on it, it was so beautiful.

Everything else was white, compliments of Draeman stone. With the exception of the gold accents along the top and bottom, the walls were white, coated with a clear substance that insulated yet let the natural color of the stone show through.

The High Counsel rose from his seat at the center of the high table and greeted them as RuArk was directed to the place of honor at his right hand, with Rhia next to him. Linc sat on the High Counsel's left and Joan at his side. Sharyn didn't sit or talk, but took up a position behind RuArk, surveying the growing crowd and closely watching the ambassadors from the neighboring provinces of Maine and Balear as they were seated.

Though the hall was huge, meals here were typically small fairs with just Rhia, her father, the commanders of the Society of War along with the top ranking members from the Society of Physics and Space, all talking about the usual events of the day or upcoming collaborative projects for new weapons or gear. Tonight, so many encroachers came to preen in front of the High Counsel's special guests that extra tables had been brought in just so the usual diners could have seats at all.

Rhia ground her back teeth—all of the Council of Seven had come. Dressed in the typical Draeman tunic and trousers done in silks and velvets in the colors of their Societies and Houses, they strutted into the hall with the sigils of their colonies practically plastered across their foreheads. Pushing through the throng, they seated themselves strategically among the guests at the high table. Their only goal was to wiggle their way into discussions with the visiting ambassadors on behalf of their individual colonies. Blasted parasites.

Rhia gave RuArk a nudge and subtly motioned

with her eyes for him to follow her line of vision. Well, they quietly agreed on one thing—nothing was more annoying than jockeying nobles. Perhaps the false rumor that he'd come to sign new trade agreements paid off too well.

At exactly six o'clock, the High Counsel sounded three chimes on a fine crystal bell etched with the Greysomne sigil. The hall fell quiet.

He raised a glass to RuArk and said, "In honor of our guests, we'll enjoy something seldom had since the great lady of this house passed on. A traditional Gaian meal." The entire hall sent up a collective gasp, some in great expectation of savoring such rich fare, and others in disgust as they imagined what was in the stuff. Rhia had to side with the ones whose stomach clenched with terror. Gaian food cooked by Draeman chefs? Yuck.

"Good evening to all. Cheers!"

Hearty "cheers" rang around the huge room in response to the High Counsel. The bright chime of crystal touching crystal sounded as neighbors turned to one another in toasts as the Houseman brought out the first course.

◊ ◊ ◊

Rhia groaned inwardly at the arrival of Brita's brother, Ricard. In his infinite wisdom—snark—and amazing lack of good sense, he strode into the hall with as long a stride as his short legs would allow. Unfortunately, he found himself up against a very determined, though quite subtle, Sharyn. Oh, and Sharyn's very sharp, discretely wielded blade.

"Who is he, Rhia?" RuArk whispered, appearing to concentrate on the plate of food in front of him.

He smiled at her, but the intensity in his voice

didn't sound happy at all. The man looked so at ease, nobody further than half a table length away would think anything of importance was being discussed. She was very good at hiding her thoughts behind her eyes, but she conceded that RuArk was better.

"He's Brita's brother. Tell Sharyn to stand down, RuArk," she hissed back.

"No need to worry," RuArk said. "Most of these people believe she's greeting the High Counsel, not protecting us."

"What do you mean 'protecting us'? My father's men, *my* men, wouldn't allow anyone in here they didn't know."

"Irrelevant since we suspect the person behind the plot to kill you is someone you know and know well."

Well, she couldn't dispute that, so time to get back to the whole 'stranger' thing.

"I deal with strangers on a daily basis, RuArk. Draema is full of people from other provinces. How am I to go about my duties? You're the Protector of your province, and I'm a diplomat and ambassador for mine. Surely you understand."

"What I *understand* is that your duties have been given to others."

Her mouth dropped open. RuArk winked and popped a wonderfully fragrant piece of smoked fish into his mouth, and then grimaced. "I've never tasted anything quite..." He coughed discretely and gulped down half a glass of water. "Uh, quite like it."

She was sure he hadn't. There hadn't been a Gaian to direct the chefs in the correct way to prepare their native dishes since her mom passed cycles ago. Not to mention there might be plenty of crystal clear water in the High City, but they were for leisure. There wasn't a stocked lake in the entire City, and the occasion was too last-minute to have anything imported from the border colonies. She didn't even want to know where the chefs had gotten the fish from.

Turning back to RuArk, she watched him flash a discreet hand signal that looked like he was trying to get crumbs off his fingertips. Sharyn backed up, smiled and shook the High Counsel's hand as if they'd shared a joke. Her father, being the tactician that he was, went right along with it, his smile easy and the relaxed posture of his body genuine. Sharyn then resumed her position without the slightest sound. She ignored Ricard, all together.

And RuArk was right—nobody seemed to think anything was out of place.

But poor Ricard stood there wide-eyed and trembling. He managed to regain his composure after a few moments of having his person free from the threat of that blade to his balls. This time, as he took the final steps to reach the High Counsel, he moved much more slowly. Rhia felt sorry for him.

"Greetings, High Counsel," he stammered, recovering from his near bout with the inability to ever bear children.

"Hello, Ricard. How are you? Well, perhaps I shouldn't ask you that just now," the High Counsel chuckled. Motioning to RuArk, he introduced the two men. "RuArk of Gaia, this is Ricard Shae, an old friend of the family. He's brother to Rhia's companion, Brita."

"I remember Brita. Ricard, your sister was always kind to me and my relatives when we came to visit when I was a small boy," RuArk said, inclining his head politely. But Ricard wasn't looking at RuArk.

Instead, his eyes were plastered on Rhia.

She groaned inwardly as RuArk's answering expression made it clear Ricard was just a bit too dreamy-looking for his tastes.

Ricard, like Bryan Collaidh, was another who'd always fancied himself in love with her. The difference was she actually liked Ricard and considered him a friend, even if he did believe he was the most spectacular man walking. He was actually a genius, and responsible for many of the more recent discoveries in Draema and his native province of Balear. At the same time, he was forgetful, clumsy and oblivious of others. Kind of like right now.

"Greetings Rhia."

"Hello, Ricard. Won't you have some dinner?"

Ricard sighed with awe and attempted to squeeze between RuArk and Rhia. It was quickly obvious RuArk wasn't moving, and Ricard certainly couldn't move him. He looked condescendingly at the mighty warlord, fully expecting him to give up his seat. Rhia bit the inside of her cheek to keep from grinning when her inner bitch became curious as to how annoyed RuArk would get over someone as silly as Ricard. After letting the posturing go on for a few moments, RuArk's jaw began to tick.

Uh oh.

"Um, Ricard," Rhia stepped in deftly.

"Yes?" he sighed dreamily.

Good grief, poor idiot.

"RuArk is a guest of honor seated by the High Counsel himself. I'd be happy for you to join us, but you'll have to sit down there," she said, pointing to an empty seat some four or five places down from hers.

"Isn't there any way I could sit next to you?"

RuArk rolled his eyes. Rhia smiled sweetly while gritting her teeth. He was a dear, dear man, but damn he was obtuse. She was tempted to spill that she and RuArk had been mated this morning, knowing Ricard would hop back a few feet in disbelief. Maybe the surprise would shock some sense into her old friend.

Doubt it.

Unfortunately, or fortunately, depending on how one looked at it, their mating was a secret to everyone except her father, Mannon, RuArk, and his men.

"Ricard, you know I've always been fond of you, but I'm sorry. The High Counsel chooses who has the seat of honor and RuArk is a guest." *And my lifemate.* "Oh look! There's Brita. She's waving to you."

Ricard turned, caught his sister's eye and literally wilted like a hothouse flower that had received too much iozene light. Rhia touched him lightly on the sleeve and said, "Brita really missed you while you were away visiting your parents in your homeland. You know how much she means to me and I don't want her feelings hurt. So sit with her and be nice, okay?"

At her touch, Ricard's demeanor brightened considerably. He kissed her hand and swaggered away with smug satisfaction.

Rhia watched him go, relieved a confrontation had been avoided while still saving Ricard's feelings. RuArk hadn't appreciated the intrusion and she didn't even want to guess how close the man had come to making his displeasure known. Young RuArk would have popped Ricard in the lip. Grown up RuArk? Who could say?

"Why make the man believe you care for him?" RuArk growled, barely moving his lips.

"But I do care for him," Rhia replied sweetly.

"You are playing both sides Rhia." His voice was calm, but the gritty bass of his words screamed *pissed off*. "Know right now that I do not share."

She wondered if he realized that his words gave him away. 'You are' instead of 'you're' and 'do not' instead of 'don't'? Yep, he was quite annoyed if he'd slipped into what the Draeman considered stuffy, old fashioned speech. As a man who traveled to many lands, RuArk was a master at using the dialect of whatever people he was visiting.

But not right now. While his annoyance was clear in his speech, Rhia wondered if she could get him to cuss like a Draeman once he slipped back into Draeman common? Maybe it should be on her list of things to do.

She giggled and quickly regretted it when he stiffened.

"I'm First Heir, RuArk. What good is it to be a diplomat of Draema if I can't be diplomatic?" She smiled, stabbing him playfully in the back of the hand with her fork. "And by the way, Gaian, I don't share either."

She didn't bother trying to hide a completely unashamed grin at getting the last word in. Wouldn't be the last time, either. He growled, low in his throat, eyes locked with hers.

"Be nice RuArk. It's so much easier to diffuse a situation when you're sweet about it," she crooned. He growled some more.

"There is nothing sweet about me, Rhia. But it is a word I would use to describe your scent."

"I'm not wearing any perfume," she whispered out of the side of her mouth.

"Yet I smell you just the same."

Dropping his schooled mask, he allowed her to glimpse the hot, raw desire in his gray eyes as they clashed with her tawny ones. Oooh boy, this might get ugly. *Sexy*.

"Sweet and spicy, like the freshest honey and cream with a bit of allspice. I can almost... taste you." Oh. My. God. He was talking about her woman's scent! *Holy shit*. He gave her a heart stopping grin, and her color deepened. How many times had she blushed today? This was ridiculous. Even if he was such a fabulous specimen of manhood she'd have to be non-human to resist him.

Besides, she wasn't resisting him as a man. What woman in her right mind would complain about having a man like RuArk in her bed? No, it wasn't that. It was the whole "having her life snatched out of her control" thing that grated on her nerves.

And the fact that he wasn't playing fair just now.

She tried to kick him under the table. He caught her foot, untied the strap of the high heeled sandal and slipped it off. The cheerful conversation filling the hall covered up her near-squeal when she burst out laughing in the middle of the vegetable course. She pretended a cough, lowered her voice to hiss between giggles.

"Stop tickling me, RuArk. You're making me embarrass myself."

He replaced her shoe, but kept hold of her leg, draping it over his thigh beneath the thankfully long tablecloth. His hand eased from her calf to her thigh and back again. She squirmed, trying to get loose.

RuArk's fingers pressed into the muscle just short of her sex in warning. It had the intended effect. She went completely still and gave him a vicious scowl.

Damn. Must not be vicious enough considering the man was doing a piss poor job of holding in that damn devilish smile. A smile that never faltered as he teased her flesh.

And it felt... good. Fun even. Definitely unexpected.

Hell, she couldn't even remember the last time she played with a male. Actually, she could — it had been with RuArk, a bazillion cycles ago in her father's courtyard as a child.

In his most innocent voice, he said, "School your features, love. Your eyes look as if they might fall into this... whatever this dish is supposed to be from my homeland."

It was true. Her eyes felt as big as saucers. RuArk laughed some more as she cursed colorfully under her breath.

Her father looked up. "What was that, Rhia?"

Shit. Obviously not quietly enough.

"Nothing, Father. RuArk and I were just discussing a matter of... uh... diplomacy."

RuArk painted on an innocent look while her voice went all breathless and not convincing at all as he continued to stroke the inside of her thigh.

"Well, I'm glad you two are having a good discussion," said the High Counsel turning away to engage Linc. A glance at Joan had Rhia reining in her bit of undercover abandon to watch her best friend with RuArk's First Commander.

Interesting. Every time Joan tried to speak with Linc, he seemed polite but short. Was he simply not interested in anything she wanted to talk about? While they were dressing for dinner, Joan had told her about the man she'd met in the stables. The moment she met Linc she figured it must be him, but now her best friend wore a bored-as-hell expression. Perhaps Joan had simply imagined the spark earlier? It certainly wasn't there now. Rhia caught her eye from across the table and winked. Joan flashed a 'look on the bright side' smile and moved her attention to someone else.

So far they'd made their way through what Joan would have called "sort-of" meat, fish and vegetables. Spring was getting underway and fresh bio-greens with late winter tomatoes were available, served with a sweet creamy white sauce. It had all smelled delicious, even though it tasted like wood. Either way, Rhia barely noticed. Much too busy concentrating on breathing, considering RuArk never stopped touching her flesh.

By the end of the meal she was boiling hot, bothered and ready to stab RuArk with anything she could get her hands on. He'd let his hand rest on her thigh while he talked with her father. His fingers played across her skin under the silky fabric of her skirt. Gently caressed, stroked her from her knee to the top of her thigh. Though he'd stopped way short of the soft and sensitive flesh at her center, her skin sizzled and her underwear—soaked with her own dewy moisture—stuck to the heated skin between her legs.

Gritting her teeth, Rhia tried her best not to roll her hips against RuArk's questing fingers. She'd thought his earlier kisses were torture, but *this*, his touch, sent her reeling. Just when she thought the torment was done and she'd be able to make a clean getaway, the dinner crystal chimed and the High

Counsel's voice rang out once more.

"Tonight," he began, "In honor of our guests, I've requested a special dessert to be enjoyed with a short vocal performance by the Society of Choralers to end the meal. Enjoy."

The bottom or Rhia's stomach fell to the floor. Great. Go ahead and give the man more time to drive her crazy. The Society of Culinary Arts brought out an unexpected treat—a cold frothy whipped dish with what was supposed to be orange honey and berry compote swirled throughout.

And RuArk made it such an erotic experience she could have swallowed her spoon without realizing it was stuck in her throat. Every time he took a spoonful of the fluffy sweet treat he slowly licked the confection off of the back of the spoon, swirling his tongue around it while looking her directly in her eyes until she glanced away. He leaned close, only to whisper, "I wish we could announce our joining. It would give me an excuse to carry you back to your apartment. I would love to give you a Draeman wedding night, Rhia."

Oh good god.

"I've enjoyed your kisses today. I wish I could taste this sweet dessert on your tongue."

She still said nothing. Couldn't form the words.

"I've always thought you were beautiful, Rhia, even when we were young. Now you're simply breathtaking. And now that we're together again, I can't keep my hands off of you."

She turned to him, her tongue stuck to the roof of her mouth. Still, no words came to mind. Not a single snarky syllable.

All she could think about was the tingle in her

belly, the warmth of her skin as the heat flowed to her sex.

"What is it Rhia?" he asked when she groaned as he licked the spoon again. "Don't you like my tongue?" Then he described in detail what he planned to do with his tongue, all of it involving her bare skin and not much else.

"Bastard."

"Not at all. I promise my parents were married when I was conceived."

She didn't feel like laughing, damn it.

In fact, she was speechless. Breathless. Trying desperately to give the appearance everything was fine. Oh blazes, she was going to combust if she didn't get away from him soon. And the hotter she got, the angrier it made her. Her libido careened out of control and she didn't like it one blasted bit.

Rhia was a walking, talking, semi-orgasm. But she was an orgasm with a plan. RuArk said he'd give her some time to get used to the idea of being mated, right? Well, she would use that time wisely. Wisely indeed.

RuArk moved swiftly up the winding tower stairs, Linc close on his heels. He pressed his key to the wall lock outside his apartments and watched the door slide smoothly open with a patience he most certainly didn't feel. RuArk moved through the living area and disappeared momentarily through the tall archway that led into his bedroom.

Returning with his gear bag and two arms full of

clothing, he called out quietly and Sharyn came quickly through the adjoining door.

"These documents," he said, producing three thick documents bearing the official seal of the Protector of the Realm, "are to be given to three captains of your choosing. Each one will take a ten-man fireteam. The first to the new holdings in Province Springs, the second to our warriors who remained behind in the Borderlands, and the third to my Grandfather in Gaia. They ride within the hour."

"Tonight?" she asked.

"Yes, tonight. Meet me in the stables as soon as your orders are given and we'll see them off."

"What of the other fireteams? Have you orders for them?" Linc asked as he watched Sharyn tuck the documents into her quiver, then sling her bow across her back and head for the still-open door.

RuArk tilted his head as Linc watched his fellow First Commander. His eyes remained plastered to the jade green sarand draped sensually over her lithe form until she disappeared from view down the wide stairway.

"Linc?"

No answer.

"Linc!"

"Wha... yes, sir?"

RuArk's thick black brows rose. Linc was discomfited—an uncharacteristic state for a Gaian warrior. The man who was known for his cool-headed demeanor and cynical outlook on everything, especially women, now seemed to be enthralled by one.

"Why don't you approach her, Linc? It's obvious to all that you are taken with Sharyn."

Lifting his chin, his green eyes glittered, and

with an offended drawl, said, "Warriors are not 'taken'. They take." He cleared his throat and added, "Sir." Though the rising color in his cheeks revealed his true emotions, Linc's expression remained unreadable.

RuArk yanked his gear bag open and set it on a small table.

"And warriors do not lie. Not even to themselves," RuArk replied without looking up from the clothing he neatly folded and packed with practiced skill.

Linc's already flushed face deepened to an even darker shade. When he finally opened his mouth to speak, RuArk was honored to be one of the few to whom he would dare reveal any weakness. Linc's gaze turned back toward the stairs as if a thought could bring back the woman who'd just descended them.

"I do not deserve her, Wind Storm. I have nothing to offer. Except my hard warrior's body." A half smile kicked up at the side of Linc's mouth and RuArk snorted. "A life of roaming from place to place is not good enough for her."

"She chooses this life, Linc. It is not put upon her. If you speak with her, you may be surprised at what you learn in regard to what she wants." Knowing the other man was uncomfortable with such exchanges, RuArk changed the subject.

"Contact Marth. Tell him to finish his hunting and head to Neine as soon as possible. He is to bring his catch with him when he leaves here, but the fireteam stays behind to surveil. Everyone else will travel with you, Sharyn and me when it's time. Give the orders and then meet me and Sharyn in the stables."

"Why are we leaving today? I believed our plan

was to go to the new holdings after the Draeman ceremony your lady requested."

He rolled a pair of buckskin leggings, stuffed them into his gear and dropped the large leather bag at his feet with a loud thunk. With a deep breath, he revealed the reason for the hurry. "I had a Vision last night. What we do now is because of that Vision."

"A Vision? You have never expressed that Gift before."

"I was sure I was too old to manifest any true Gifts, though the Grandfather did speak of it the last time he walked the Dream with me."

"The Gift of Vision? That is a rare thing."

"Yes, and until I learn to master it, keep it between us."

"I understand. What did you see?"

"I saw my lifemate on the road to Province Springs. It was so real I could have reached out and touched her. I could almost smell her."

"But if you saw her going where she is supposed to go, why are we preparing to depart early?"

"Because Rhia was traveling to our new holdings *alone*."

Linc's eyes widened in amazement.

"It may be today. It may be two days. Either way, we leave when she leaves."

"She'll be upset that her plans are derailed, Wind Storm."

"No, she won't."

With a wink, RuArk put his bag next to the door and headed to the stables.

CHAPTER THIRTEEN

"Oh come on Joan, please do this for me. Please."

"Forget it Rhia," Joan said hotly, slashing her hand through the air. Moving swiftly for the door, she could almost feel her dark eyes glow with anger. If she'd believed in a god, she would have prayed earnestly for the deity to come take Rhia away somewhere, anywhere but here trying to talk her into another dumb stunt.

"Ever since we were children I've done all kinds of stupid things for you and I always get caught. Your father's going to kill you when he learns you haven't been planning a wedding trip for the past few weeks. Instead, you've been planning to run. And don't look at me like that. I'm not going to help you, because unlike you, I want to keep my skin.

"Get in here already." She'd almost made a run for it when Rhia grabbed her by the hand and yanked her back into the apartments with a *shush*. "What if RuArk is next door?"

Joan didn't really care. Hell, she almost wished the man would overhear what this numb-skulled woman was up to.

"What if I get caught? Your father would tell my father. Or worse, he'd have me carted off to Harbor Station and assigned to one of your brother's airships. As a soldier, I don't mind the patrol part of it, but you know I hate riding in those blasted airships. On the water or flying above it, they still make me want to hurl. Bleh."

"Joan, I'm not asking you to help me leave the High City. I'm only asking you to go on this errand for my father."

"Yeah, but it's *your* errand. *You're* supposed to do it, not me," Joan fumed. Her nails raked through her curls until they stood on end.

"He's always wanted me to delegate more of my duties, right?"

"Don't even try that one on me, Ree. Forget it!"

"Come on, Joan. All you have to do is go to the Ambassador's Quarters and give the High Counsel's letter to the delegates from Eastern Maine. It grants them a negotiation session for the additional iozene they want to purchase. Just deliver it and leave."

"But I don't look or sound anything like you. What if they get suspicious?" Joan asked, not sure she really wanted Rhia to answer the question. Even thinking about it was crazy.

"They've never met me. Just put on my overcloak and keep the hood up. Oh, and uh... wear one of my outfits."

"Blasted hell, Rhia, are you nucking futs? Yes, nucking futs because you're obviously *way* mixed up right now," Joan screeched. "You know good and well what kind of trouble I could get into impersonating the First Heir. Not to mention, wearing the colors of a Blademaster when I'm not a damn Blademaster. Hell, if

I dressed up like you just to go take a pee, I'd still be breaking the laws of the Society of War. Girl, I need a drink," she muttered, as she rolled her gaze up to the ceiling.

Joan stalked over to the dining table, needing some space to think. She poured herself a healthy glass of deep red wine and sat a moment, studying the fine circular mosaic that made up the dining area floor. Even the wine was against her, the sweet, fruity liquid was nowhere near strong enough. After numerous deep breaths and sighs, she finally cleared her head of visions of leaning over the side of a rocking, rolling airship, gliding along the river two stories up from the waters, feeding the fish with whatever she'd had for breakfast. When Rhia sat down across the table from her, Joan spoke up.

"All right, Ree, let's cut to the chase. What's with all the secrecy and sneaking off? Why can't you just go on to Draema Neine and live happily ever after? Even if you didn't want RuArk, which you *know* you do, there's one small issue. You're *already married*!"

Rhia hesitated. Joan moved in for the kill.

"Look woman, your honor requires you to keep your word. You said you'd go to Province Springs in Neine without a fuss, and that's that."

"I *am* going to Province Springs," Rhia replied quietly.

"Then why do you want me to put my head on the block and impersonate you?"

"Because Brita and I are going to Province Springs alone. Not me, the big guy, his mistress, and…"

"Oooh-hoo-hoo!" Joan crowed, unable to keep the mirth out of her words. "You've got to be kidding.

You're jealous of that gorgeous First Commander woman who's always with your man? What's her name again? Sharyn? Geez, Rhia, you don't even know what her relationship is to the Wind Storm. She could be one of his blasted relatives for all you know."

"I know who she is, Joan."

Joan's eyebrows inched up her face in wonder.

"Wait, let me get this straight. You *are* jealous?" It was too much. Joan set the glass of wine on the table, stood up and wrapped her arms around her belly. After a minute of fighting to hold back her chuckles, she practically hit the floor laughing. The First Heir of the most powerful province in the world was beautiful, had the body of a goddess and held the rank of Blademaster on top of that. But she was mad because her lifemate kept company with his own First Commander?

Ri-damn-diculous.

"Oh shut it, Joan. I am *not* jealous. I just feel trapped. Everywhere I go, RuArk is there. Isn't it enough I'm forced to spend the rest of my life with him? Do I want him? Yes. But not like this. I just want to get away to get my head together. I need out of here. Besides, there's no law that says I can't go where I want to go when I feel like going."

Joan, still bent over holding her stomach, still chuckled as she sucked in great gulps of air trying to get her breath.

"And if you fall over laughing I'm going to kick you in the ribs."

"I'm sorry Ree. Well, actually, I'm not sorry. Think about it, girl. You've been waiting for a man like this forever. He's right here, and married to you. He's even allowed you to royally avoid him for weeks, giving you time to get used to the idea of mating when he would have been within his rights to take you right then and there. What *is* your problem?"

"He and my father think I need him to protect me, but damn it, I can take care of myself. Besides, I have yet to challenge him, and no, that muddy stint in the pavilion didn't count."

"Rhia, he deliberately held back. It was obvious to me, if not to you, that he won fair and square. Besides, you're married Rhia. You know, joined? Mated? It's common courtesy to let your man know where you're going."

"I don't recall those Gaian vows requiring me to get his okay to do what I want, go where I want. And don't say it. The military is about orders. I know that, considering I give them every day. But this is... This is something else. I will not be controlled like this."

"Ree, what are you afraid of?"

Silence.

Then finally, "Joan do you really think I want a wuss for a mate? I mean, maybe you were right when you asked..."

But Rhia didn't have to finish. Joan remembered exactly what she'd said, standing in this very room, in fact. *"You're so used to running things, could you really handle a man you can't push around?"*

"It seems I've been raised to deal with every kind of diplomatic or military threat. But I have no idea what to do about reconciling being a mate with being, well, me."

Aw hell, Joan thought as her heart softened at Rhia's genuinely miserable and confused countenance. *Sigh.* She was such a sucker. "Well, I see I've hit a sore spot," Joan said softly, feeling sorry for the sadness in her friend's eyes. "I'll run the errand for you, but I must be a total idiot for doing it."

Relieved, Rhia hugged her tightly and sighed, "I love you, Joan."

"Yeah, yeah. Let go of me, Ree. I'm smothering here with my face smashed up against your big breasts."

"It's not my fault you're so short," Rhia chided.

"And it's not my fault you're so tall. Even for a half-Gaian female you're a blasted beanpole."

After stuffing one of Rhia's outfits into a small gear bag, Joan turned to Rhia. This was her best-friend, and she wanted her to be happy. There was no doubt in her mind that RuArk could give that to Rhia, but for now, a hug and a smile would have to do.

Shit.

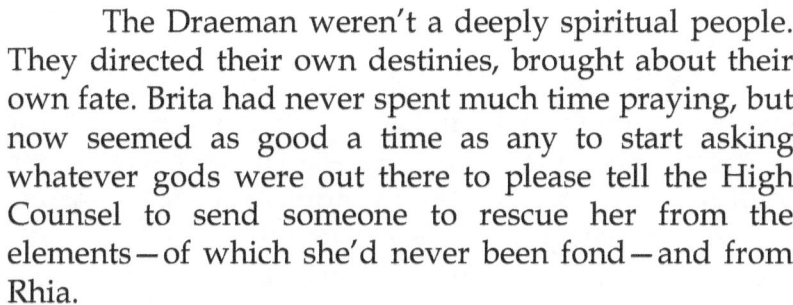

The Draeman weren't a deeply spiritual people. They directed their own destinies, brought about their own fate. Brita had never spent much time praying, but now seemed as good a time as any to start asking whatever gods were out there to please tell the High Counsel to send someone to rescue her from the elements—of which she'd never been fond—and from Rhia.

Her ass hurt from riding a blasted horse—something she hadn't done in more cycles than she cared to count. And with the full onset of spring, the clear skies allowed the bright sun to bake her to the back of the animal. It was too warm to ride with a cloak during the day, and now that the sun was setting, it was too chilly to ride without one. The day's sweat had dried on her skin. She was itchy, stained, and she cringed at the thought of being none too clean.

"We shouldn't have left without telling someone, Rhia. No one will know we're out here if something happens to us. And I don't see what was so bad about RuArk that made you believe high tailing it out of the High City was your only option. We've been riding forever and I want to go home."

Rhia dismounted and tethered her borrowed gelding to a budding low-lying branch and turned to watch Brita struggle to dismount. Rhia replied with a lopsided grin and Brita wanted nothing more than to pummel her. She was never grumpy, but it seemed to be her middle name these days and it was all Rhia's fault.

"Brita, we've only been riding for three days."

"And a half, Rhia."

"Fine, three and a half days. But the weather is perfect. Fresh air, blue skies. What more could we ask for?"

"What more? I'll tell you what more," Brita bellowed hotly, swinging down off her horse with a dexterity she certainly didn't feel. The soreness of her backside and thighs briefly forgotten, she stalked toward her charge, her salt-and-pepper shoulder length hair ruffled by the breeze. Correction, the few dry strands that weren't stuck to the side of her face, were ruffled by the breeze.

"Look, I came along because I didn't want you riding into who-knows-what alone. Not to mention, if you got injured I'm the only one you'll let anywhere near you that can treat wounds, though I'm tempted to feed you an enema right now. What more could I ask for? I could, for your information, easily ask for a soft bed, a hot bath, some decent food along with your father to come riding along in a nice enclosed hover. To. Save. Us!"

Rhia's face split with a cheeky grin. The urge to smack her rose exponentially.

"You know that hovers don't work way out here, Brita."

"Well, we could have taken the fucking train!"

"Did you just curse at me? Oh my god, did you really? I haven't heard you curse since I was a kid."

Ignoring the question, Brita yanked her pack off her damn horse and let it drop to the ground, uncaring whether she'd broken anything useful or not.

"Yes, goddammit, I'm cursing! Fuck! Shit! Damn it, damn it, damn it!"

Brita fairly bristled with anger. Her fair skin felt hot and red, but from the sun or her temper, she couldn't tell and didn't much care. Hell, she could almost feel her freckles threatening to get up and leave her face for the way she was mistreating it out in the wind and sun.

"You're actually yelling at me?"

"Yes, damn it, I'm yelling! Ow!" Stomping her foot sent a wave of pain up her left butt cheek. That did it. She really needed to throw something. Now. Reaching down, Brita snatched up a good sized rock and hurled it for all she was worth—which wasn't much, as tired as she was. Rhia didn't even have to dodge the flying object that went careening off to her right.

With only enough energy left to throw her words at her charge's back, she added, "Every colony has at least one train station. We could have taken! The!

Fucking! Traaaaaain!"

Then she promptly plopped onto the nearest log and immediately regretted it when both sides of her butt spasmed.

"Damn horses," she grumbled.

Damn Rhia.

Damn everything.

Grrrrrr!

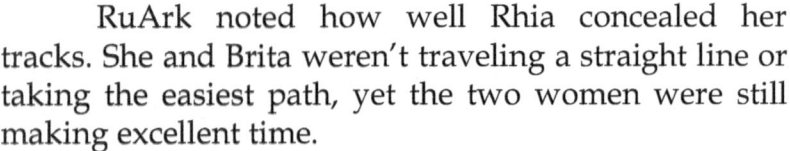

RuArk noted how well Rhia concealed her tracks. She and Brita weren't traveling a straight line or taking the easiest path, yet the two women were still making excellent time.

As he packed his gear for the day's ride, the Grandfather's words resonated in his head. *"Your Gift of Vision will not fail you."* And the old man had been right. The manifestation of that particular unexpected Gift while meditating one night was the only reason he'd been aware of Rhia's plan to run. In fact, though he'd been sitting on the floor in his tower room with not a soul around, the Vision had been so clear, it was as if she'd been right next to him.

"Wind Storm, we have discovered something."

Dalmore was a young warrior, solid, broad shouldered with stern, dark eyes, and high, chiseled cheekbones. His long, dark brown hair was pulled back in a thick ponytail of soft waves. His boyish face was tight and drawn, the pallor of his skin not its typical light, golden hue, but a sickly green.

Though he stood well over six feet, like all Gaian warriors, he was not as tall or thickly muscled as

RuArk. There were few, Gaian or otherwise, who were. RuArk used it to his advantage as he rose to tower over the man. Pinning him with a hard glare, RuArk's gray eyes pierced the younger Gaian to the quick. RuArk knew that only something deadly serious could shake the countenance of one of his men, but if the man could not face his leader, he certainly could not face an enemy.

"How long have you been in my service, Dalmore?" RuArk spoke softly, his words clipped, his tone menacing, and his face a picture of chiseled stone.

Completely still, head and chest held high, Dalmore locked eyes with the Protector of the Realm and refused to look away as he replied.

"This is my first assignment, sir. I was sent just as you departed the Miwatani Capitol for the northern borders."

"Show me what you have found that makes you afraid."

Dalmore's stern expression slipped. "The Protector insults me by suggesting such a thing," he said calmly, yet with all the assurance expected of one counted worthy to serve the Wind Storm of Gaia. "I am a Gaian warrior and fear nothing."

Just the answer RuArk was looking for.

"Come then, Dalmore, show me." Falling into step with the younger man, RuArk was led to the shady side of a knoll of huge trees with trunks so large that four men couldn't circle them with their arms outstretched. On the other side of that knot of trees, hiding from the setting sun, sat a form covered with a thick white cloak.

"We were scouting ahead of the lady Rhia to make sure her way was clear when we came across this," Dalmore spat. He gestured with repulsion toward the figure rolled up in a tight ball on the ground.

Noman.

But why? Their kind never ventured far from their own lands in the high country near the border they shared with Gaia. The few who did were usually driven back by the warriors who protected the caretakers of the priceless coffee fields nearby.

Lately the Noman packs seemed driven by something other than their need to feed. For this reason, RuArk had dispatched several fireteams of elite fighters to tackle the problem. In fact, he'd been on his way to join them when the Grandfather had appeared in the *Dream* with the warning about the plot against Rhia.

Now he stood in front of a creature that should be several hundred leagues away.

"How is it possible that it can track in daylight?" RuArk wondered aloud, his voice a tight hiss as he slowly paced in front of the spitting, angry creature that bared its fangs as it tried to keep itself covered.

Dalmore yanked back the hood and snatched a dirty, but sturdy, formerly white piece of cloth from around its eyes and handed it to RuArk. The creature howled as its skin quickly reacted to the rays of the afternoon sun.

"It used this to shield its eyes. The filth says it can travel during the day if it stays out of direct sunlight and keeps itself well covered. It had no wish to be seen, let alone captured, but its covering was not sufficient. It sought shelter beneath the trees and became separated from its pack."

Noman weren't the smartest creatures in the

world. Brilliant, nocturnal pack hunters, but their intellectual pursuits ended there. They simply weren't interested in anything other than the thrill of the hunt and the taste of blood mingled with sex.

"When are the other scouts due back?"

A voice rang across the clearing. "We are here, Wind Storm."

RuArk turned to see several seasoned warriors melt through the trees so silently not even the leaves stirred beneath their boots.

Getting straight to the matter, RuArk asked pointedly, "Osgar, how many?"

"No more than ten. We wanted to engage them, but did not wish to give away our position. It would hardly have been a worthy fight anyway." He was a tall, bulky giant with a permanent stern expression and a black-as-midnight fall of white streaked hair. "Our six against their ten? They would have shed tears about how unfair it was."

They got a good laugh out of that, but it didn't last long. They despised *Noman*. Vile, inhuman blood drinkers. And tracking his woman? RuArk had been concerned before. Now, he was downright angry. All of them were.

"How long did you track them?" RuArk asked.

"We came upon them yesterday afternoon. Tracked them until a few hours before dawn."

"Yesterday afternoon? What did they do once the sun began to set?" RuArk asked.

"They kept watch. Never left their positions, not even to hunt. They did not approach the lady, Rhia, in any way," Osgar said.

Noman that sat and watched their blood prey rather than eat it?

Turning to the young warrior, RuArk instructed, "I want to know why they are tracking her, Dalmore. For now, this one lives." He nodded toward the bundle of flesh trembling on the ground at his feet. "I want answers. Until I have them, it travels with us. Sharyn, you take a team and watch over Rhia for now."

Sharyn nodded, silently pointed out eight warriors, and departed without a word.

"Osgar, take your team, find the rest of this one's pack and draw them away from my mate. They cease breathing. Today. Track after us and catch up by nightfall."

RuArk left the knoll and headed back to his tent, swearing to himself and the Ancestors that by this evening, this cat and mouse game he played with Rhia was over.

CHAPTER FOURTEEN

Chuckling under her breath at Brita's disdain for the great outdoors, Rhia left the other woman in the clearing. She enjoyed her huge bathing tub and big comfy bed as much as the next woman, but she'd always held a fondness for being out where she could see, smell and touch nature. She felt as if she were part of, and connected to the flowers, the wind, even the sky. When laying under the stars she could swear she heard the earth sing to her, lulling her softly to peace.

And a little peace was just what she'd needed, though the answer it brought wasn't exactly the one she wanted.

Thinking back on the questions Joan had asked her before she'd left the High City, Rhia mumbled to herself, pulling her brows down into a frown so deep she felt the beginnings of a headache.

"Can you handle a man you can't run over?" she mimicked in a high, totally non-Joan-like voice. But now she realized she'd been more upset by the fact that she couldn't answer the question, than by the question itself. In fact, Joan had been right about one thing— Rhia had waited for the right man to come along forever. Now he'd appeared, larger than life, and suddenly she wasn't sure what she truly wanted anymore.

Perhaps because she'd always expected to marry someone from her own province? Being only half-Draeman had never mattered until now because life as the First Heir to her province was all she knew. Draema was all about position in the various Societies. Rank and status was all.

A Draeman husband would expect her to continue to live her life as she always had, even keep her own separate apartments in her father's home if she wanted... with the added benefit of sex on demand, of course. She didn't know what to expect from RuArk. Perhaps he'd want her to be glued to his hip? Then again, what if once he got to know her, he decided that leaving her to herself was better than spending time with her?

Rhia's gut clenched at the thought. Rejection was a dry, bitter pill to swallow, and even harder to choke down if it came from someone you actually cared about. It was something she had plenty of firsthand experience with.

She'd never run from a challenge before, but then again, she'd never had a challenge where she didn't know the rules or her teammates. As a realist, she knew that constantly fighting her marriage would get her nowhere but miserable fast. But as a soldier, how did she *not* fight when it was all she knew how to do? The female side wanted nothing more than to fall for RuArk, to simply let her guard down and let him in.

Nah.

Well... maybe.

Hell, she had no idea.

Either way, the feeling that her time away from

RuArk was running out had grown with each mile she'd put between herself and the High City.

Still, five more days to Province Springs in Draema Neine, if she'd calculated correctly. The image of Brita throwing rocks at her, with her skin flushed an alarming hue, while her hair stood on end flashed behind Rhia's eyes. In the midst of her inner turmoil, the thought brought a smile to her face.

She passed through a tall stand of trees and knelt at a gurgling stream so clear that several small schools of little fluorescent fish could be seen swimming along with the current as it ran swiftly over piles of huge rocks. Should be just the thing for drinking. Squatting, she washed her hands in the chilly flow before cupping them to take a taste.

Whew, this is cold.

But it was also sweet and refreshing, a welcome treat after a long, hard day of riding without the benefit of the cooler pack she'd chosen to leave at home.

After a few moments of breathing in clean, cool air, Rhia stood.

Time to get back to my grumpy companion.

As she turned toward the campsite, the fine hairs on the back of her neck kicked into a dance. Keeping her movements easy and relaxed, she eased her hand toward the blade strapped low on her hip. She heard only the typical sounds of the forest, saw only the shadows caused by the sinking sun. But her eyes and ears deceived her. Something was there. She could feel it.

Definitely time to go.

Rhia took a single step back toward the stream and walked into a long, very sharp blade as it made contact with her neck just beneath the jawbone.

———◆———————◆———

"So, my mate is found?"

The second she heard that voice, Rhia didn't move a muscle, except for the sharp pink one in her mouth.

"I was never lost. And just how did you catch up so quickly? You're not supposed to be here, blast it."

"Neither are you." RuArk removed his sword from the furiously pulsing vein in her neck. The sharp point sank into the mossy ground with a quiet *schnick* as he leaned on the pommel.

"I was going where I'm supposed to go."

"Without the protection or permission of the man you belong to?"

"I belong to no one," she ground out as a single finger stabbed at the middle of his chest. She seemed to like poking that particular spot.

Unmoved, he said, "Do you not, Rhia? Just as I belong to you?"

Her eyes widened as her head tilted to the side. Ah, this must be one of those Gaian things she'd never learned, where mates were a part of each other—two wholes that made an even stronger, larger entity, and accountable to one another.

Since her mouth wasn't moving, perhaps the woman was so surprised by his statement her tongue glued itself to the roof of her mouth while her brain sought something to say.

"You're talking old fashioned, RuArk. Um, so I guess you're pretty pissed."

RuArk bit back a grin, but said nothing more.

His anger at her reckless behavior had melted the moment he saw her safely drinking at the stream. Stabbing fear for her safety was replaced by plain and simple need. His arm shot out, grabbed her around the wrist and pulled her to him. The moment her body touched his, chest to chest, the desire to touch, to know she was truly whole morphed into the need to taste.

A flare of concern filled him when she went limp.

"Rhia? Are you ill? Are you injured? What is…?"

A foot hooked behind his ankle as Rhia gripped his cloak, yanked him forward, then gave a small shove back. He went down like a piece of falling timber. It would have worked beautifully if he'd released his grip on her wrist. Instead, she went down with him, causing the air to whoosh from both of them. With a sigh, he unwrapped their limbs and pushed to his feet.

"I did not come here to fight with you Rhia, but since that is all that is ever on your mind, let us do it and get it over with." Exhilaration swirled through and around him as his cloak and overcloak landed in a heap, along with scabbard and all manner of hidden daggers and blades. Meanwhile, leaning against one of the many towering tree trunks, Rhia crossed her arms over her chest and put on what must be her negotiator's face. Then, the expression slipped as she spoke.

"You are just so damned pretty to look at," she said. "Damn, I didn't mean to say that out loud."

Satisfaction bloomed in his chest. Pride in the fact that she truly found him attractive joined the excitement of moving to the next level with his stubborn mate.

"Uh, I mean what do you want if you win?" she asked, her voice as steady as the tree she leaned against, but a deep blush gave her away.

"*If* I win?" His hearty laughter was rewarded with a cat-eyed glower. He had no intention of losing this round of what was sure to be the first of many challenges between them. Though she deserved to be punished for running, his admiration for the woman kicked up a notch. "You are the first woman I have ever wanted who has such a stout heart. You have proven to be quite resourceful. However, I am not pleased with how you have chosen to use that resourcefulness."

A tangle of emotion skipped across Rhia's face. Was it anger or wonder? He couldn't tell, not yet. But from this day forward every moment he could spare would be spent getting to know her... In every way possible. And Gods, he so looked forward to it. That last thought had the blood thickening in his veins and quickly heading South. No, he could not stay on that path or the fight would be over before it began. An erection made sparring incredibly difficult.

Finally, she said, "Wait. If I'm the first woman you've wanted with heart — and who's to say you really want me at all — then does that mean you don't want..."

Her words skidded to a halt, and so did his anger. She wasn't just being difficult. Rhia honestly thought he had someone else in his heart?

"Don't want who?" he asked.

"Never mind," she mumbled. Looking away quickly she found an interesting spot to study on one of the rocks near the water's edge.

"Who, Rhia? I don't want who?" he pressed. No answer. His mind took a quick spin through his time in

Draema Proper and at the Citadel she called home. For the life of him, he couldn't think of a single female that he'd paid any attention to, other than her.

"Rhia?" he asked again. She glared, but still said nothing. Fine. Time to get on with this. "My terms are when I win, you will stop fighting me. Go where I go, sleep where I sleep, stay at my side unless I say otherwise. And most importantly, you will do what I ask when I ask."

"Are you out of your fucking mind?"

"I do believe so," he muttered. "Consider it a learning time. You choose how long. After that you are free to live the normal life of any Gaian woman, though I honestly hope you choose not to."

"That's an awful lot to expect, big guy. I guess I'll just have to whip your ass." Her lips pressed into a grim line as her cloak hit the ground, but she didn't draw her blade.

Shoulders squared, her lovely face full of determination laced with caution, his little soldier had a few terms of her own.

Big surprise there.

"If I win, I want to go home to Draema Proper, back to the High City. Alone."

"Not possible. We're mated, Rhia. The fact that we have not shared sex makes no difference. Besides, we both know that you don't want me to lose this challenge. You are known for your honesty. Be honest with me, and with yourself."

He wanted to reach out and rub his thumb along her bottom lip as her mouth pressed into a thin line. She was adorably flustered. Waiting patiently, he wondered which choice she'd take—lie, or come out swinging from the corner he'd just backed her into.

"All right, fine. I'm ridiculously attracted to you, but I want you on my terms. Mine. I don't appreciate having no say in the matter, regardless of how perfect my new husband might be."

RuArk resisted the urge to tilt his head to the side in question. Did she really think he was perfect? Rather than asking, he clamped his own lips tight, determined not to interrupt her.

"I didn't even have a minute to think about marriage. Yes, I know taking off was wrong, but I needed some space, some time to think. And yes, I needed to think about how to challenge you. It's a matter of honor for me."

Honor? Now that was something he understood perfectly.

"I am giving you a way to learn who I am by being by my side while still satisfying your honor when you lose." He took a step forward, lightly stroked a long finger up the smooth skin of her arm and watched a trail of goosebumps rise.

The sincerity of her words combined with one little touch was like lighting a stack of dry brush, then slowly adding larger and larger pieces of cured wood. Just like that, he was on fire. Gods, he wanted her.

Another step closer. Her eyes widened as he spoke in a deep voice that sounded strained even to his own ears.

"I saw you in a *Seeking* before I returned to the High City. My spirit and the magic in our blood recognized you as mine. Not only in the *Seeking*, but the moment I saw you that first night in the tower. Even while you ripped me to shreds with your tongue, I knew you were mine. Your father had his reasons for calling me to you. He wants more than a protector for you, Rhia. He wants you to enjoy being a woman, and I am more than capable of making sure you do indeed enjoy it."

There was a profound beckoning in his dreamy grays. His voice had gone all soft and deep, making her belly quiver in response until butterflies dive-bombed the pit of her stomach. Just what she needed before a fight—a stomach full of insects on high-grade hypnotic pharmaceuticals.

She recognized the truth in his words, knowing her body reacted to the mere sight of him. Her skin tingled wherever he touched. Her blood burned and bones melted with his kisses. She'd never had this reaction to anyone. Ever. If that didn't make her feel like his woman, she didn't know what else could. But that wasn't enough, was it? She could never just lay down who she'd become because it felt good. Feeling had never gotten her anywhere but a one-way trip to disappointment.

"It will be dark soon, Rhia. Let us get on with it, or do you forfeit?"

"Forfeit? In your dreams, big guy."

"How long?"

Without hesitation she responded, "Thirty days, if I lose."

"Choose your weapons," he challenged with a half-grin.

"No weapons," she countered proudly and dropped into a perfect stance of one of the old hand-to-hand combat styles lost long ago. She didn't know of anyone in the entire Society of War that had mastered it, except herself. Adrenaline and all-out joy spiked at the thought of the coming fight. She loved sparring, was damn good at it. Hell, she'd take a good old fashioned knock-down, drag-out fist fight over a laser pistol any day.

Rhia's confidence faltered for a moment when his body coiled into the same pose. Did RuArk really know this style? Or was he just mimicking to throw her off?

Not that it truly mattered. As soon as the fight started, it was over.

Every blow she'd attempted to land was blocked. Each strong combination was reversed until she found herself defending instead of attacking. Considering she was well-studied in martial arts, that was really saying something.

Then he'd pulled out some moves she'd never seen before. The man basically kicked her ass in less than sixty seconds.

RuArk waited patiently as she caught her breath. Hell, he wasn't sweating or even panting. Anyone observing would assume he'd just taken a stroll through the woods while she was down and truly out for the count.

Blasted man.

"Fine. You win, RuArk. Now get off me." Her voice quavered a bit, but she was silently relieved it was over. He'd challenged her and won, fair and square. Her pride might have just taken a beating, but a part of her, a deeply buried part, couldn't be happier.

"Not quite yet." Then he lowered his mouth to hers and kissed her thoroughly.

The evidence of his arousal pressed into her

belly and ignited a blaze in her own body so hot that the cold ground beneath her back was refreshing rather than chilling.

Breaking the kiss, he groaned against her lips. "You taste like springtime, Rhia. I believe it has become my favorite season."

She blinked. Then blinked again as he stood. RuArk stepped back, as if he understood that she wanted, *needed*, to get up on her own just now. Rhia gained her feet with a sheepish grin and wobbly knees, snatched up her cloak and then turned to head back to camp.

"Your thirty days begin right now," he said as he reached out and took her hand. The triumph in his eyes dared her to pull away, but it wasn't necessary. She was too tired to fight with him anymore. Besides, she was a woman of her word and she would keep it.

Oh joy.

CHAPTER FIFTEEN

On the way back to camp, Rhia marveled at how much her life had irrevocably changed—correction, how much her life had irrevocably changed after a muddy sparring match, a few quick words over some strong red wine in her father's study, and a second challenge.

Oh, hell, her father. He was probably worried sick and furious with her at the same time. Damn. How was she ever going to explain her way out of this one?

A slight tug on RuArk's hand got his attention.

"Any chance my father knows I'm safe? I also need to get a message to Joan and…"

Instead of a true answer, all he gave was a deadpan stare and a quiet, "We'll talk about it later."

"Look, you don't understand, RuArk. I asked Joan to…"

"Rhia. We will talk later, in private. Right now, there is pressing business we both must attend to."

Okay, fine. Play hardball, why don't cha.

They passed by what RuArk indicated was *their* tent, and continued on through the other side of camp. As they walked, it dawned on her that holding hands with this man felt… comfy, though her palm had begun to sweat a bit from the remnants of adrenaline. Rather than pull away, she simply tightened her grip.

No surprise to see a horde of men milling about knowing that wherever RuArk was, so were his warriors. They were all busy, yet everything was quiet and settled. Even the horses were silent.

Brita and Sharyn sat on a big rock stirring a pot of something that smelled deliciously like meat stew. *Real* meat stew that made Rhia's stomach grumble loudly. Was it dinner time already? Her mouth watered in anticipation of tasting whatever it was.

Just then, Brita looked up and called a greeting while Sharyn tended the fire, cleaned her knives, and instructed Brita in the cooking, all at the same time. Rhia responded with a half-hearted wave, but didn't leave RuArk's side. She'd given her word to be gracious about getting to know him. No muss. No fuss.

"Where are we going? Any chance we can eat soon?" she asked.

"We can, but first, I want you to meet someone."

A rugged-looking, older, large warrior—well, that didn't mean much considering they were *all* large—with streaks of gray shot through jet black hair, moved toward them with an air of authority. He was a stocky, boulder shaped man and oh so easy on the eyes.

"Lady Rhia, it is an honor and pleasure to meet the First Heir of the Draeman province and her seven colonies. I am Osgar."

Wow. What a charmer.

"Rhia, this is one of my most trusted warriors."

"Is he a First Commander, too?" she whispered. The male smiled but deferred to RuArk.

"His rank is similar, but his duties are... unique," RuArk replied. To the charmer, he said,

"Explain to the lady what you saw."

Gaze now firmly on her face, the man's expression hardened enough to still the rumbling of hunger in her stomach and replace it with anticipation of the worst kind.

"My fireteam has been tracking you. As well as those on the hunt."

On the hunt?

"I don't understand," Rhia replied. Instinct declared impending doom. Dramatic sounding, yes, but it couldn't be helped just now given the buzz of foreboding energy suddenly swirling through the air.

"We have been tracking and eliminating, when necessary, the Noman that hunt you."

"Noman? You mean the ones in children's stories?" she asked disbelievingly, having only heard of the things in fairy tales.

"They are creatures who live in the dark caves far to the north. They live on the blood of men and prey on the weak." Osgar spat fiercely upon the ground when he finished speaking, as if it would wash the taint from his mouth from merely talking about them. Realizing what he'd done, he apologized quickly, but without much remorse on his handsome, chiseled face.

"Dalmore," RuArk called to a younger man nearby. "She needs to know what hunts her."

Brow furrowed and a knot of apprehension tightening at the base of her spine, Rhia listened closely, grimacing as Osgar and Dalmore described what happened to the northern folk who were now called Noman.

"The Noman were once common people of the northwestern lands. The mountainous region stretches from western Draema, across the land bridge to border northwestern Gaia. After the Breaking, their homes completely destroyed and the earth rearranged, those people sought shelter in caves in the mountains.

"They did not know the caves contained a dangerous substance. Before the quakes it was safely buried deep within the ground, but became exposed by the heaving of the earth. This substance, a glowing rock infused with an uncommon energy, is called radium. It provided them with heat and light. But the people did not know that when men are exposed for long periods of time, they are changed. The histories call the energy emitted from this rock, gamma rays.

"Many of the people died of a sickness from the rock. When those who survived came out from the caves, the plants and animals that were exposed to them died. Even now it is a barren wasteland where nothing grows. Those who survived death began to change, their bodies accommodating the poison and taint of the rock. Their eyes and hair became an unnatural white and their skin lost its pigment, taking away their ability to tolerate the warmth and light of the sun."

"They developed an allergy to sunlight," Rhia stated, coming to understand the sad history of these Borderlanders.

"Correct, Blademaster. Their bodies could no longer hold its own heat so they became wholly dependent on the glowing rock for warmth. Unable to farm or rebuild land during the day, only at night could they venture from their caves to hunt. Over time, even their teeth changed to accommodate their new unnatural diet."

Rhia felt sorry for the people who had walked into those caves seeking shelter only to be condemned to a living hell. It happened a long time ago, but the result of those events lived among them today. Hunted them. Hunted her.

"How is it they became dependent on blood?" she asked Dalmore, unaware she'd instinctively sought RuArk's hand, twining her fingers with his, seeking his solid strength.

"There was no food as their livestock perished along with their lands. They began to eat their dead, but the flesh and organs rotted quickly and contained lethal amounts of the taint. They found that if they could extract the blood just before a person died, it sustained them. And the blood of a healthy human was even better. To this day they drink only the blood of the living. The entire society became known as the Noman, for they were no longer men."

"They sound like the vampires of ancient legend."

"There are differences," Osgar said. "Those legends speak of supernatural forces. These are people who simply sought refuge in a place that they should not have gone. Noman mate and bare young the same as any other species, passing the mutation to their offspring. Noman cannot be 'made' by being bitten, nor are they immortal. Centuries ago, they began to migrate from those original caves to spread out into the Borderlands. Some of their ability to retain body heat has returned, though their colorless features, allergy to sunlight, and need for blood remain."

"What happens if they do bite you?"

"Their bite introduces the taint to your blood, like a bacteria or virus. You would be dead within days, if they did not bleed you dry first."

"What do they look like," Rhia whispered. She

didn't know whether she should continue to pity them or be revolted.

They led her a short distance into the trees, when Dalmore stopped short.

"They look like this, Blademaster." Dalmore pulled a canvas sack off a large lump of something on the ground. It was a man, or something like a man. With pale skin, as white as Draeman stone, its lips were thin and bloodless with a bluish-gray tint, and the eyes were an indescribable white with a thin ring of light blue around the iris.

As soon as it laid eye son Rhia, it snarled and growled at her, twisting and pulling against its bonds.

"You. He comes for you," it said. "You will not escape."

Gleaming yellow teeth showed as it ranted, with canines like the teeth of a wolf. A man with fangs? It was the most eerie thing she'd ever seen. And what the hell was it talking about? Someone was coming for her?

This was no frail creature trying to get his hands on her. This was an animal. But Rhia was no shrinking violet. Standing her ground, she snarled right back at the thing as RuArk and his warriors made a half circle around her, guarding her back.

Osgar tossed the sack back over its head while it continued to thrash about, letting out a bloodcurdling scream at having its prey so close yet still out of reach.

"They move like the wind, but are easily killed. Only as strong as the average man," Osgar said.

"We Gaian warriors are far from average," RuArk whispered for her ears only. "And it seems that my mate is as well."

—————◆———————◆—————

"You've failed me," Rama Collaidh hissed through clenched teeth.

"I think not. The men you sent to capture Rhia failed you. One of the foreign giants got to her first and carried her off before the idiots could finish the job. She is probably on the way to Province Springs by now. So do not think to lecture me on failure, old man."

Behn knew there was next to nothing that could be said to dispute the facts. It had been Collaidh's idea to have Rhia kidnapped at the Ambassador's Quarters—an abysmal failure since Joan Rouillard, who was now missing, had been the one to go meet the delegation instead of Rhia. Never mind the fact that there *was* no delegation from the eastern provinces who wished to secure iozene from Draema.

"So, dear Father, I have set other plans into motion."

"What other plans?"

"Do not concern yourself."

"Don't concern myself? How dare you, you white haired Noman freak. You will inform me of these plans immediately," he hissed through gritted teeth. Red-faced and angry, Collaidh tried to keep the upper hand, not realizing Behn already had it. "Tell me, right now. Otherwise, we can end our business dealings right here, right now. And you can go back to that rock pile you call the Borderlands. So spill it, Behn."

"Well, finally, you address me by my name." Expression calm, cold, he settled into Collaidh's own chair, stretched his long legs out before him and crossed them at the ankle as if he planned to stay awhile.

The older man painted on a bland expression he spoke in the most bored voice he could conjure.

"I have work to do, so tell me now or leave."

Examining his neatly trimmed, too-white fingernails, Behn said, "Rhia is to be taken. Plain and simple."

"Taken from where?"

"From wherever she is. I have others keeping a very close eye on her. There is no place she can hide from me."

"But I thought you couldn't get into her *Dreams*, you idiot."

"And I cannot, yet as long as there are weak minded Ungifted available," he sneered, delivering a pointed look. "Our plans have a chance."

Collaidh left his desk, stomped to the door and yanked it open. "Fine. That will be all. You may go."

Like the specter of death that he was, Behn rose without the slightest sound, unfazed by his sire's disdain.

"And Behn, bring her unharmed and unspoiled. No fucking or feeding on her."

"I said, do not concern yourself." The words brought quite a bit of frost with them as Behn flung them over his shoulder without breaking stride. "You promised me the woman, and I will have her for reasons of my own. Feeding is not one of them."

At Collaidh's dismissive nod, Behn faded into the blackness of the unlighted hallway. But there was one more thing that needed to be said.

Collaidh had obviously been flustered considering he'd forgotten to close the door. Behn watched him cross the room and grab a bottle of amber liquor off the sideboard with a muttered "shit".

When he turned back towards his desk, Behn was right behind him. Close enough to feel his breath waft across his nose as they stood toe to toe.

"And, Father?" Behn bared gleaming incisors with emphasis on each icily delivered word. "Since humans are the only species that will turn on their own pack, it would be wise to never forget I am half human with a human's ruthlessness and ambition. Never call me an idiot again."

Behn left Collaidh's office and made his way out into the night. He would continue to play the semi-subservient role until he had what he wanted, then he would do away with the old bastard. Slowly and with great relish.

To think his sire actually asked, no *demanded*, that he keep his presence, his very existence, hidden when he'd become an expert at it, having spent almost thirty cycles playing around the edges of this pathetic, weak-minded society.

Later that night, as a lovely human female slept in his arms, Behn closed his eyes and stepped into the realm of the *Dream*. In short order, he found the thoughts of a man, who like himself, was held in equally high disregard by Rama Collaidh. The man would remember the instructions given to him while unknowingly carrying Behn's awareness along with him.

"*Over the next three days,*" he whispered into the mind of his unknowing accomplice. "*You will discretely gather twenty men loyal to you. Ride for the township of Province Springs in Draema Neine on the morning of the fourth day. One day's ride outside the township you will meet some of my kin. In your eyes they will appear to be typical human men. You will see no differences. They will help you capture the First Heir. Kill RuArk of Gaia who now protects her. Bring the woman to me unspoiled and unharmed."*

CHAPTER SIXTEEN

After a simple but delicious meal of meat stew, some kind of sweet bread and ice cold water from the stream, RuArk and Linc left to discuss some of their super-secret warrior stuff, so Rhia took the opportunity to slip into their tent. After a quick wash-up, she changed into a set of light leggings and matching shirt, and slipped into bed.

The low flames of a fire pit in the center of the tent served as her only source of light as Rhia lay in the dark. She listened to the quiet of the camp, the rustle of the wind through the quickly budding trees, the hushed, almost imperceptible conversation of the men. At first, she'd been relieved to have some time to herself, but that relief quickly turned into something she hated — uncertainty.

She had to shake it off, had to try. She might not be prepared for this new life she was thrust into, but if she were honest with herself, she wanted it so very badly. Wanted to be the center of someone's world. To mean something more than status to someone. To be loved. Truly and deeply loved.

But damn it, she just didn't know how to be *that*. So, that meant she had to learn. It was just another challenge, right?

Riiight.

And then there was Joan to worry over. Had she made it to the Ambassador's Quarters without getting caught? Was she in as much trouble as Rhia surely was? Add the Noman threat to the concern over her and her best friend, and there was no doubt her head was going to explode with all the unanswered questions swirling around in there.

Rhia stilled the moment she sensed him there in the dark. A lovely shiver slithered beneath her skin at the sound of clothing hitting the floor.

"RuArk?"

"Yes, sweet," he whispered.

Naked, he slipped under the thick blankets, wrapped strong warm arms around her body and pulled her back against him.

Without thinking or even knowing why, she scooted away from the scalding heat of his body as if she'd been burned.

"Rhia, you won't ever get used to sleeping with me if we don't actually lay together. I am willing to let you work up to the sex, but believe me, it will happen. And you'll like it."

"Why can't you just let me go to sleep?" Her yawn finished on a squeak when a thick, muscled arm snaked out in the darkness and wrapped about her waist.

"And I told you, I would have you in my arms tonight. You asked for sleep, but I don't recall granting that request. At least not just now. Ease back this way and lay against me."

She did, and with his taller frame now cuddled behind hers, Rhia didn't miss how his body seemed to mold perfectly around her. The curves of her backside fit into the contours of his larger frame like a key in a lock, like she belonged there. And it felt good.

"I understand, RuArk. Having to ask anyone's permission to do anything, especially sleep, is something that's going to take me a minute to get used to. Surely you understand."

Yep, that was her story and she was sticking to it.

Her breathing accelerated, in agitation or arousal, she wasn't quite sure. But she did know one thing—his breath tickled as it played with the fine hairs at the nape of her neck. Rhia didn't even resist the urge to be in a romantic mood. She was honestly and truly tired. Wiped out, in fact. Not to mention she just couldn't quite wrap her head around the idea of letting him ride to her rescue. The struggle to hold onto herself was in full force in her head even if her stupid body was ready to give up the fight.

She'd had more to say, but the words floated away when his skilled hands smoothed up and over her stomach to stroke the valley between her breasts.

"We will talk for a short while."

Talk? With his hands learning her skin, she didn't think she could string a thought together and hold it long enough to push it from her brain down to her mouth.

He sat up, taking her with him. Rhia huffed, puffed, and grumbled, but still found herself neatly arranged exactly where he wanted her—straddling his massive thighs, palms planted firmly against his chest as she glared daggers.

The fire pit in the middle of the tent cast a soothing, warm glow over his features, transforming his skin to molten gold. He was so thickly muscled and hard everywhere. Especially *there*. No mistaking the ginormous arousal pressing up between her legs. The pulse of his thick cock called, and a deep, flaring ache centered at her sex, answered. RuArk eased her forward and pressed her cheek to his chest, while his fingers stroked through the thick curls of her hair.

His fingers worked magic as he dug into tense knotted muscle. The good kind of pain created a hum in her belly. The sound worked its way up through her throat as she responded to the attention.

"You will relax now, Rhia," he whispered softly into her ear.

She'd been doing just that until thoughts of her friend came to mind and tension leached back into the very places he'd just rubbed it out of. This wasn't right. How could she relax when she had no idea whether Joan was okay? She bit off the rumble of pleasure in her chest and forced it to dissipate as if it had never been.

"Will you stop telling me what to do already? Besides, I have no right to relax when my father is probably worried out of his head and Joan..."

"Someone tried to take her, Rhia."

"What?" Rhia bolted upright, her voice a high pitch she'd never heard herself make. Ever.

"Someone attempted to kidnap her. They thought she was you. We believe it to be the same men behind the plot we've been investigating."

"Oh my god..." Her stomach lurched. She was going to throw up.

"Joan is safe."

"How the hell does kidnapped equal safe?" She tried to raise her head so she could look him in the eye.

"I said *attempted* kidnapping."

"But…"

"Shhhh. Let me ease you. Joan is well. One of my men intercepted those who tried to take her."

"Where is she? Oh blazes, *how* is she?"

"You will see her again soon."

"What? When? Where?"

"No more questions tonight. I only share this news because I am selfish where you are concerned, and I want your attention focused right here. And your horse will be here in the morning. You can ride him the rest of the way to our new home."

"Seriously?" Another unfamiliar squeak came out of her.

He laughed. "I said I want your full attention, not half of it, which is what I would have if I allowed you to needlessly sulk and worry for Joan and your horse day and night."

"I don't sulk, damn it." She tried to snap, but the way his fingers soothed the tense muscles in her neck caused the words to slip out on a wispy moan. He was bossy, bossy and more bossy, yet held her in his arms and rubbed away her worry.

And it got to her, damn it.

She wasn't sure what to think when RuArk retrieved a small brush from one of several small leather pouches hanging from one of the tent poles near the bed.

Her eyes drifted closed again and words ran together as she murmured, "Whaddar you gonna do wi-dat?" She floated closer and closer to what she knew would be sweet dreams. She'd almost made it when her eyes popped open with surprise when a firm but gentle stroke guided soft bristles through the thick locks of her hair. She soaked up the sweet calm that enveloped her until she was a boneless heap of '*aaah*' from her scalp clear down to her toes. Hair brushing certainly never felt this good when she did it herself.

"Tell me of your growing up time," he said smoothly.

"Well, you were around for most of the beginning. Where should I start?" She sighed, not bothering to keep up the fight with her eyes. They wanted to stay closed, so let 'em. But now her mouth didn't want to move either. All she wanted was to keep her forehead against his chest, listen to the strong thump of his heart as the brush slid through her curls until she was dead to the world asleep.

"You may choose what you wish to share."

Huh? Share what? Oh, yeah, he wanted to talk about her childhood.

Bleh.

She yawned. "After my mother died, I continued blade training. I made First Blade well before my sixteenth birthday, then I..."

"No. I wish to hear about your life, not your duties."

"RuArk, once my mother was gone, my duties *became* my life."

"Do you spend all your time thinking on your duties?"

Okay, his questions were making her think, which made her more awake. Damn it.

"Yes. I mean, no. I don't know. Sometimes I wish I could just be somebody else, somebody with no responsibilities and no title. Maybe join the Society of Equine Breeders, or Basket Weavers, or anything other than be tasked with the safety of all of Draema province."

She started when his deep, rich laughter resonated through his chest and up her arms. It made her fingers tingle. The bass of his voice traipsed along the nerves where her hands rested on the sculpted slabs of his pecs.

"You handle a blade well enough, yet it would be interesting to see you weave baskets, Ree."

He called her Ree? Nobody called her that but Joan. She decided she liked it, but balled up her fist and thumped him lightly in the chest with a scowl anyway. He chuckled some more while parting her hair down the middle with the brush before pulling the mass of curls over her shoulders to play in it. His fingers felt as good against her scalp as the brush had.

"I'm glad you like to joke. I wouldn't want you to misunderstand my teasing and become upset."

Huh. In truth, she hadn't expected this man, this hardened warrior, to care the least bit about her being upset.

When he planted a soft kiss at the base of her neck, she knew exactly where this was going.

Time to say or do something to change his line of thinking or she would lose control of the situation entirely. Then again, given the sweet hum in her belly perhaps it was already too late.

"RuArk, that's nice and all, but I really don't expect anything from you." But there was no heat behind her words, and barely any breath. In fact, she sounded like a damn wimp.

Rhia bit her lip to keep from moaning when his fingers left her scalp and eased lower to massage the knots from her shoulders. Mmmm. Maybe being a wimp wasn't so bad? Surely wimps were good people, too? Raising her head, she looked deeply into his eyes and tried to solve the mystery of how she could want a man so much while not *wanting* to want him.

"Of course you expect something from me," he crooned softly with a bit of gruff mixed in. His response overflowed with intensity hot enough to melt the steel. "You want what all women want. To be taken and well loved. It matters not what a woman says outside the bedroom. Once inside, she wants to be mounted." He licked the side of her neck. "And tamed."

Enjoying the massage much more than she would ever admit, Rhia snorted rudely. "A bit presumptuous on your part, don't ya think?"

"What? Do you believe that when we make love you'll give nothing of yourself? Just move coldly through the motions? Mmmm..." He nuzzled her ear. "Not quite, gorgeous. I think you're going to like it rough."

Instinctively, Rhia knew, *knew* that he'd just told on himself and said exactly what he'd been doing whenever he'd lain with a woman. He'd taken his pleasure, but left nothing of himself behind. Had never opened his heart, nor shared a single hope or dream with any of his former lovers. And here he was, in a marriage he'd never intended with a woman he'd never dreamed of being with. But if her intuition was correct, they both wanted the same thing—more.

Now, how this resonated in her heart, she had no idea. But the knowledge was there all the same.

"When we have sex, Rhia, you will gladly give me whatever I ask," he whispered, slowly stroking the pulse point along her collarbone. "And I will do the same. Give it to you when you want it, how you want it. For as long as you want it."

"And when is this supposed to happen, big guy?"

"When you ask me for it. I would never make love with an unwilling woman."

"Cheeky bastard."

He chuckled deep in his throat. Her body shivered in response. Even as tired as she was, there was no helping the response to the contact of the strong fingers traipsing along the tops of her thighs. She was so sensitized that his hands seemed to singe the hairs off her skin through her clothes. Her stomach muscles clenched, butt cheeks felt damp underneath where sweat began to gather. But she certainly wasn't going to *ask* him to have sex with her, husband or not.

Blasted man.

She almost sighed with relief when one hand left her thigh. It took a few seconds for the heat to dissipate from that particular spot. He stroked his chin and gray eyes twinkled as he lifted his gaze toward the ceiling of their tent, contemplating. The side of his so-sexy mouth quirked up as he said, "Actually, I don't believe I've ever met a woman that refused to sleep with me."

She wanted to smack him. Hard.

Tiredness disappeared in direct proportion to the ignition of her temper. So, there'd been plenty of other women, eh? Just how many women was he talking about here? This was *her* husband and she'd skin any other female creaming, uh, screaming for him.

"So, what if I don't ask you, RuArk? Then what?" she snapped.

No longer a boneless heap of longing, Rhia couldn't keep her upper lip from curling. Spine ramrod straight, her anger flared enough to light up an iozene lamp.

RuArk only shrugged and resumed stroking and teasing her body.

"Does that mean there are plenty of others who'd take my place between the sheets if I don't ask you to fuck me?"

Still no answer.

He's playing me, letting me wonder. Bastard.

His fingers gently skimmed along her forearms, the clean, tidy nails lightly tickled the smooth flesh from her wrists all the way up to her shoulders raising gooseflesh along the way. The butterflies in her stomach came out to play. She snarled at them until they flew the hell away.

"Look at me, Rhia."

She didn't want to.

When she finally lifted her gaze, it was to be surprised yet again by the raw longing in the deep gray of his eyes. No longer steely with flecks of silver throughout, these were now stormy, wild and raging seas she wouldn't mind being shipwrecked in. And all she had to do was ask.

"I will never force you, but we can still learn each other, and what we like. Do you like when I touch you, Ree?"

Oh, how she wanted to lie. Instead, she nodded and let her eyes drift closed.

"No, no, look at me, love. I want to see your eyes as I touch you. Watch them darken from light honeyed amber to dark smoldering embers."

When she complied, he said, "It's been too long. Kiss me again."

CHAPTER SEVENTEEN

He was so much taller that even sitting in his lap, she had to scoot up to the juncture of his thighs so she could reach his lips. It felt a bit naughty that he was completely naked while she was fully dressed. Lifting her lips, she initiated a kiss for the first time since they'd been reacquainted. Instinctively, her hips pressed down harder over him, and she found herself rocking against the thick ridge of his straining erection even as his lips moved over hers.

RuArk tightened his arms around her. His softly moaned pleasure urged her to part her lips and set her tongue into a duel with his. Surprising herself, Rhia gave no tentative, shy strokes. No, this was hot and unrestrained, wet and decadent. God, she'd never tasted anything so fulfilling yet unsatisfying. The more she got from RuArk, the more she wanted.

Wrapping her arms around his neck, Rhia leaned into him, needing the brush of hard, chiseled pecs pressed, and then sliding against her swelling breasts. Frustration taunted her when RuArk removed her arms from around his neck where she wanted them most, and made her sit exactly the way he'd arranged her before, palms flat on his chest.

She broke the kiss on a strangled sigh. Then again, maybe she'd simply strangle him instead. "RuArk, let me move."

"No," he said, feathering kisses along the plane of her jaw. "And no more wearing clothes to bed, Rhia. The tunic and light leggings, off." She squirmed as his tongue played with her earlobe.

Remove her trousers? What? It was bad enough he wanted her to ask for sex. She'd held out so far, but if he managed to get her completely naked in her present state of horny-ness, she'd be a goner. After what felt like a cycle's worth of moments, Rhia croaked out a sentence as her mind raced for a solution. Maybe she could stall?

"Uh, I have to move my hands to take the clothes off." Then, perhaps she could run for it.

RuArk smiled. The sight chilled her even in the near-dark of the tent—now *that* was a predatory grin if she'd ever seen one—leaning forward until his lips were barely an inch from hers.

"No need for you to move, Rhia," he said, his mouth swooping over hers again, taking his time, and devouring her until all trepidation dissolved to little more than dust. He was all spice and lust as he proceeded to strip her naked, ripping the finely woven garment right down the seams, followed by leggings and silky, itty bitty, drenched underwear.

She yanked her mouth away and half-heartedly grumbled about boneheaded warriors not caring how difficult it was for a woman her height to acquire leggings in that particular color. The protest died in her throat as he licked a path up the column of her throat while grinding his hard naked flesh against the slick folds between her now bare thighs.

RuArk was so sinfully handsome, skin so golden, and all that thick, black hair like so much silk on his head. Other than a sprinkling of downy hair at the base of his cock—and an imposing sight *that* was—there was no hair anywhere else on his body. None on his sculpted chest, his ropy defined forearms, nor the firm thighs she straddled. Just miles and miles of smooth, bronzed skin stretched taut over bands of thick muscle.

Her breasts screamed for attention and he didn't disappoint. Rhia relished the feel of his warrior's hands moving over her body. The calloused fingers teased her sensitive spots as he explored the planes of her back and hips, sliding around to the fluttering plain of her tummy, and back up to her breasts. She snatched in a quick breath, determined to maintain some semblance of control.

If she had to give up breathing to keep from begging RuArk to fuck her, then so be it. Her head spun as the air whooshed into her lungs. But even as she breathed once more, her head continued to whirl with delicious pleasure as her mate's talented hands became more insistent.

No longer circling or teasing, but plucking, pulling, exquisitely torturing her flesh until she couldn't have suppressed her sighs of pleasure or still her squirming hips if her life depended on it. Blazes, it felt so good. The sensation reminded her of the sound sharpening stones made when stroked against a blade.

Zing! Zing! Zing!

Pressing his own hips up to meet her, his hands full of her sensitive breasts, his rigid flesh seemed even harder under her ass than it had been only moments before. Well, at least RuArk wasn't immune to what he was doing to her. She liked knowing that almost as much as she liked the sensations he wrung from her body.

The blaze between them crackled and hummed just below the surface of her skin when suddenly she was consumed by the need to reach down and touch him. To wrap her fingers around him, feel every hard inch. To see if he was a huge as he seemed pressed so intimately against her tender folds. But RuArk had other plans.

"Lean forward, Rhia. Let me taste your beautiful breasts."

She shivered uncontrollably, licking her lips, barely able to stand what he was doing right now. A fleeting thought crossed her mind that he could have simply ordered her to make love with him and she would have had to obey.

Instead, he'd promised her that she would have to ask him for it. Sworn he'd never force his way inside her body.

"May I have your breast, Rhia?" It was a hiss. The words, harsh and untamed. Needy. Sexy as hell.

Shaking her head, silently begging for mercy, Rhia leaned forward at the same time RuArk lay back, taking her with him. She practically panted with anticipation, but the man didn't suckle right away. He licked slowly from the base of one achy mound all the way to the tip of its throbbing nipple.

With full, carnal, open mouthed kisses, his tongue slid up, down and all around until she reeled from the pleasure of it. Finally, he suckled in earnest and pulled the entire crown into his mouth and drew hungrily. It was hard, rough, as if he wanted to eat her all together. Rhia yelped, then moaned loudly as sharp white teeth nipped one sensitive tip, followed by the soothing lave of his wet tongue.

He was right, I like it rough.

She wanted to demand that he bite her again, but it came out a strangled cry. The rosebud between her thighs bloomed and throbbed exquisitely. Rocking back and forth against his massive erection only seemed to make the hunger worse, but it was impossible to keep her hips still. A fine sheen of sweat soon covered every inch of bare skin from her neck down to the backs of her knees. God, she needed more. And if she didn't get it now she would simply keel over on the spot.

"RuArk. Oh god, please, do something." She'd never begged for anything in her life. Guess there was a first time for everything.

"Ask me for it," he crooned, the slightest whisper in her ear.

"No."

"Ask me for my cock, Rhia," he growled, his arms tightening around her again.

"I-I can't, but I need…" She wasn't sure why she resisted. Perhaps she'd give it more thought later. Right now she only wanted, needed release.

"I'll take care of you." He reached down between their bodies until he found the bundle of nerves peeking out from its little hood. Pressed gently at first and somehow knew it wasn't enough. Fingers circled hard. Then harder.

Yes.

Rhia soared. His demand that she stay still was completely forgotten. Her hands tangled in the thick silk of his hair as she smashed his face to her breast, and ground wildly against his questing fingers. One long digit slipped into her tight sheath, followed by another, stroking deeply. She was so wet and ready, honey overflowed until it mingled with her sweat and dripped down the inside of her thighs.

To Rhia, everything suddenly seemed so far away, as if she floated outside herself, watching someone else enjoy these luscious sensations.

Her head fell back, body trembled as RuArk's fingers sank into her again and again. His thumb grazed her clitoris in an enticing pattern that made her sex tighten. Rhia was done for.

"RuArk, oh yes," she gasped.

The pleasure on Rhia's face when she fell apart in his arms was the most beautiful thing RuArk had ever experienced. Her release was explosive, like blinding splintered light or the shattering of the sun lighting up his typically-gray world. After her body quieted and the trembling subsided, his wife tumbled into sleep spread out on top of him.

The woman was completely oblivious of the blood pounding in his ears. RuArk was so stiff and hard, he dared not move, afraid he'd accidentally break off his cock by doing nothing more than rolling over in the bed.

He sighed and tightened his arms around her slumbering frame. Tonight was just the beginning. Tomorrow night, he would teach her something new. And the next eve, yet another lesson in passion. Four more days and nights to Province Springs—nights spent touching his mate without taking her. It would be the sweetest torture he would ever endure, and the hardest thing he'd ever *not* done.

When the time came to make love, or *fuck* as Rhia would say, she would come to him willingly, trusting him completely for that loving. And the mating would be more than worth the wait.

RuArk was awake the moment the quiet footsteps sounded on the mossy ground outside his tent. Fingers wrapped instinctively around the dagger under his pillow just before Linc's barely-there whisper broke the early morning silence.

"Wind Storm, I have news from Marth. He has finished hunting and is on the way to the proper meeting place with his quarry."

Unwinding his longer limbs from around Rhia's sleek ones was torture. The raging erection from last night was now the unholiest morning hard-on he'd ever experienced in all his life. He buried his nose in the dark, red-streaked curls tangled around her head as she slept. Her scent had him closing his eyes on a ragged moan as his head was filled with the recollection of the sounds she made when receiving pleasure at his hand.

From the soft intakes of breath as he'd suckled her dusky nipples, to the sharp gasps when she'd come around his fingers, all imprinted in his mind forever. The thoughts created a clenching in his gut as he fought the desire to slide between her legs.

Instead, he eased out of bed, careful to move quietly so as not to wake her. She would need all the rest she could get with the pace he planned to set today.

Once outside, any remaining sleep was whipped

away by the crisp breeze blowing through the camp. The sun was rising quickly, revealing a crystal blue sky.

For no apparent reason, he was… happy. He would take some time to meditate later and examine exactly what was going on with the sides of his mouth as they lifted into a triumphant grin. Linc tossed a questioning glance his way, then smirked as if he knew something RuArk didn't.

"What?"

"Nothing, sir," Linc said, but that smirk turned into a full blown smile. Humph.

"How did Marth's hunting go?" RuArk asked quietly, taking a few steps away from his shelter. Rhia didn't need to overhear this particular conversation.

"Marth has bagged a wild one. Joan is giving him quite a time of it." Linc's green eyes gleamed and twinkled under the quickly fading moonlight. "He has also gotten word to the High Counsel with assurance that his daughter is safe."

"Good. Tell him to issue new orders to the men keeping watch in Draema Proper. I want to know what is happening at all times."

"Yes, sir." While Linc appeared to look directly at RuArk, his eyes took on a familiar faraway expression as he fired up his Gift and linked his thoughts to those of his brother. RuArk was always amazed at how well the twins used their Gifts, even at great distances.

A few seconds later Linc regained his own wry expression and said, "Marth did so several days ago. He also wants you to know that his quarry made it necessary to depart the High City earlier than anticipated. There was quite a lot of activity the day we left and someone had indeed been following Rhia.

Several somebodies. My brother says he looks forward to telling his story."

A moment later Rhia ducked out of the tent in a flash, ran smack into the middle of RuArk's solid back and grunted as she bounced off and stumbled. Her gaze caught his, clearly puzzled. He reached out a steadying hand.

"RuArk, I felt it again. It was exactly the same as last time."

"What was exactly the same as last time?"

"The weird goose bump feeling that makes the hair on the back of my neck stand on end. An awareness. Like someone near me, but in my head. I don't know how to explain it."

"This has happened before?"

"Yes. On the way to our first dinner together in the Citadel, remember? I'd just met Linc and Sharyn and we were walking toward the main hall. I felt this weird sensation. I stopped in the hallway and looked around to see if I could tell where it had come from. You asked me what was wrong, but I really thought I'd just caught a chill or something."

RuArk did indeed remember. Marth had just contacted Linc as they'd been walking to dinner in the great hall. Now that he thought about it, the sensation Rhia described was exactly what he experienced whenever Sharyn healed someone while he was in close proximity, or when Linc communicated with Marth using the Gifts, including their silent conversation just moments ago—just before Rhia flew out of the tent.

RuArk had spent all his life around Gifted people, so the sensation was common to him to the point where it went pretty much ignored. But Rhia's mother has passed when she was a little girl. Was it possible his mate could sense the Gifts in operation, but just didn't know it? If so, she may very well have a Gift of her own. A Gift she'd never been taught to touch or control. She was, after all, half-Gaian.

But this wasn't a conversation they could have just now. They were still being tracked. Safety first. Talk later.

"Go back inside and get a cloak Rhia. It's cold." She looked as if she wanted to fuss, but disappeared through the tent door instead. He called after her. "You have time for a quick bath and breakfast. We leave in one hour."

Hands full of gelsoap, towels, a brush and a change of clothes, Rhia flipped open the tent flat. The moment she stepped out she was swept up into a good morning kiss that curled her toes inside her boots. Strong arms wrapped around her, warming her inside the cloak she wore as RuArk's mouth covered hers in a hungry kiss. Mmm, he tasted good, like mints and fresh... something. If she had to give it a color it would be bright yellow and warming to the flesh like the rising sun.

He nipped the tendons in her neck, sending a shiver through every muscle in her back. Goodness. "Mmm, I can still smell your sweet honey, almost as if it's on my tongue."

A single finger eased its way down and over the line of her spine, awakening the nerves along each individual bone. Breathing deepened as the lush heat of his mouth devoured, pulled her into a well of need, down, deeper.

Heat that began as a subtle warmth, spread and consumed. Sizzled. God. The nipples pressed against his chest pebbled, and she couldn't help but rub against the solidness of his chest and recall the smoothness of the skin that covered the muscle there. Her sex bloomed, ached as his hands sank into her hair and gently tugged to angle her the way he wanted.

"Can't wait to have you in my arms tonight. Perhaps you will ask for what you really want? Or maybe you will beg for what you need? And…"

Nip, lick.

"I am not afraid…"

Suck, nibble.

"To admit that I do indeed need it."

Okay, she was going to melt. Right here. Right now. If he didn't back up she would ask now rather than wait until tonight. This kiss was too much, yet not enough.

Then, in an act of mercy, he ended the torture, eased his arms from around her and stepped back just a bit.

"Lucky for both of us, we have to clean up and get ready to ride. I'll have your gear loaded onto your mount. Go greet him. I do believe he's missed you. See you in the clearing in a standard hour."

With a final loud smack, lip to lip, her mate turned and went about his duties.

She'd been so consumed with RuArk, that she'd completely forgotten he'd mentioned that her horse would be here this morning. Something about having a scout bring him…?

Hell, she could hardly remember any conversation from last night, not when most of her brain has been bombarded with nothing short of a sensual onslaught. And it had been so, so good. But right now it didn't matter. She didn't have much time for anything more than a quick hello to Moonlight, thankful someone had groomed and watered him already.

She pondered as she walked toward the spot where they'd eaten last night. She hadn't expected RuArk to leave her to herself today. After all, they were supposed to be glued at the hip, right? Not one to question something that should have been a relief, Rhia threw herself into a routine that was surprisingly familiar — breakfast, bath, move out.

Only today she was headed to Province Springs rather than to a meeting, a training session, a Council of Seven conference or some other such task. Feeling surprisingly well rested and comfortably full, Rhia set her empty bowl on a large rock, scooped up her stuff and began the short walk toward the stream.

A hint of soreness between her legs sent a blush to her cheeks. RuArk had spent quite a bit of time... there.

By the time he'd finished with her, she'd been begging him to stop rather than take her. Even now, her sex softened, then filled until a dull throb pulsed beneath her clitoris at the memory of his hands and mouth on her skin. *All* of her skin.

During her single days, she'd stroked and palmed her breasts and imagined what it would be like to have someone else's hands caress her. But since there was nothing to be done for it, she'd typically ignored her arousal. Now, things were different. She had a mate to associate with carnal longings. And now she knew one thing she'd only guessed at before — his hands felt a hell of a lot better than her own.

CHAPTER EIGHTEEN

Moving quietly toward her goal, her thoughts remained on her new husband. In a rush, her head filled with RuArk and her consciousness seemed aware of him in a way that was indescribable. She pictured him with clarity as if a vid played in her head. The image was crystal clear, from the flex and bunch of his biceps to the position of his wrist as he moved a black diamond encrusted stone across a blade with sure, even strokes.

Her eyes mentally crossed when the image's long black locks were brushed back over his shoulders like a thick curtain of silk falling over the wide expanse of his bare back to whisper against the skin. A few random strands fell forward and obscured the strong set of his jaw.

He straddled a large log near the edge of the clearing, partially concealed by a clump of evergreen brush.

Rhia blinked and looked around. RuArk was nowhere around, so how did she know he was servicing his blades when she hadn't seen him, nor heard the zing of a sharpening stone meeting metal?

Yet she *felt* him. Saw him in her head. Felt the

weight of his office press down on his broad shoulders. Felt his concern for those in his charge… and she was at the top of the list.

How did she know all this? Know how he felt, both the good and the bad?

Rhia turned the corner and suddenly he was there, sitting on the same fallen tree her mind had conjured. She met his gaze and stopped dead in her tracks. The strange awareness grew exponentially, slammed into her heart at the exact moment her tawny eyes met his deep grays. So strong it was almost tangible.

RuArk sat perfectly still, a black diamond sharpening stone paused over one of several blades spread out in front of him. Rhia's head tilted to the side, brow furrowed and body tense, trying to see inside him, through him.

Warmth infused her skin, limbs, and muscles until it settled in her blood. A subtle pull somewhere deep inside her body made her want to touch him, kiss him, wrap herself around him. As if their destinies intertwined… just as he'd said he'd seen in the *Seeking*.

Still, this was just weird. Besides, she was supposed to be upset about this whole sham of a marriage thing. Her father meant well, but that wasn't the point. Was it?

As abruptly as she'd halted, she changed her direction.

'Oh, please don't let him come after me right now,' she implored under her breath, stomach quivering under a wash of emotion. Desperate for him, yet terrified, afraid to accept what could turn out to be the gift she'd wanted most — RuArk.

She almost stopped and turned to look back to

see if he followed. Then the sound of the stone on metal made it clear he'd returned to his task instead. With a little distance between them, relief flooded her mind and body as the tight bands around her chest loosened and allowed her to breathe again.

Sitting next to the stream on a large rock, Rhia splashed cold water on her heated cheeks. Everything was a jumble—her mind, her thoughts, everything. She knew she'd eventually cease being surprised at her physical reaction to RuArk, but this wild inner whatever-it-was occurred with barely a thought, then burned out of control when their eyes met. More like when their *minds* met. Sure, she'd felt an insane attraction to the man. Always had even when she was a girl. But this... this was something new. Something more intimate, as if he'd burrowed a layer deeper beneath her skin, and she, beneath his.

She might not understand all this lifemate business, but it didn't take a scholar from the Society of Physics and Space to tell her that this was a true connection. A deep one.

RuArk forced himself to finish seeing to his weapons, shaken as the blaze of what was obviously a new bond with Rhia died down to a subtle glow. He sat and pondered her escape into the forest, and there was no doubt it had been an escape. Her need to distance herself from everyone, even her friends, when she was troubled seemed so out of place for a woman, a soldier, with such a dynamic personality. What had happened to make her believe the only way she could survive was to do it alone? The pieces of the puzzle were there, but he had no idea how to put them together.

But damn it, she was his. And if it killed them both, he would see her taken care of. Though it seemed to be the last thing Rhia wanted, he instinctively knew it was exactly what she needed.

Rhia rose from the stream, dressed and turned to head back to the clearing. She skidded to a halt as an annoyed growl formed low in her throat. It was unusual for her to dislike someone, especially someone she didn't really know, but for some reason this Sharyn person got under her skin.

Sharyn eyed her up one side and down the other, boldly measured her until her gaze came back 'round to meet eye-to-eye. Finally, the woman offered a greeting, but her tone was as icy as the clear stream she stooped next to as she cleaned her teeth.

Was it a challenge?

Rhia did some measuring of her own. Forget being intimidated, especially by a woman who wore scarves for clothes.

"Your face says you do not like me, Rhia. Are we of like mind?" Sharyn asked, her voice calm, sure and hard as stone as she rinsed her mouth and spat.

"Maybe, maybe not," Rhia replied with a bit of edge, but honestly it was all the edge she had left. There was too much on her mind and she just really didn't feel like doing this just now. "Look, right now I..." her words ended on a sigh. The urge to explain vanished as she felt herself crashing, almost caving in on her own soul. Being left alone rocketed to the top of her "need" list.

Sharyn seemed to sense the shift in Rhia's posture and let her own guard down, but just a bit.

"Let us come to an understanding, yes?"

Rhia really wasn't in a giving mood, but it was obvious Sharyn wasn't taking the hint to go away. She crossed her arms over her chest and leaned back against the rough bark of yet another huge budding tree. Resisting the urge to tap her booted foot on the loamy ground, she waited for the other woman to get the burr out of her drawers and get to the point.

"I understand you have a certain feeling, an awareness at times."

Whoa, what? The tree forgotten, Rhia sprang to attention.

"How do you know about that?"

"I am a First Commander to the Wind Storm. Why would he not share something of importance with me?"

"This is considered important? Why?"

"Because you may be Gifted, Rhia."

"Of course I'm gifted. All Blademasters are gifted with the natural ability to—"

"No, Rhia. You may have the ability to touch the Source that allows the Gifts, given by the Ancestors, to operate. It may also be proof of the beginning of a strong bond with your lifemate."

"Bond? Look, I'm not into that kinky stuff."

Sharyn laughed outright. Humph. There was obviously more to this Gaian-style mating business than Rhia had been told.

"We must explore your abilities. Perhaps you have the Gift of a Sensuan," Sharyn drawled, a gleam in her eye.

Rhia couldn't tell whether it was snark or good natured humor. Whatever it was, this was a side of the woman she'd never seen. Cocking her head, she studied her, sensing a familiarity and camaraderie of sorts. What was Sharyn to her? Rhia may not like her just now, but she did believe she could trust her. No idea why, but it was there all the same.

"A Sensuan? You're crazy. All Sensuan are Gaian."

Rhia almost flinched at the 'duh' look she received, then laughed at her own ridiculous words. Of course they were Gaian. Just like her, even if she was only half. Geesh. Floundering, she muttered, "Well, okay, but Sensuan don't really have...uh, they only, well..."

"I can see you have not given much thought to how they do what they do, though you are half Gaian," Sharyn stated matter-of-factly.

Ouch. That stung, but it was no less true. In fact, by the time she'd finished making the rounds with RuArk last night, meeting his men and such, Rhia had been thoroughly embarrassed. Every man, whether they'd ever set foot in Draema before or not, had knowledge of her home. They knew Draeman history from before the time of the Breaking. They knew the languages, laws, social structure and many of the customs. Even the layout of the lands and location of the borders of all seven colonies that made up the province of Draema.

What did she know about Gaia? Beans, is what, and she'd never even had a naturally-grown one of those, either.

RuArk's terms for their agreement were

suddenly quite important now. She needed to learn, about him, their people, and even about herself. Damn, she hated running to catch up.

"So what about this bond business?"

"Those of us with Gifts can sometimes sense others that carry them," Sharyn said. "As for this *bond business*, we can also sense those we have joined our lives to. It is called a mate bond."

"I don't understand. How does this bond form?"

"It requires only the acceptance of the joining in your heart, not the sharing of your body. Sometimes it happens between mates without their admitting it with words. But the heart knows. It is all that is required, just as the mating itself. It is a magic of sorts."

Those words came back to her. RuArk had said something about 'the magic in their blood.' Hmmm.

Rhia shook her head in amazement. How could her heart accept something without her head being involved? This was way beyond her realm of knowledge or experience. But the pulsing hole in her gut told her Sharyn was on to something.

"Tell me about the sensing thing?" Rhia asked.

Thankfully, Sharyn obliged.

"First, I must know how acute this feeling is you've experienced. It is an awareness of someone or something around you that you could not see? Or perhaps a tingling on your skin, as if something fleeting had touched you? There was no fear, but a knowing someone was near?"

Rhia nodded, eager to understand.

"When you think of the Wind Storm, you begin to sense him because the bond is invoked."

"By thought? It's that simple?"

"It is the simplest explanation. However, sensing

the Gifts is different, less precise than the bond. It requires no thought, and happens when you are in the presence of another who is touching their Source. The Source can be touched without actually engaging your Gifts."

Really? Not only had she experienced what Sharyn described, but had felt it many times since encountering RuArk and his warriors in the High City. It was a tingling that began in her scalp and slipped down the back of her neck, especially around Linc. A passing presence, like a shadow brushing against her mind. Just then, the hair on the back of her neck stood at attention as she became aware of a subtle *something* that seemed to press against her very spirit.

Sharyn.

"You are using your Gift right now, aren't you?"

"No, but I am touching my Source. It is what allows mates to invoke their bond, and allows me the ability to use my Gift. Can you feel it?"

"Yes, I can feel it. And I'm not sure I like it at all."

"Why? Because you cannot control it? Because it is something of which you are not an expert?" The words were calm, but the heat, the blatant attitude in Sharyn's gaze was purposely present. It pushed a button that sent Rhia's temper flaring.

"Just who do you think you're talking to like that?" Rhia took a step forward, hands on hips, but the other woman's words brought her up short.

"I am speaking to you, Rhia. I respect you because you are lifemate to the Wind Storm. I will protect you with my life because it is my duty to protect RuArk and you are now a part of him. I protect him from danger, his enemies, and from pain. I will shield him from anyone who would cause him harm. And should you choose to be a source of hurt, I will include you among his enemies."

Holy shit.

"I would never hurt him," Rhia blurted before she could hold back the words, but knew they were true. Silently, she scolded herself for simmering just below a boil while Sharyn was as composed as the finest Draeman noble taking afternoon tea — yuck.

"It is important you understand that I am your equal, not your student. I do not take orders from you unless the Protector demands that I do so, or I choose to swear the oath to you. So far, you have earned nothing."

Rhia was appalled. No one had ever spoken to her like this. But she had no retort because Sharyn's words rang true even as the hardness left her voice.

"I am not your enemy, Rhia. You can learn from me, from all of us. We have been places you have never been. I am familiar with things of which you have little knowledge. The Gifts and the bond to your mate are examples of this. You would do well to remove your nose from the air and accept that you are not in charge. Not here. Not for the moment."

Well, at least the woman is straightforward. Sharyn picked up her bow and slung it over her shoulder.

"Besides, I do not compete with you for RuArk's affection, Rhia. He loves me."

And just when I was starting to respect the bitch, Rhia snarled to herself.

"But," Sharyn continued, "he loves me as he would a sister. He is my cousin, though we are not related by any blood. This is something you would know had you bothered to simply ask. You have his heart, though neither of you seem to realize it. You fight your need for him, but there are many women who would take your place if given the chance."

"Have you ever slept together, Sharyn?" She just had to know. Braced herself for the answer.

"We have slept together under the stars." She paused. "With thirty or forty other people around us. We have never shared our bodies, if that is what you mean. But if he ever asked me, I would gladly give myself to him. I owe him my life and I would do anything for him."

Uncomfortable silence stretched between the two proud women. Both stood their ground, neither looked away. Rhia was impressed with Sharyn. It would be much better to have her allegiance than to be a foe.

"I believe you are a wise woman, Rhia Greysomne, but are you wise enough to accept what cannot be changed? To embrace what is now a part of you, meaning your mate, and quite possibly a Gift? I can help you learn the ways of our people. I will even help you understand your mate. Well, whenever he is not teaching you, of course."

Though Sharyn's mouth was a straight line of seriousness, her eyes seemed to smile anyway. Rhia knew it was as close to an extension of friendship as she was going to get. Insight into what made RuArk tick? An advantage into this new life of hers? And the chance to make a friend? She'd be crazy to turn away.

"I would like your help, Sharyn," she smiled, extending her hand to the other woman. For a moment, she wasn't sure Sharyn would take it, when with a swift movement the other woman reached out and wrapped her fingers around Rhia's forearm. Touching the fingertips of her free hand lightly to her own lips, she kissed the tips and placed them on Rhia's skin next to the fingers that gripped her firmly.

"This is called the Sister's Kiss."

Rhia wasn't sure what to do when Sharyn continued to stand there with both her hands on either side of Rhia's forearm, holding fast. When Rhia mirrored her actions and lightly kissed her own fingers and placed them on the skin of Sharyn's forearm, the dark haired warrior woman nodded, closed her eyes.

The energy, the connection was so intense Rhia's skin practically ran away from her body. Surely every hair stood on end as a door inside her own mind opened wide and Sharyn walked through. Wow. It was exciting and humbling to have this strong woman be willing to share something so intimate.

Rhia had good friends in Joan and Brita, but she now realized that it was more than friendship that she'd been missing since her mother had passed. No, it was the inner-joining she'd just experienced with Sharyn, that she'd also had with her mother—a touch of her Source energy. Sure, she had a father and a brother, but...

She didn't want to think about it just now.

Instead, she focused on the flow of her Source. After it slowly vanished, Rhia suddenly found herself pulled into a fierce hug.

"You are now my sister. We are family, Rhia, with a bond of our own. Nothing quite like what you will develop with your mate, but we will be close, you and I."

The thought was comforting, calming and thrilling all at once, but she kept quiet, careful not to interrupt as Sharyn explained the significance of the little ceremony they'd just completed. This was a rare honor, especially for a non-Gaian. If this conversation had gone any better, Rhia would have floated clean away.

Sharyn's smile rivaled the blinding sun as pride and accomplishment shone in her dark brown eyes.

Now, it was time to hit the road. With a skip in her step she didn't bother to hide, Rhia headed back to camp with Sharyn's light-hearted chuckle sounding in the light breeze behind her.

CHAPTER NINETEEN

Dalmore came forward to assist her with mounting. Before she could wave him away, one look at the raised eyebrow of her lifemate changed her mind.

Sigh. Nothing wrong with letting the man be a gentleman.

She painted on a smile, then realized she was genuinely in a good mood, and allowed Dalmore to help her up into her saddle. RuArk eyed her askance, but said nothing.

As they rode, their entire party, as large as it was, remained quiet, carrying on silent conversations with their hands. With all her military experience, she'd never seen anything quite like it. Warriors rode both in front of and behind them. Some traveled well off the road and into the forests on either side. They were flanked on all sides, but could easily be mistaken for a small party traveling alone. The Noman she'd exchanged growls with the night before was conspicuously missing.

Their pace was leisurely, but she detected the hum of anticipation, of danger as they moved. Yet, her mate was a solid and calming presence. After riding in comfortable silence for a couple of standard hours, she finally whispered, "Why is everyone so quiet?"

He nudged his mount close enough for the supple gray buckskins stretched over his large thighs to rub against her leg. That simple contact blazed clear down to her toes, but she shook it off and forced herself to concentrate on his words instead of his strength and the hardness of his muscles, what they felt like skin-to-skin. And his full, tempting lips. God, and all that sinfully soft hair.

Sigh. He turned a soft smile in her direction before it was pushed away and replaced with a granite seriousness she wished he didn't have to wear. Ever.

"You are being hunted, which means," he said, motioning to the men surrounding them, "*we* are also hunted."

That explained why they weren't all traveling on the road together.

"Can we talk at all?" she whispered.

Nodding, RuArk indicated with his hands for her to be as quiet as possible, then casually produced a wickedly curved dagger and began polishing it as they covered the distance at a leisurely pace. Now *that* was an impressive weapon. She just had to touch it.

Holding out her hand, she asked breathlessly, "May I?" His answering smile melted her bones. She lowered her lashes, hid a demure smile of her own and held in a gasp of anticipation as he placed it in her hand.

Both the blade and handle were jet black and made of a metal alloy she wasn't familiar with. The hilt was covered with a tacky almost sticky substance that she imagined would stay in a soldier's hand even if it was coated with blood. She flipped the razor sharp weapon over her hand and across the backs of her knuckles testing its weight and balance. Except for the color, his knife was very similar to the one she always wore strapped to her thigh that had once belonged to her mother.

Next, he removed several more knives from hidden sheaths on his body and explained how they differed from her Draeman weapons. Assassin's blade, long knife, bowie knife, and more. He even let her play with one of his armor plated wrist guards she'd never seen him take off before. She couldn't remember enjoying a conversation with a man more.

Suddenly, Rhia longed to have more in common with RuArk than a mind boggling attraction, or a love of weapons and tactics.

"Have you ever been in love, RuArk?" As soon as the words left her lips, his expression became as hard as Draeman stone. Too bad her teeth weren't sharp enough to bite off her tongue. Damn.

Surprisingly, there was no hesitancy on RuArk's part. Not necessarily a good thing.

"Once. It was the most idiotic thing I have ever done."

Ouch.

"Who put the thorn in your side to make you so jaded about love?" she snorted cynically. To her surprise, RuArk didn't hesitate to tell his story, but with so little emotion he could have been talking about his horse, or a trip to see the snow up on the highest peaks of the Borderland's mountains.

"My thorn, as you say, was called Ansla. She was to be my mate. I was young and thought she was the great love of my life." Now it was his turn to snort. "I was so naive. Father tried to warn me, told me his thoughts on the woman, but encouraged me to make my own choice. It was his way of trying to guide me without making me feel incapable of making decisions on my own. A man named Shiel, a fellow clansman, told me I should listen to my father. I found her in his arms the night before our joining ceremony."

Rhia scowled and opened her mouth to defend her sex, but snapped it shut as his schooled features slipped with his next words.

"You appear to be a woman of honor."

He seemed surprised at his own confession, as if he'd discovered something he liked, but would rather it be unpalatable. Rhia rolled her eyes and laughed at his disgruntled expression, earning a deep scowl from him.

"Yes, I have honor, RuArk," she said, falling silent until she felt him begin to withdraw again. She wanted to continue the conversation. "We both seem to be carrying some baggage."

He raised a brow, prompting Rhia to explain.

"I just think we've both been scarred by our pasts," she explained. "But I'm not Ansla and you're not Bryan. Do you believe we can change our way of thinking?"

Perhaps love each other?

He didn't say a word. The very air seemed to thicken as the space between them filled with unease. But who was uncomfortable? Her, him, or both of them?

Needing an answer, *any* answer, she pressed. "Well, once we get to know each other better I'm sure we'll care for one another as much as we care for everyone else."

"Make no wagers on that, Rhia, for I have no wish to care for you as I do everyone else."

Laser pistol fire to the gut would have hurt less. How the hell did he fake such a wild attraction to her? Last night he'd touched her as if she were more precious than the old histories, as cherished as cut gems or an iozene mine.

Brita had explained to her that men were different from women. They could be content with just sex and attraction with no need for any emotional attachment. Is that what was going on here?

Like hell.

Rhia spoke quietly, each syllable laced with fire… and pain.

"Fine. I could care less. I could never love you anyway. You're not my type. You're just an oversized babysitter chosen by my father. I may want you, RuArk - what woman wouldn't? But I never said I needed you. And I won't. Ever."

Not exactly how he'd intended the conversation to go, though he'd spoken the truth.

He'd always kept a healthy distance from everyone. As a leader, a Protector, he'd never allowed anyone to get too close, couldn't afford to care too much, to put another person before his duties. But now, in such a short amount of time, he'd come to realize his error of his self-imposed loneliness.

As a man, he was meant to love, meant to have a mate he could share himself with. And gods, he could barely keep his eyes off of Rhia as it was. He wanted to live in her blood, make her crave his touch. But beyond the physical, he wanted to share her hopes and dreams, listen to her problems and try to fix them for her.

When she was close, the wind carried the fragrance she used to rinse her hair, and the faint juicy scent of spiced apples from the gelsoap she lathered over her toned body. And the more time he spent in her presence, the more he was tempted to forget his plan to let her adjust to their mating and seduce her with every skill he had.

Care for her like he did everyone else? Not a chance in all the hells. He wanted more than that between them. Much more.

Obviously, he'd botched the telling of it.

RuArk watched stoically as a fuming Rhia clamped her lips shut and pulled ahead to ride point with Sharyn, determined to ignore him. He took in the way her legs gripped her horse, the curve of her hips, how the sun illuminated the fiery highlights streaked through the natural curls and waves of her soft, dark hair. Keeping his Protector's face firmly in place, RuArk silently recited the most boring Gaian history he could think of and thanked the Ancestors for self-preservation—it was the only way he was able to appear aloof.

He'd felt the faint stirrings of their life bond when they'd exchanged the words in her father's office. This complex woman felt something for him, but right now, the boil of anger in her gaze said she'd rather shoot a Draeman laser pistol at his head than admit she cared. One thing was clear—Rhia was emotionally engaged.

But so was he.

She was proud, yet vulnerable, just like the woman he'd seen in the *Seeking*. The stiff-necked female claimed she didn't need anyone. By the time he was finished with her, she would indeed need him. All of him—heart, body and soul.

Gods knew he already needed her.

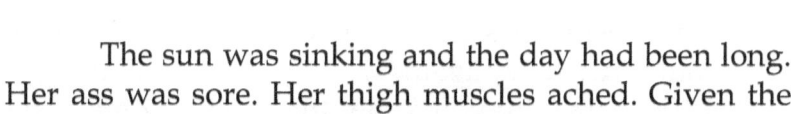

The sun was sinking and the day had been long. Her ass was sore. Her thigh muscles ached. Given the fact that they hadn't stopped, except for the one time where she swore she would die if they didn't, Rhia was bone tired.

Soon they would all settle into an easy camaraderie, with quietly told stories, laughter and plenty of good natured ribbing. But enough was enough. A few more minutes and she'd fall face first into what was left of her dinner.

She stood and stretched, then handed her plate to Brita. After a big jaw-cracking yawn, she said, "I'm not up to socializing tonight, RuArk. I'm going to bed."

RuArk's gaze took her in from head to toe, his expression a mix of blatant heat with a dash of humor. A quiet *ahem* reminded her of her challenge-imposed "yes, RuArk" days. Shit. She was supposed to be asking, not ordering.

Bleh.

His annoying gesture of raising his left eyebrow a good inch conveyed a wealth of meaning. Good grief, she'd only taken two steps. Surely that didn't count as a breach of promise, right?

"Uh... I mean... oh, never mind," she grumbled, thankful none of the warriors visiting around the low-burning fire paid any attention as she tried to ease her sore butt back down, but couldn't quite manage it.

RuArk chuckled. Rhia glowered. Sharyn frowned as she watched from beneath the shadow of a nearby tree.

"RuArk, I'm tired. I'd like to retire now. May I *pleeaasse* go to bed?" Hands clasped in front of her and eyelashes fluttered outrageously.

"Sarcasm does not become you, Rhia. Perhaps you would care to try again?"

"Oh come on, you know this is killing me," she gritted through clenched teeth.

"All the more reason to do it correctly the first time, then the killing of yourself could be avoided."

"You unmerciful, blasted... All right, all right, fine!"

As soon as RuArk stood, the warriors closest to him left their places around the fire and backed up a few steps. Sharyn stepped out from under the dark shadows of the oak with a grin as wide as the Coalrado River. As quickly as her mate had risen, he was seated again with such fluid grace he seemed to melt onto the log.

Damn it, now she really was on the spot and immediately mad at herself for it. Nobody had paid the least bit of attention to her conversation with RuArk before. Now, everyone listened. Her cheeks blazed as if the heat of the campfire had jumped from the coals and given her a hot kiss. When would she learn to control her tongue? Right now, it seemed the answer to that question was *never*. Head lowered, teeth gritted, she tried one more time. Sincerely.

"RuArk, husband, I'd like to wash and head to bed. Do you mind?"

He rose again, slowly this time, and took her

hand to plant a gentle kiss in the center of her palm. She met his gaze and the awareness hit her again squarely in the solar plexus.

Emotions that had seeped through their bond all day swirled around them so thickly, she expected it to solidify and hide them from the world. All the longing of his soul washed over and through her, the will to please her yet take her in hand if needed. And he was thinking about... spanking? God, it was an aphrodisiac to the senses.

Yep, I've lost it. I'm insane.

He leaned in, cupped her cheek in the hollow of his palm, and gave her the gentlest of kisses. So at odds with what she knew he felt, it was impressive he controlled it all.

"You may go, but not to sleep. I will join you shortly. There is something I wish to share with you."

And based on last night in his arms, she could just guess what that was.

Her stomach did a giddy little twirl and her gaze slid away from him as she tried to hide the excitement that lit her up from head to toe.

When he joined her a few minutes later, he walked straight to the bed and began to expand on the sensual experience she'd endured the night before. Oh, he was so wonderful at pleasing her. He left no part of her body untouched, feasted on her breasts until she arched up off the soft, silken bedcovers. The man knew just how and where to touch. His fingers, followed by his mouth, relished every inch of her body until the very hair on her head seemed electrically charged.

Her breath whooshed from her chest in sharp pants, and her body shuddered when his teeth came into play, nipping her here and there. Everywhere. Kisses rained on her neck, down her back and along the tingling globes of her butt cheeks. From her eyebrows to her toes, he kissed, nipped, sucked and played her like the finest antique stringed instrument. He hovered at the juncture of her thighs, and blew over the damp skin.

"RuArk. Please." She rolled her hips. "Please kiss me there."

Her wish was his command. Her sighs filled the space, followed by desperate moans when suddenly, she felt what he felt, wanted what he wanted. Saw how her pleasure made him wild, and knew the more he gave her, the more he wanted to give.

"Not fair," she gasped the moment their newly forming bond flared to life.

"Can't help it."

He was pouring himself into her, and it was nowhere near enough. The merging of their inner selves needed a conduit. Rhia's moan became raw, wild screams as she yelled his name, uncaring of who might hear.

She begged him to surge inside her wet, willing channel, and end the sumptuous torture. Her body anticipated the moment when his hard length would stretch and fill her until she saw stars.

"Please!"

Instead, he rapidly circled her clitoris with the tip of his tongue, and then outright feasted on that little bundle of nerves.

After a shattering climax, she lay sated and trembling in his arms. When her wits returned, it was morning and she didn't even remember falling asleep.

CHAPTER TWENTY

Rhia was surprisingly well rested, even though she'd spent each night in RuArk's arms, panting and writhing until the early hours of the morning. He'd stroked her until she melted in sweet release, but she still burned with the need to be filled. And after pleasuring her to the brink of insanity, RuArk had held, soothed and comforted her until her eyes drifted closed. God, she hoped she hadn't snored like a horse with a bad cold.

It amazed her how his assurances that he'd never take her until she asked, freed her to enjoy learning his body and allowing him to learn hers. Too bad asking the man to forget the 'honorable' business and get on with taking her wasn't an option. Tempting, but she just couldn't bring herself to do it. Besides, a soldier and Blademaster wasn't supposed to be this damn gaga over anyone. It was ri-goddamn-diculous.

Peeling her gaze away from RuArk's handsome, strong profile, Rhia marveled at the rugged mountains ahead to the West. The terrain had become noticeably steeper a couple of days back, but the peaks towering before her seemed to pop up out of nowhere as if the legendary Breaking that formed them so long ago had indeed broken the world.

Off in the distance to the west, a huge gated archway was set into a forty-foot high stone wall. That arch marked the end of Draema province. The farther one traveled from the High City, the more rural and natural the land appeared. Even the well-worn trails and wide pathways crisscrossing this part of the province didn't tame the beautiful wildness of this green and lush place. It only gave it a bit of an uncivilized order.

"Wow," Rhia breathed in awe. Amazed at the bare, sharp mountainous cliffs that soared above the sparse tree line, she asked, "What's out there on the other side of the outer wall?" Emotions high, a mix of excitement and uncertainty trickled down her spine. She had a feeling that anyone with common sense would know to be careful of what lay over those mountains.

RuArk rode to her side and spoke into the silence. "That's the Borderlands. It's a wild and untamed place, windswept and barren. Mostly sand and rock."

As they rode closer, Rhia took in the myriad browns and reds, so vivid the landscape appeared painted.

RuArk pointed toward the soaring rock she was staring at. "Up here, the Land Bridge juts out from those cliffs and crosses high over the river to the north where the Borderlands continue on the other side. The vast lands of Gaia also begin there. Over the mountains to the west, is the sea," RuArk said, his voice low, deep with what seemed a certain respect. Perhaps even awe.

"Through the western arches, can you see where the land slopes downward? It's a break in the peaks that forms a natural gateway where the sea flows into a sound. It's the beginning of the River Dee. From there, the waters run upstream into the harbors at Province Springs, our new home."

"So why does the land fall away like that?" Rhia asked, holding up her hands to shield her eyes from the early morning sun.

"From this distance it appears to be a sheer cliff, but it's really a steep slope that leads down to a flat, sandy beach."

"You've seen it before?" She now realized how sheltered her life in Draema Proper had truly been. She'd never seen anything like this, yet here it was, just outside of her own province.

"Many times. The waters are deep and wide and the beach is a wonderful place to play in the water."

"Play in the water? Why would anybody want to do that?"

"Because it's fun, Rhia," he teased, with that damned dark eyebrow winging its way up his forehead. She wanted to smack him. "Can you swim?" he asked.

"Of course I can swim," she sniffed. *Yeah, in the bathtub.* "I just haven't done it in a while. It's not one of the things I spent a lot of time studying while growing up."

"I am fully aware of how you spent your time growing up." The words tickled her ear as he moved in so close he may as well have been on her horse with her. "Fighting, training, followed by more fighting, Rhia. But I will enjoy teaching you to simply enjoy being a well-loved woman."

Heat rushed into her cheeks.

"I love the way you blush. It turns your

cinnamon skin into a burnished brown, like melted caramel over red apples. Delicious." It was said with a purr that sent a flash of warmth through her stomach to set the butterflies playing there on fire. Rhia nudged him away with a slight lift of her shoulder. Why did he have to go and mention loving?

"After we settle in, we can ride down to the beach if you wish."

"But that's outside the province. Is it safe to pass through the arch into the Borderlands?"

There went that brow again, rising at what he'd obviously thought was an insult.

"RuArk, I didn't mean to imply you can't keep me safe. I haven't been outside of my own lands since I was too little to even remember the experience. I've read about the oceans, but I've never seen one. Harbor Station leads down to the ports where you can sail out of the bay, and then out to sea, but I've never done it. Never needed to."

"You've had more than enough of your share of duty. Time you learned to play, love."

There went that blasted blush again as her head tilted in wonder at the endearment. A big palm reached out and gently teased her cheek. Her eyes closed briefly at the caress and her mind drifted to all the ways that particular hand had stroked and teased her until her skin crackled with anticipation.

Both the touch and the twinkle of RuArk's silvery, gray eyes conveyed a wealth of meaning that she couldn't quite deal with in the light of day. Instead of falling into the depths of his gaze, she squashed her feelings and pulled an attitude around herself like a cloak.

RuArk's hand fell away as Sharyn and Linc

approached. The warmth of his fingers was immediately missed.

"Scouts report the way is clear all the way to the gates of the township, Wind Storm," Linc reported brusquely. But the man hadn't spared RuArk a glance yet. Linc's gaze remained glued to Sharyn while he spoke to RuArk, but Sharyn ignored him and gave all her attention to Rhia instead.

Interesting byplay between the two First Commanders.

RuArk nodded at Linc, and the warrior kicked his mount into a gallop and thundered away. Yet Sharyn stayed behind, speaking softly with Rhia and Brita. Something was obviously up. She'd be sure to needle Sharyn about it later.

Their party reached a crossroad and turned East, heading away from the Borderlands. As they approached the entrance of Province Springs, Rhia noticed that a few Draeman soldiers were on duty, but the rest of the patrol was made up of huge, hulking, giants—Gaian warriors. Hell, anyone would think twice about storming this place.

The epitome of calm, Rhia discretely admired the picture they made standing up on that wall and suppressed a shiver as every one of their handsome almond-shaped gazes plastered themselves on her.

Then she had something else to marvel over. After the initial creak and groan, the gigantic gates eased silently apart and disappeared into the very stone with nothing more than a slight hiss.

Do these people do everything in silence?

Even the gates of the High City, the most technically advanced spot in the region, sounded like amplified claws scraping over hammered metal when they hadn't been moved in a while.

Once through, their large party traveled well-groomed roads with views of rolling meadows dotted with clear green ponds. Row after row of towering trees dressed with amazingly long branches spread over them in a living canopy. They were still somewhat bare because of the high altitude, but the last remnants of ice had melted and the small buds that would become leaves, flowers and fruit were growing rapidly. It would be a lovely grove come late spring.

Other than traveling to Harbor Station to see her brother every now and then, Rhia hadn't been out and away in a long time. She'd forgotten how beautiful and lush the land was. The budding trees and the wondrous signs of the coming season reminded her how abundant and prosperous her homeland truly was.

A half dozen honed and devilishly handsome warriors rode to meet them. Each golden-skinned male sported dark locks from inky black to chestnut brown, their bodies covered in leather. Amazing. Leather, *real* leather made up their buckskins and tunics, either of suede in a natural golden color, or dyed in the color of their houses.

RuArk seemed to be the exception as far as height and brawn went. Both taller and wider than his kinsmen, he was certainly the biggest warrior Rhia had seen so far. All sported strong, angled features and straight, white teeth. But RuArk's smile was more charming. While the Draeman had eyes that spanned the colors of the rainbow, Gaians had eyes of the deepest, darkest brown to the lightest, golden amber... just like hers. But RuArk? His eyes could only be described as stormy gray. An enchanter's eyes.

The leader of this drool-worthy pack of masculinity was obviously a kinsman of RuArk's. Rhia was quickly introduced to RuArk's cousin, Drefan, then the two men slipped into the Gaian tongue, sharing an easy camaraderie. Sharyn had already taught her a few words as they'd ridden, but she was nowhere near fluent enough to keep up.

She watched Drefan's expression grow more and more bemused as he listened to what she assumed was a short accounting of RuArk's journey. It was obvious the man couldn't believe RuArk had taken a lifemate because he kept looking from RuArk to Rhia and back, with both eyes and mouth wide open in what could only be described as shock.

Well, Rhia had her day's quota of being gawked at.

"Excuse me, gentlemen. It's rude to speak in a tongue unknown to your guests." The much-too-sweet smile plastered on her lips faltered when forty mouths snapped shut. Every face became a blank mask as hardened warriors turned all their eyes on her.

Great, just what I didn't want.

"Why didn't you kick me before I opened my mouth?" she whispered to Brita.

"What? And miss all this?"

"You are a wicked, wicked woman, Brita Shae."

"Payback for making me ride until my ass feels like it's going to fall off, Rhia Greysomne."

"You're a damn medic who's been stitching me up forever. I know you have an ass repair kit in your gear somewhere."

Rather than answer, Brita winked, then bit her lip to keep from laughing.

RuArk spoke in perfect, sarcasm-laced Draeman.

"Drefan, this is my lifemate, Rhia Greysomne, First Heir to the Province of Draema. Though she is half-Gaian, she is in need of lessons in proper Gaian etiquette. I am sorry, but she simply does not know any better."

"What? Excuse me..."

"Come again, Rhia? Were you going to say something?" RuArk asked, with the smirk from hell firmly in place.

Rhia gritted her teeth as the stony expression fell away to reveal an unashamedly huge grin. Even his eyes dared her to respond. Too many days of cooperation remained on her challenge loss, and the last thing she wanted was to add more time to her "Yes, RuArk" days. Lowering her eyes in a manner she prayed was demure, Rhia gritted her teeth, clasped her hands in her lap, and said not one blasted word.

Obviously satisfied that she wasn't going to open her mouth, RuArk nodded his head at his cousin. Drefan and his fireteam escorted them through the township, clear to the other side. As they rode, he reported the goings on in both Province Springs and the Realm of Gaia. Or at least that's what Sharyn whispered her way since the boneheads spoke quietly in Gaian again as they occasionally cast winks Rhia's way.

Blasted men.

Blasted gorgeous, charismatic, *too*-everything, men.

The township was much larger than expected. In fact, it felt more like a full-blown city, just without the polish and gleam. More natural, untouched, and to her surprise, cleaner. Rhia was immediately at home as they passed through the bustling town center where the people went about their business. She admired the balanced mix of paved and graveled roads, and vast parks full of evergreens and grassy clearings. There were neat rows of homes, shops and Societies all along the way, and not a speck of dirt anywhere. She hadn't expected to see so many buildings in the traditional white stone this far from the High City. The place was absolutely thriving.

They passed through an open gate set into low walls, then up a cobbled path into a courtyard at the bottom of a gracefully sloping hill. RuArk dismounted and handed his reigns to a smartly dressed Groomsman. He stepped over to a still mounted Rhia. She didn't need help dismounting, but when her husband reached for her, she was certainly smart enough not to gainsay him.

"This is our new home, Rhia," RuArk said proudly, holding Rhia about the waist as he pointed to the top of the hill. She was floored. It was a four story, pure white, sprawling, bloody palatial, villa!

Hand in hand, they walked up a stone-inlaid path to the main steps. She stood at the bottom of those wide stairs and admired the beautiful latticed gallery that spanned the entire length of the front of the villa.

Her eyes glowed with appreciation of the small details that added to the opulence of the place. Stone terraces and balconies were bordered with lifelike carvings of vines that twisted and twined up tall columns.

RuArk took her by the shoulders and turned her to face him. He looked deeply into her eyes and rocked her world.

"Rhia, this house is your joining gift from me. I've had the deeds all prepared."

"What?" She snatched her hand away, took a step back. Emotions spun wildly out of her control. How could he do this to her? Oh, that's right, she was simply a means to an end. Fist planted in the side of her hip, she took a single step forward.

"Rhia did you hear me? I said, this house is…"

"I heard what you said. How can you give me this place? My father gave *you* this house. No, wait, this entire blasted township just to get you to marry me. How could you throw that in my face?"

RuArk said nothing. His warriors took one look at his face, and left to find their own lodgings. His expression was cool granite, impassive and hard. And she didn't give a blasted damn.

Rhia gestured toward the villa. "Thanks for being an insensitive thoughtless jerk. What do you even call it when someone gives you a gift, and you give it right back to the person, or daughter of the person who bribed you with it?"

Rhia gasped when her chest was suddenly against his.

When her gaze clashed with the hard glint of his eyes, her mouth snapped closed all on its own. No one interfered with the dress-down of a Blademaster. Correction, no one interfered with a Blademaster… except this warrior.

RuArk stood quietly, and looked down at her. The only dead giveaway to the extent of his anger was the large vein pulsing furiously in his neck.

He spoke slowly, voice low, controlled and as icy as a midwinter wind. She winced, wishing he'd just yell at her instead. She could handle his passion better than cool disdain.

Barely a growl, each word bitten off at the end.

"In private, say whatever you wish. But you will not carry on in front of my men. *Our* men." He gave her a moment to respond. She said nothing. "You. Will. Not. Disrespect. Me." He gently released her and took a step back. "I vowed to protect you, and to care for you, and so I shall. Now, the Head Houseman will take you to our rooms and offer whatever assistance you need."

He dropped her gear bag at her feet, turned on his heel and stalked back down the hill. She was instantly contrite and annoyed with herself. Even though she was still pissed at the whole "sold into matehood" thing, it didn't change the fact that as a Blademaster of high ranking with the Society of War, she knew how important it was that a leader maintain the respect of his men. She would have skinned anyone who'd dressed her down in front of her soldiers in the High City.

Even as annoyed as she was, she couldn't help but notice the play of muscle in his strong thighs visible through his trousers as he walked. The man moved with the grace of a feline and even pissed off, he was magnificently gorgeous. Too bad she hadn't noticed about five minutes ago.

Rhia called after him. No response. No look back.

Damn, her first day in their new home and she'd blown it already.

Way to go, Rhia. Way to go.

CHAPTER TWENTY-ONE

With a weary sigh, Rhia hefted the bag over her shoulder and walked up the steps to the double doors. A short, stout man dressed in typical Draeman trousers and a short jacket appeared.

"Good morning, First Heir. I'm Lunis, Society of Hospitality and steward of the estate. Please leave your gear. I'll send someone to get it. Now, if you would come with me?"

Lunis was friendly and polite. He offered to take her directly to apartments she would share with RuArk, but Rhia opted for a tour of her new home, instead. As they walked, he explained how the estate and its grounds covered several acres of fertile land. The villa's stables alone housed twenty mounts. There was an armory and barracks, gardens, groves, a stocked lake, several storehouses and such. A low wall surrounded the entire grounds of their private home. The rest of the township was just outside the low gates, which usually remained open.

As she walked beside the Houseman, exploring the rooms along the wide hallways, Rhia marveled at the finely carved marble, stone and tile. Each room, each piece of furniture, even the colors, were to her liking. And the entire place was hers — every piece of thick carpet, every mirror, everything. She was both elated and disappointed.

On the way to the dining hall, she passed a Gaian warrior in buckskin tunic and leathers accompanied a Draeman soldier in uniform. Side by side, the two men carried large bundles of sparkling white linens and disappeared into the kitchens as Lunis steered her into what he called the great hall.

Rhia took in a sharp breath. Now she was *really* impressed. It was something out of one of the history books for sure. The room was huge, dominated by a gigantic fireplace and filled with large round glass-topped tables. A long, half-moon shaped affair served as the head table. Much to her liking, it wasn't elevated above the others.

The floor was covered with icy white marbled tiles, and the walls were smooth semi-transparent stone. A polished gilt framed mirror took up one whole wall, and made the space appear twice its size. The gleaming piece could only be described as exquisite.

A soldier came into the great hall, and placed a frosted glass vase in the center of each table. A warrior watered the large potted trees growing in the corners of the room. What the hell was going on here?

"Lunis, why aren't there any women in the villa? I haven't seen a female since we entered the place and we've been walking around for a good hour now."

"We received specific instructions that every person with duties inside the estate grounds must be a fighter. Basically, everyone who serves here is a soldier of Draema or a warrior of Gaia. He wanted to be sure you were protected."

"Smothered is more like it," Rhia grumbled

under her breath while running a finger over the fine details of the mirror's frame. She was immediately contrite. Her fingerprints remained behind, smeared across the glass.

Changing the subject, she said, "It's hard to fathom those huge Gaian setting tables, washing linens and cooking the meals."

"Isn't it the same in the High City and every other colony of Draema?" Lunis asked.

Rhia cocked her head in thought as she used a corner of her shirt to wipe at the smudges she'd left on the mirror. Now there was more dirt on the mirror from her travel stained clothes than from her fingerprints.

"Our province," Lunis continued, "especially in the High City, has male and female soldiers, housemen and horse breeders, right? Sex has never been an issue in regard to one's profession. That hasn't changed under the new steward. After all, this is still Draema."

The man had a good point. She decided to drop it. Sort of.

"So, if everyone who works on the estate is male, what do the women do? Are there any female soldiers?"

"The Society of Bankers, Science and Technologies and Farriers have full branches here and are run by women. Actually, the women pretty much run everything, if we men are honest." Lunis chuckled. "You'll see when you go into town. As for the Society of War, there is no branch way out here though we do have a few soldiers assigned to this place. None female, though. Anyway, they report back to the nearest branch clear on the other side of Neine. Well, they used to, anyway, but The Protector has…"

"The Protector?"

"The Protector of the Realm. It's a Gaian designation for Mr. Miwatani, but it's still his job even if he lives here now. Plus, it sounds all ominous and important, so many of us use that title for your new husband."

Rhia quirked a brow, but didn't interrupt.

"Anyway," Lunis continued, "not all of the soldiers work here on the grounds. Some are training on both the inner and outer walls with the new arrivals. There are also plenty of other Societies, shops and businesses to be run."

"What do you mean by new arrivals, exactly?"

"Under orders of The Protector, dozens of warriors showed up weeks ago to help us with security around the town and to get the villa and stables ready for you."

That would have been right after the ceremony in her father's study. Wow.

"I think that many of the men who crossed the river to help us now plan on staying. This house was once used by our Councilman who sits on the Council of Seven whenever he visited. He unfortunately doesn't make it out here too often."

So, the warriors she'd seen on the wall were going to be a permanent attraction? RuArk's people had always held to themselves since the Breaking. Yet it made sense if he was to be responsible for both Gaian and Draeman holdings, that he welcomed both cultures. Rhia had no doubt he would keep to his old ways while accepting that others might not. If anyone could integrate the two societies, it was RuArk Miwatani.

The same guy you called an insensitive jerk? Yeah,

that guy.

Rhia wore poor Lunis out, roaming up and down all four floors. Two and a half hours had passed before she realized the only rooms she hadn't seen were her own.

She opened the heavy doors, stepped inside, and stood frozen to the spot in a breathless stupor. It was beautiful.

The gasp of pleasure faded to a tired sigh. Locating her gear bag just to the right of the threshold, Rhia sat down on the floor next to it and brooded. She'd embarrassed RuArk and herself twice today. It was completely out of character for her to be so undisciplined. Even when she and her father disagreed, it was never done in public. Would she ever be able to control her temper around RuArk?

Restless and angry with herself, she got up from the floor and wandered around her new apartment. There were four large, spotless and finely appointed rooms, all done in her favorite shades of gray and peach; a large living room centered by a huge fireplace, a study complete with a big marble topped desk, a spacious master bedroom with the largest platform bed she'd ever seen positioned right in the middle, and a bathing room fit for a queen.

All of the rooms had plush, thick carpets and large floor to ceiling windows that led out to terraces. Strategically, it was brilliant because she could reach any room in the apartment from the terrace.

Finally, she made it into the bathroom and felt like even more of a jerk. In the center of the floor was a deep bathing pool sunken into a gray and silver platform. There was a sitting table with mirrors as well as a soft, plush daybed near a bay window where she could recline after a good soak.

To her delight, the tub had already been filled with steaming hot water and some kind of oil that smelled faintly like her own favorite scent—cinnamon. Perfect. A hot relaxing bath was just what she needed. It wouldn't undo her blunder, but it would sure feel good. Then she'd find RuArk and apologize for her less than heir-like behavior. Sorry wasn't something she had to say often, but she certainly wasn't too proud to do so. Any good leader could admit when he was wrong. Didn't mean she had to like it.

———————◆———————◆———————

"Come on now, out of the tub."

Startled out of a deep doze, Rhia cracked an eye open and gazed groggily up at the owner of a gentle, soothing voice and met a pair of stormy, gray eyes framed by long, black lashes.

In front of her stood a woman who looked so much like RuArk, Rhia blinked a couple of times just to make sure her vision was clear. But where RuArk's skin was deeply tanned, hers was almost creamy with a hint of a warm blush. The woman was older and wore a jade green sarand interwoven with silken, silver thread.

Both she and her outfit were splendidly beautiful. Finely arched black brows were set over high honeyed cheekbones. And her hair was to die for. It hung gloriously dark, bone straight, and past her hips to brush against her thighs, covering her body in a veil of secrets.

"Good afternoon, Rhia."

"Hello." It was then Rhia realized she hadn't

been breathing. The woman's beauty and quiet air of authority made Rhia feel like a little kid in her presence. Strangely, a very comfortable kid.

The woman smiled sweetly, held up a towel and motioned her out of the tub to the window seat. Heat infused her chilled skin through the window courtesy of a bright yellow sun. A sigh slipped past her lips as the woman vigorously rubbed her head with a scented towel, then took on the duty of taming the tangled mass on Rhia's head that was supposed to be hair.

"Good morning. You may call me Mila."

"Thank you. It's so very nice to meet you. I remember hearing your name often when I was little. You must be RuArk's mother."

She smiled down at Rhia as she worked a brush through the tangles and said, "RuArk? Sometimes I forget he has a Draeman name. But yes, I am mother to the Wind Storm, and queen of Gaia. I am so looking forward to getting to know you. Most of our people have dark, straight hair, but yours is wavy, just a shade lighter and alive with little flames of red. The curl comes from your father, I am sure, but your beauty is your mother's. By the spirits, you look so much like her."

The shock that this woman had known her mother was followed by the realization that she shouldn't be surprised at all. Mila had never travelled with RuArk and his father to visit Draema when she was a child, but that didn't change the fact that Rhia's mother had come from the same land.

It would have been stranger if they *hadn't* known each other. A wash of melancholy flowed through her. After all, she'd begun a new life, had a mate now, yet here she sat, sharing the moment with someone else's mother while hers was gone forever.

She forced away the sorrowful grip that tightened her throat.

Instead of tears, think of something positive, Ree.

Be grateful, her father had always told her. Good time to remember it.

Mila herded her toward the bedroom.

"Your mate has left a Joining gift for you."

Rhia wasn't sure she could take another gift. The last one had seen her yelling at her husband before she could even get into their new home.

Arranged on the silken, gray covers of the bed, lay a cream-white sarand. She'd never seen an outfit quite like it, and in such a beautiful color.

Rhia marveled at the sheer number of little blue beads in various shades sewn in intricate patterns over the top, along the yoke, sleeves and hem. Mila helped her slip into the sarand. The bodice revealed a hint of her smooth belly, and the bottom was slit up the sides and fell in a wisp of luxury against her legs. Her skin peeped with each step as the weight of the beads caused the fabric to swirl around her limbs just a bit when she walked.

White, soft leather *moccs* were decorated with the same blue beadwork and fit her feet like they'd been made just for her. A choker, earrings, and silver combs, all embedded with rare blue lapis stone, completed the ensemble. It was the most stunning set of clothes Rhia had ever laid eyes on that wasn't in a history book. It was Gaian, through and through.

The queen settled Rhia on the platform steps of the huge bed and secured the sides of her hair with the silver combs. The weight and coolness of the jewels against her skin were such a delight all she could do was touch them, smile and touch them some more.

"It's so beautiful."

"Yes, it is beautiful regalia. I wore this very same dress when I joined my life to the king. And you will wear it today for your own joining ceremony."

In front of a full-length mirror, Rhia's mouth dropped open. Blazes, she'd never felt so feminine in her life. It was strange. Not unwelcome, or odd, just different. Warm. It was all so lovely, given to her as a gift by someone who had no motive. Given because she wished to, and not because she wanted or needed something.

When Mila nodded her approval, Rhia beamed.

"Are you ready to go, Rhia?"

Wait. "Go? Go where? To do what?"

Another surprise? She certainly hoped not.

Mila's smile calmed Rhia, like a balm of soothing oil over her frazzled mind. She liked her new mother-in-law and paid close attention as the queen explained.

"I mentioned a joining ceremony, remember? A traditional Gaian joining occurs when a warrior takes a lifemate by giving his vow to protect her."

Rhia thought back to that day in her father's study. RuArk had indeed pledged his protection, and his life, to her. Their days and nights together, getting to know him, learning who he was as a person had been... enlightening. One thing was for sure—he took his responsibilities seriously.

"Since you could not have the ceremony you wished for in your father's study, my son sent word for us to prepare a traditional joining ceremony for you here in Province Springs."

When the hell had he done that?

"But I don't know much about Gaian culture.

Who should I expect to see at the ceremony? What am I supposed to do?" Her heart lodged in her throat at the thought of being pushed onto a stage where she didn't know her lines.

"Do not fret, Rhia. The king and I, with our People, came up from the harbor not long before you arrived early this morning. Our family, now your family, has come to celebrate with you both, to support you, not to have you anxious."

Rhia's mouth dropped open. The king and queen of Gaia had come to Province Springs just because RuArk told them she wanted a wedding? And the queen had brushed out her hair and helped her get dressed? It was extremely humbling.

"The Wind Storm is our son, but you are also very special to be chosen as his woman. We feared he would never take a mate."

Yeah, right. I'm so special my father conspired with that big guy you call 'son' and bribed him to marry me. And I pissed him off within ten minutes of being here.

Rhia clamped her lips shut to keep the words from spilling out.

They left the villa and headed for the stables. Brita, Sharyn and a man she immediately recognized, stood waiting—the king of Gaia. He didn't look any older than he had the last time he'd brought RuArk to the High City on a visit to see her father. Queen Mila was beautiful, but the king was, and had always been, breathtakingly handsome.

His hair was thick and black as night, with strands of silvery gray peppered throughout. His skin looked firm and deeply bronzed with not a wrinkle to be seen except at the corner of his eyes with a gaze of light amber, just like Rhia's. She wondered if that was how RuArk would look in thirty cycles.

He wrapped her in a warm, easy hug. "It has been a long time, Rhia. It is so very good to see you. And even better to have you as part of our family."

Damn. The tears that had threatened before, returned, knocking at the back of her eyeballs to be let out. With a deep breath and even deeper resolve, she held him tight, then squared her shoulders as she stepped back a bit. "It's good to see you, too, sir."

"Sir?"

Well, yeah. As a kid, she'd always called him sir or your majesty. It was polite to treat elders with respect.

"Sir is not required. Call me Àn, and if you wish it, you may call me Father." He smiled warmly, showing straight white teeth and deep dimples. Blazes, if she and RuArk had a son who looked like this, she'd have to beat the women off with a stick.

Àn planted a gentle kiss on her cheek and mounted a magnificent gelding. His wife approached and when he leaned down to kiss her, it was so intimate and stirring, Rhia had to look away. With that, the king departed, and Mila took Rhia by the arm with a smile. As they walked past the private stables of the estate, down the hill and through a budding forest, Rhia was suddenly drowned in a sea of colorfully clad women.

So many new aunts, cousins, and clansmen, there was no way she'd remember them all. She was overwhelmed, not just by their numbers, but by the sincerity in their faces as they affectionately patted her on a shoulder, gave her flowers or gently tapped her hand as she passed. By the time Mila quieted the crowd, Rhia was juggling armfuls of fragrant wildflower bouquets.

"We have waited anxiously for this day, but let us make it more comfortable for my new daughter by speaking the Draeman tongue while she is learning our language."

Immediately the chatter started again, and Rhia now understood every word as they confirmed their well wishes and welcomed her to their family.

Family. What a concept. Her father and brother were her blood kin, but for so long, she'd felt that Joan and Brita were all she really had in the world until this very moment.

Not because her kin didn't love her, but...

All thought fled as she took in the line of warriors waiting on the other side of the clearing, practically hidden from view as the women gathered around Rhia and chanted a song that resonated in her bones. It felt ancient, meaningful. And just for her.

When the singing was finished, Rhia stared as RuArk stepped into view. He stood next to his father, and waited. The ladies gently nudged her forward until she was moving through the now parted crowd. She kept walking until he was a mere breath away.

My goodness, he's beautiful.

Dressed from head to toe in sparkling white buckskin leathers with matching tunic, RuArk seemed to gleam. Much like her outfit, he wore intricately beaded, soft-soled *moccs*. His long, black hair hung loose, the sides adorned with little braids threaded with tiny sparkling white shells that tinkled when the ends caught in the easy breeze.

He reached for her hand as she stood with eyes wide, and her heart in her throat.

CHAPTER TWENTY-TWO

"Are you pleased?" he whispered for her ears only.

Rhia took in the scene around them and gave him a wooden nod. Pleased? She was flat-out floored. No one had ever done anything like this for her in... well, ever. How the hell was she supposed to respond?

RuArk spoke in hushed tones as his father began speaking to the crowd and began the ceremony. "We are to be joined in the Gaian way. Our family, friends and relatives are here to witness."

"Your mother explained, but I just didn't expect... RuArk? How did you manage all this?" she whispered back.

"Everything is possible with a sound strategy, Rhia. And I must admit, it pleases me to make you happy."

He laid a heart-stopping smile on her, and she saw his satisfaction with her pleasure shining in his silvery grays.

She reached out to him, but stopped mid-hug. Not wanting to embarrass herself by kissing her husband before she was supposed to, she bent her ear instead and listened intently. She smiled with genuine joy until she thought her lips would freeze in their upturned position. The king spoke, breaking into her thoughts as he said her name.

"Rhia Greysomne, I stand in your father's stead. From this day forward you are my daughter." He looked to RuArk, and said, "Son?"

RuArk nodded, then addressed his father, repeating the words he'd said that fateful day in the High Counsel's study.

"From this day forward, I pledge myself to you as a son and a protector of your line. I accept Rhia as my woman and will protect her until I am called to join my ancestors at the sacred council fires in the spirit world. I acknowledge her as your most precious gift and vow to keep and protect her always."

She listened closely this time and would remember these words, this moment, always.

After the vows, they shared a kiss, waved to the crowd and the festivities began. The afternoon was filled with games and feasting on dishes so richly delicious, Rhia almost wished for some bland Draeman food. Almost.

The evening was spent in one of the tree-surrounded clearings near the water. Drummers and singers had come over from RuArk's home across the river to play for them. Each beat of the drum, each high-pitched note sank into Rhia's soul, made her feel as if she'd recovered something lost so long ago.

Rhia sat around the edge of the dancing circle with Sharyn and Brita. She rolled her eyes at the two women determined to get her up to speed on Gaian custom, language, and running her household rather than the Society of War. Maybe they'd plan a trip across the river to Windsong to spend time with her parents-in-law?

RuArk and Linc returned from a sweaty fast paced game of Knock Ball and joined in the conversation.

Rhia started when a woman danced so close to their seats she almost stepped on Rhia's feet.

There was no missing the devilish gleam in the woman's eye when she planted herself firmly in front of RuArk and rolled her hips in time to the music.

Whoa. What the hell?

Oh yeah, this was a clear invitation, all right. The woman's pale, pink sarand floated dangerously high as she twirled and spun. Hell, why didn't she just climb into RuArk's lap and rub her breasts all over him and get it over with? Just when Rhia thought she might, the other woman slipped away, only to make her way around the circle and back in front of RuArk. The cow's movements became bolder, if that was possible.

"Who in blazes is that?" Rhia hissed at her husband.

For the second time that day, RuArk's face hardened to a golden block of granite. "That," he ground out, "is the thorn in my side."

Sharyn whispered, "That is Ansla."

That was RuArk's ex-fiancé? Wow, she hadn't seen that coming. A flash of jealousy hit her in the center of her chest along with a bit of relief. Right now, she didn't even care about the circumstances of her marriage. Only that this woman hadn't managed to get her claws into RuArk.

RuArk held out his hand for her. "The Elders wish to see us."

With a nod, she slipped her fingers into his and let him guide her into the night.

The evening was warm and humid as they walked. Moisture in the air kissed and cooled her heated skin, dewy from all the dancing, laughing. Living.

They stopped at a large tent erected over the area where they'd received the blessing over their mating earlier. RuArk stepped to the small round door and motioned her inside without a word. Rhia stood silently while her eyes adjusted to the dim light of a small fire in the center of the lodge.

She looked from one Elder to the next. She'd met them all earlier. All except one. Her eyes widened in surprise as she faced the man who'd visited her dreams and driven away the nightmares until RuArk arrived in Draema Proper to claim her — the Grandfather.

Buried memories surfaced the moment her gaze locked with the old man's. Dreams she hadn't been able to remember. Conversations they'd had in her sleep that she hadn't believed real. And now he sat right in front of her, his warm smile as familiar to her as her own.

"You remind me so much of your mother, only she was not so stubborn." The Grandfather chuckled and the other Elders added bits of humor to their companion's jest. After all, she'd heard that her mother had been well known for her, uh, *steadfastness*.

Rhia blushed, but couldn't help smiling. In the next moment, the Grandfather straightened his back, expression solemn once again. He motioned to a spot directly across the fire pit.

"Sit, child."

She settled gracefully on a soft covering spread on the floor. A brief shiver of concern slithered beneath her skin when RuArk left her side and went to sit with the Elders.

"You understand why you are here?"

Rhia nodded. On their way over, RuArk had explained that she was to be brought before the Elders to receive her Gaian name. This was warrior business and she was more than a bit anxious. Few were granted the honor of standing before the Elders.

The Grandfather continued, "Your manner and character will compliment your lifemate well. Therefore, you shall be known by a name similar to his. But your name also says much about you and who you are. You have the ways of a warrior woman, full of fire and courage. From now on, among our People, you shall be known as Fire Storm, first lifemate of the Wind Storm."

"Excuse me?" She didn't bother hiding her scowl.

He cleared his throat and added, "*Only* lifemate of the Wind Storm."

They shared a moment of humor when she rose, crossed to where RuArk sat and showered his wide chest with playful blows as he teased her saying, "Well, I am unsure about the 'only wife' part, Grandfather."

By the time their visit with the Elders was done it was well past midnight.

"Rhia, I must see to a few things. Moonlight is tethered near the edge of the clearing. I'll walk you to him. Head back to the villa and I'll join you shortly."

RuArk knit his brow, puzzled when she pulled away and squared her feet as if she were ready to fight.

"I just remembered something you said before and finally put two and two together. Why is that Ansla woman here? She's the one who slept with your best friend that you called a thorn in your side. Why is your so-called thorn at our wedding?"

"Joining."

"Whatever."

RuArk slipped on his stoic façade, then changed his mind. This was his lifemate. The Ansla business was a matter of honor for her. Instead of keeping his feelings from her, he reached for her hand to soothe her.

"Rhia, I am sorry Ansla is here. I have no wish to see her any more than you do, but that woman and her family have lived in Gaia since before the Breaking. Many of her male relatives are in the Protector's service, *my* service, and have given their blood for our people. I would not dishonor them by forbidding them to bring her to a royal joining. Her actions don't change the fact that her family is honorable."

Something in the back of his mind said she shouldn't be this upset. Rhia was a rational woman, a seasoned diplomat with the patience of an ass... hmm, then again, maybe that wasn't a good thing given her stubbornness. But this thing about Ansla didn't make any sense.

Wait, was she jealous? Pleasure pooled in his gut at the prospect until the woman's anger flared and her mouth was suddenly moving faster than her brain.

"You would rather dishonor your mate than some cheating ex-girlfriend? Didn't you see the way people looked at me when she challenged me by dancing practically on top of you?"

He simply stood there unable to answer because

he *hadn't* seen the way people looked when Ansla danced close to him. He'd shut Ansla out of his life and out of his mind cycles ago. No matter how seductively she danced, it hadn't aroused him at all. His eyes had been full of Rhia.

"Rhia, she means nothing to me."

"Do you still love her?"

His gray eyes narrowed dangerously. He couldn't believe what she'd just asked him. His lifemate, his woman, didn't believe him. He turned on a silent growl and left her standing alone under the moonlit sky. For the second time in a day she called after him. And again, RuArk ignored her.

Damn again.

On the road to Province Springs, RuArk had told her that Ansla was a woman of his past—a past that he'd buried long ago. Rhia believed him, but she hadn't *told* him that she believed him. No, she'd ranted the moment the puzzle pieces about the other woman had snapped together in her brain.

She'd have to show him that she'd taken him at his word. Show him that she appreciated how he'd made sure that her arrival here had been special, from the house, to the joining, to the naming.

She was so lost in thought that she didn't even mind the two warriors that tailed her all the way back to the villa.

After a long, hot soak in her now-favorite bathing pool, Rhia walked into the bedroom and met a gift so elegant and wholly feminine, it was truly an expression of the sensuality RuArk had aroused in her.

Rhia scooped up the garment, hurried back to the bathroom and found the nearest mirror. There, she donned yet another wedding present from her husband. She slipped into the dainty garb and relished the silky slide of it against her bare skin. The exquisite material of the winter white confection cast her shape in an alluring silhouette.

The nearly see-through gown was made of soft, light silk that sparkled like crushed diamonds. A matching cape trimmed in thin gold braid covered the spaghetti straps at her shoulders, and fell gently to the floor.

Wow.

She thought about the events of the day and how her husband had gone out of his way to make her happy. She'd been completely surprised at having a ceremony at all, since she'd fled her own home to avoid one. She was offended about the house at first, but it didn't change the fact that his men had to have ridden like maniacs to get back and forth between wherever-the-hell and Province Springs to get everything ready in time.

And her? Well, she'd been pretty much a brat, but woman enough to admit it. So, tonight she would also admit that she wanted him—his body, his presence, even his love. In exchange, she would give him the available pieces of herself. Could she give him her all? No, because she didn't' feel quite whole, though she wasn't sure why.

Yet, knowing that her happiness and protection held the top spot on RuArk's list of important things, had begun to fill in all the empty pits and cracks of her soul. The fear of losing herself simply wasn't as vast or terrifying as before. Was it there? Yes, but the abject terror was no longer present.

He really had no reason to trust her. Fleeing the High City when she knew they were already married saw to that, though he'd never thrown it in her face.

Sigh.

Just another example of the kind of man he was.

Her mind reached for the close memories of the careful attention showered on her since their first night together under the stars. She could still feel the molten trail his fingers had taken as he'd touched her in places no other hand, but her own, had been allowed. Rhia remembered his sensuously, full lips on hers, the touch of his hand on her thighs, the strength of his arms about her waist, and his fingers playing in her hair. With every thought, she took a breath, but the next thought of RuArk simply took it away again.

And now, she was ready to accept these new roles — mate, lover, perhaps even friend. Well, as ready as she could be at this point anyway. Every change of heart had to begin somewhere.

She took one last look in the mirror and drew a deep breath. "Okay, big guy, here I come", she whispered to the image that stared back at her with equal parts eagerness and trepidation. Tamping down on nervousness, she commanded her dinner to stay where she'd put it as she made her way back to the bedroom.

RuArk still wasn't there. Used to Housemen coming in and out of her space at home, Rhia noticed a small tray next to the bed with a chilled carafe and two crystal glasses filled with crisp sparkling cider. She grabbed one and then sipped while reaching for calm.

Unfortunately, calm was nowhere in the room.

Almost spent with anticipation she practically jumped out of her skin when the drapes billowed. Something stirred in the dark out on the terrace. She peered out into the night and spied RuArk looking up at the night sky. He wore a scrap of leather about his hips and nothing else. His broad back and midnight fall of hair were set aglow by the moonlight. She could see him a million times dressed just like this and never get over the sight of his magnificent body.

And there's a decent man inside of that skin, Rhia. Remember that.

CHAPTER TWENTY-THREE

RuArk watched the dancing orange glow of the distant bonfires. The shadows of the tents stretching across the large meadow made him think of home. Home made him think of his new mate. He let out a tired sigh. Rhia could be as stubborn as a freeborn mule. She was angry with him for something well beyond his control, yet he smoldered for her touch. He'd been in a state of arousal all day just from the sight of her. She was so beautiful, sensual. Yet she resisted her very nature with all the strength she could muster.

He was unfamiliar with rejection, but accepted the emotion for what it was when Rhia had pulled away from him as if she couldn't stand his touch. Pulled away from him over Ansla, a woman who was less than beneath her notice. He'd thought Rhia was beginning to at least care for him, though she would probably never admit it in a million cycles. Would pride always be an issue between them? And what of trust? Was she afraid he would betray her, though he'd given her no reason for such mistrust?

After all, RuArk had seen Rhia in a *Seeking*. He had gone to the High City for *her*. Was now here in

Draema Neine with *her*. Mated to *her*.

Perhaps this wasn't about him at all. The woman had had more than her fair share of dealing with idiots, like that Bryan person he'd enjoyed tossing headlong down Rhia's stairs. But even with Bryan's recent return, something in the recesses of his soul told him that whatever this was with Rhia was deeper, something more ingrained in her than just a bad prior relationship. At times she seemed genuinely afraid to mate with him, afraid to accept him, as if he'd try to make her into something other than what she was.

Yet that still brought them right back around to trust.

RuArk didn't hear Rhia come out onto the terrace, but there was no mistaking the apples-and-spice scent that floated on the evening breeze as she watched him from the glass terrace doors. He went still, knowing she wore the wedding present he'd ordered Lunis to leave on their bed. Turning, he took in the image of his wife. She was beyond lovely in the silken perfection that hung loosely to just above her knees. The deep tone of her skin set off the color of the gown and he willed his body into submission. He hoped he would be able to embrace her and leave it at that, if that was all she wanted.

"RuArk?"

Mouth glued shut, he simply swallowed and drank in her beauty. The silhouette of her shapely body under the sheer gown was more beautiful than he could have ever imagined. Her face was... flushed? She seemed to be doing a lot of that lately. The woman blushed almost as often as he had a raging hard on for her.

He cocked his head to the side and wondered

what caused her coffee-and-cream skin to burn. She flushed deeper under his stare, but her eyes held an unmistakable hint of something wholly feminine, seductive, sensual and determined.

He quivered as her gaze took him in slowly, from his feet up to his hips. Her gaze lingered at the top of his breech and became something primal. Deeper. That look sent chills up his spine. His cock responded immediately, and his breech rose up to meet her.

He gulped.

"Do you like it?" he asked, referring to the gown.

"I love it," she purred, never taking her eyes from his. "Thank you."

Desire shone in her eyes, and with each word spoken, he could almost taste the spicy, heady flavor as she stepped to him with an oh so *not* subtle sway to her hips.

Just like in my Seeking that seems so long ago now.

He flexed his thigh muscles and tried to shake off the potent effect that was Rhia. His arousal was heavy and full. Ready. Almost needy. The self-control he'd exercised as they'd traveled together over the past several days was all but spent. Seeing her dressed like this, knowing she was his, and with the huge bed visible behind her was almost too much.

He was dying with need, yet he would wait for her acceptance if it killed him. RuArk forced himself to continue to stand there.

Perhaps they could talk. Yes, talk!

Talk would help get his mind off of his cock.

"You look beautiful, Rhia. I—" That was as far as he got.

Rhia attacked.

He was almost shocked into inaction when she threw herself into his arms and boldly kissed him, but he recovered quickly when she began to take, demand. She thrust her tongue into his mouth, tasting him, not bothering to hide the deep moan of pleasure as she took what she wanted.

"Mmmm, you taste like chocolate and coffee. Gimme."

He was so astonished he started to take a step back and make sure it was really her, but couldn't tear himself away from her soft, warm body. He closed his eyes as she stroked his back, then moved her hands down and around to caress his thighs. The muscles jumped at her touch, impatient for her warm fingers to make their way around his hips and slowly massage the pulsing ridge between his legs.

She threw her head back and arched into him, allowing him access to whatever he chose to take from her. Pleasure bloomed in both his body and mind as he realized that she did indeed want him. Right now.

Gods, it was as if the woman pulled his response from the depths of his soul with a need so strong he had to will himself not to take her right there on the terrace. She rolled her head on her shoulders, then said them—the words he'd longed to hear for far too many nights.

"RuArk, I'm sorry."

"Rhia…"

"No, just hush and listen." Calloused fingertips, a testament of just how much she worked with her weapons, pressed against his lips. There was no helping it—he opened his mouth just enough to take them inside. With a gentle bite, her words came out in a hiss.

"I... oh."

RuArk almost smiled, but the smoky haze in her eyes brought him up short and all he could do was stand there, listen and *feel*.

"I've been a total ass today. Thank you for all you've done, all the gifts, the joining. Just... everything."

"Rhia, I do not expect you to try and repay me for..."

"This isn't about repayment. This is about what I want. I want a mate, a true mate." Arms wrapped around his neck and pulled him down into a deep kiss. "I want you. Now."

Time stopped, and he would remember this moment forever. Her scent, the taste of her mouth, the heat of her hands on his bare flesh. The weight of her full, firm breasts, the silken skin covering the toned muscle of her bare arms. The throb of his erection as he pressed against her belly and his fingers drifted in lazy circles along her butt cheeks.

"How much do you want me, Rhia?" The words were ground through clenched teeth.

She didn't hesitate, but looked him square in the eye. "Desperately."

◊ ◊ ◊

RuArk carried her inside, walked up the wide steps to their massive bed and tossed her into the center. She felt so sexy as she reached above her head to grab handfuls of the soft bedding, writhing as the softness welcomed the weight of her body. RuArk came over her, kissed her with agonizing care from neck to knees until every nerve sizzled, every pore of her skin tingled and breathing was practically impossible. His mouth sought hers, and his tongue probed hungrily.

She savored his unique flavor. Delicious.

He kissed the smooth lines of her neck while his fingers played in her hair, tugging lightly. She gave him what he wanted and tilted her head back. His lips moved along her throat and shoulders. Strong, white teeth released the clasp on her gown and freed her aching breasts from their silk prison.

"Rhia, you are so beautiful," RuArk whispered harshly as his fingers trailed behind the sheer material, sliding it down around her waist, raising gooseflesh along the way. A shudder worked its way through her body when he finally touched her. Lungs filled on a gasp and released on a sigh as he encircled and tugged the swollen tips of her breasts. When a scorching tongue replaced his hands, Rhia was utterly and happily lost.

He suckled with slow, tortuous circles. Rhia arched frantically off the bed when he drew the entire crown into his mouth. By the time he finally gave his attention to the other breast, she was wild with need.

He'd touched her like this while they'd been traveling to this place, but she knew there would be more. Tonight, he would give her the part of himself she'd only looked at and touched in wonder. Fantasized about. And she couldn't wait another moment.

She clutched him around the waist, and snatched at his breech. She needed to be closer. To be part of him. But he took his time and she died just a little because of it. Her blood scorched the insides of her veins. Oh god, from head to toe she boiled, but wanted the heat turned up until she exploded. The sheer anticipation had her moaning, aching to be filled. Her body dripped with need. It was torture.

Pleasurable, blazing, torture.

"RuArk, please."

Rhia licked her lips, eyed the deep ridges that defined the muscles of his body. They flexed and bunched as he dipped his head, moved to another angle, licked, sucked at her flesh. Golden and gleaming, his abdomen was like the tide, rolling in waves over his belly without the slightest trace of fat. She marveled at the fine outline of his thighs and calves. He was large, solid and splendidly lick-able, like someone had poured melted honey over a hardened, steel-corded frame.

He eased back on his knees, gave a sharp tug and let his breech fall free. Her gaze settled on a thick, swollen erection and held. It was beautiful. Pulsing. And it beckoned to her. She was anxious. Wanted to feel his hardness inside of her, the girth sliding into her moist heat. The room swirled and spun as she gave herself up to the urgency in her belly. But RuArk wasn't moving. Instead, he stroked himself and watched her as she watched him right back.

So he was playing the tease, eh? Fine, two could play that game. Lips almost lifted in a wicked grin as she considered what to do next.

She looked deeply into his eyes while her tongue slid sensually over kiss-swollen lips. She spread her legs wide and slipped a single fingertip into her own scalding heat. Oh, that felt good. She ground her hips in a deep, slow circle, inviting him to come inside.

RuArk looked as if he might just swallow his own tongue when Rhia's fingers disappeared inside her velvety folds. He dove between her legs and urged her thighs to fall completely open. The little nerves that ran up along her inner thighs caused the flesh to ripple and jerk at his touch. As he rubbed his cheek back and forth against her skin, the air thickened with the sweetness of her arousal. He inhaled deeply and she thought it was the most erotic thing she'd ever seen.

The hair was clipped short on her mound, and shaved silky smooth just below. Rhia almost flew from the bed when she felt the playful touch of his tongue on the folds of her sex. *This* was something he'd driven her crazy with on those endless nights to Province Springs.

"Oh, shit!" she shrieked, not sure whether she wanted to scramble away or grab his head to press him closer. Had she lost her mind? Blazes, she certainly hoped so. Decision made on the best course of action, she said, "More, please."

"Whatever you wish, however you wish." He licked her cleft from top to bottom. "As much as you wish." A little nip of her outer lips had her growling. "As often as you wish." Now he delved deeply using his tongue to penetrate her drenched sex.

She was a woman swept away, carried out to sea, drowning in need. Her head thrashed from side to side, nails sank into the downy softness of the bed as she sought an anchor for the madness. Her hips instinctively sought more of the madness caused by his mouth. As he lapped and feasted, he pushed a finger into her clenching heat. Her womb pulled unbearably tight, coiled like a spring.

Suddenly the spring released and she exploded in a burst of rapture. Eyes wide, she came all over his hand with an intensity that caused the room to spin as sparkles ignited behind her lids.

Her scream gave way to incoherent mumbling as he gently laved the folds of her tender blossom, lapped her relentlessly until she lay naturally intoxicated.

Finally, when she was sure she could take no more, he slid up her body and kissed her so she could taste herself on his tongue.

She came up for air just long enough to speak four words.

"RuArk, please. Take me."

The words came out on a labored breath. Her soft pleading to be filled with him was almost more than he could bear. RuArk looked into Rhia's half closed, misty eyes. Lips parted in desperation as she lay trembling uncontrollably beneath him.

"Now. I'm aching... please."

He positioned himself at her slick opening, but still waited. Sweat beaded across his brow, and he clenched his teeth. Every muscle across his upper body bunched and trembled. She may not have a hymen, but he knew she'd never been with a man. A visit to the Society of Physicians to remove a little piece of skin was not the same as having sex, and certainly not sex with a warrior. RuArk was willing to take as long as necessary to make it as painless as possible for her, even if it killed him.

Hard as his cock was, he thought it just might.

"RuArk, I swear I'll peel your skin off very slowly if you don't fuck me."

He guessed he would just have to oblige her.

The engorged tip of his thick cock throbbed against her tight entrance. RuArk held his breath as he probed gently, working himself into her inch by torturous inch. When he was almost seated, he held still a moment, then pushed in until he was there. So *there* she had to feel full to bursting.

She was slick and primed from the orgasm he'd already given her. Her walls held him so tightly, it was his turn to squeeze his eyes shut. The feeling of her heat closing around him was exquisite and sent him reeling. He grimaced in an attempt to smile, and then began a slow, rhythmic grind that scalded his sac with a barely contained release.

"No, RuArk, don't go slow. Move."

RuArk lost himself in her tantalizing body. Her fingers dug into the thick muscles of his thighs and back, and her strong legs squeezed him in the same rhythm that her sweet honeyed passage tightened around his cock. The woman drew him headlong into the sensuous web she'd spun around them both. His name was a gasp on her lips between harsh breaths. She arched against him, and told him how she wanted it, loved it, needed it.

Her words were highly erotic, sizzling. And he was swept up in the tide. The control he'd forced himself to exert... hells, what control?

"Gods, you feel so good." He sucked hard on the soft skin of her neck, marking her. He growled and pulled almost completely out of her soaked flesh, then plunged deep. Then deeper still. Every delicious stroke brought him to the verge of utter bliss. Each plunge made him hungry for another one as she squeezed him, milked him.

Their sweat soaked bodies entwined as they climbed to the top of passion's mountain. Caught in a waterfall of pleasure, they fell headlong into deep fulfillment. Rhia screamed, and held onto RuArk's broad back as her world splintered. RuArk roared to the heavens, blasting his seed against the very entrance to her womb. He loved how fiercely she clung to him, and demanded every drop.

RuArk held her tight as he dragged in lungful's

of breath. His skin tingled from scalp to toes long after the last wave had crashed over them.

He rolled to his side and gently gathered his mate into his arms as she dozed. He watched her slumber a moment while his fingers played absently in her thick, dark hair. The loving had been extraordinary, but there was unfinished business between them. He dipped his head and kissed her softly on her forehead, then kissed her again until she half-opened her eyes and flashed a drunken smile.

She looked up at him as he balanced over her on one elbow. He was completely unguarded, letting her see the concern in his eyes.

Silence stretched between them, but the trickle of awareness was there nonetheless. It was as if a wall between them had cracked beyond repair.

Finally, she said, "RuArk, I'm sorry for getting angry today. I really do appreciate everything you have done to make this day special and to make me happy. I love the house, and your, I mean *our* family is just wonderful. I can even get over Ansla." She reached out and traced the outline of his jaw, her light brown gaze falling deeply into his silvery grays. She whispered, "Can we start over?"

He cocked a brow, thinking perhaps they could start anew. Making love with Rhia had been an earth-shattering experience, more than just physical. She was his destiny. He felt the strengthening connection with her as it hummed just beneath the surface of these newfound feelings. There was no use fighting what the Ancestors had decreed. No use resisting what he'd felt since the day he'd walked back into her life.

He dropped a gentle kiss on her check, her nose, her brows. "Absolutely, we can start over, Rhia."

"Well, can we start over right now?" She slipped her arms around his neck, shimmied against his body and took his lips in a rekindling kiss, sparking the blaze between them yet again.

CHAPTER TWENTY-FOUR

After the joining ceremonies on that first day, the rest of the township was invited to the remainder of the festivities. Keeping with tradition, they'd feasted, played games, danced and celebrated for a full seven days.

Most had come out at one time or another and expressed wonder at witnessing the vibrant and colorful Gaian culture for the first time, and on Draeman land, no less.

Even Ansla hadn't ruined the fun—a few words with her in the presence of the Elders and her parents took care of any ideas she had of becoming RuArk's second wife.

The joining of the Fire Storm and the Wind Storm was the most fulfilling bout of hot sweaty sex RuArk had ever enjoyed in his life. Every morning since their joining, RuArk had come awake with Rhia's long limbs entwined with his. Streams of sunlight filtered through the drapes to cast a golden glow down her back. Her skin looked soft and infused with heat. Hot definitely described every night they'd spent together.

He stretched and Rhia shifted. The scent of

sleep-warmed woman wafted up from the covers bunched down around her waist. Even far gone in slumber, she stirred a reaction in him that he had to tamp down, knowing she would be sore from their marathon of loving last night. Brimming with energy, he reluctantly peeled back the blankets, rose, and padded silently down the bed's wide steps in the early dark of dawn.

With a final look at his woman, RuArk ducked into the bathing room to wash.

His parents and family had departed, so all that was left was to give orders to the warriors headed back across the river this morning. Afterward, he would scout on the other side of the outer wall that separated the province from the Borderlands. In lieu of a bath, a swim at the gateway just near that spot would do. He dressed quickly, snatched a towel from a neat pile of plush, laundered linens and headed out.

With the last of the boats headed safely out of the harbors toward Gaia, RuArk left the piers and passed through the center of town. Not long ago, the streets had been quiet and deserted. The sun had barely risen a standard hour ago and now it was a bustling place. People of all ages, male and female, made their way from one Society, business or school, to another.

He was pleased to see his warriors strategically positioned and keeping watch. Though focused on their duties, many still took the time to kneel down and speak with the curious children who had never seen a Gaian warrior before.

RuArk even spotted a couple of the giants sneaking a sweet or two to their little comrades. Then, with a conspiratorial wink, they slipped their calm, yet serious expressions back into place and resumed their patrols.

The men and women of the township had readily accepted his men, who had arrived to prepare the place before Rhia and he rode in. Now it was time to begin getting the people better acquainted with The Protector himself.

In no time, news flashed through the township that the Protector was in the square and he quickly found himself surrounded. Sharyn, Linc and two fireteams of warriors appeared and took up positions covering his sides and back.

"Stand down. I wish to meet the people, not scare them away," RuArk spoke quietly. The twinkle in his eyes took the sting from his words. "Let them come two at a time. And take care, you are so much larger than these Draeman townsfolk, I do not wish them to get broken." The unexpected jest rolled from his lips. Some of his warriors tilted their heads in wonder, if only for a moment. Sharyn and Linc grinned, but said nothing, and quickly took control. In seconds, the crowd was organized and RuArk held a town meeting next to a huge stone fountain in front of the Society of Justice's halls in the square.

By reputation, he was known to be a fierce fighter, but he was also just and fair. RuArk was pleased that both the Draeman, and the Gaian who would newly settle on this side of the river, all voiced their needs and concerns openly and without fear.

In the midst of a spirited conversation with the senior fellows of the Society of Horse Breeders, it suddenly became hard to concentrate.

Thinking on his lifemate caused their bond to kick in. A little Rhia-sized spot in his head was suddenly filled with her. Sure, he expected the bond to make him aware of his mate's general whereabouts, and perhaps strong feelings. But he was *not* supposed to know that she'd just come awake or what she was thinking. And she was definitely thinking about him. In fact, she dwelled on the memory of his hands blazing trails over her body. The feel of his hard flesh, claiming and filling her. His lips claiming her everywhere between her mouth and her toes.

RuArk was instantly hard.

Well, this is new and damn disconcerting.

As he thought about it, he had to admit to himself that since he'd become reacquainted with Rhia, all kinds of new and interesting things were bursting their way to the surface.

Good gods, it took an effort to focus, so he forced himself to concentrate on what the Horse Breeders were saying. He almost breathed a sigh of relief when the bond released and winked out. Good thing he'd thought to grab a large drying towel before leaving home because he used it now to hide his burgeoning erection. Promising to have another town meeting soon, he instructed Linc to hear the rest of the petitions and excused himself from the crowd.

Instead of returning to the estate stables for his mount, RuArk took off at a dead run. He waved to the soldiers standing atop both the inner and outer walls as he passed through both sets of gates. Quickly covering the two-mile stretch to the overlook, he made his way down the steep slope and sank his feet into the cool, coarse sand at the base of the towering mountains.

He looked up at the rocky formation that stood between the open ocean and the beginning of the river, and his mind drifted back to Rhia. RuArk accepted that he missed her. Actually looked *forward* to simply sitting and enjoying a cup of coffee and conversation with her.

He wished she were with him so he could take her around the other side of the mountain gate to where the soaring rock ended and the open sea began. To show her the land bridge suspended hundreds of feet overhead where the mountains had broken and fallen away so long ago, leaving the thin ribbon of rock that connected this side of the river to the other.

He suspected that Noman snuck into Draema across the land bridge to avoid his warriors who patrolled the Gaian borders on the other side. Though the area he scouted stood outside of Draema province, his warriors would keep an eye on the lands anyway. His mate and their new home was less than two miles away. He would take no chances.

RuArk shed his clothes and weapons, and placed them close to the edge of the water. After a quick wash, he waded out into the warm blue-green water. Easy waves danced over his body, and he dove deep, with long sure kicks against the easy current. Again, his mind conjured an image of Rhia slipping her long legs around his waist. He could see her so clearly and if he hadn't been underwater, he may have tried to inhale, just to see if he could smell the gelsoap she lathered through her wild curly mane.

Five. Six. Ten dives later he still couldn't get his mind off how responsive she'd been during sex. Then there was her easy smile, her admirably stout heart. Yes, she'd kicked open the door to his heart and walked right on through. In fact, he was pretty sure he'd lost himself to her the moment she'd sunk her well-controlled blade into his pec muscle in a filthy, well-prepared training circle.

So much for well laid plans. He'd set out to

make her need *him*, not the other way around. Instead, he was... smitten?

Great Ancestors, was he really? He'd need to come up for air to ponder that one. Making his way back to shore, the smile fell from his face as if someone had taken an ice-cold cloth and wiped it away.

His long legs ate up the distance and he was back home in no time. But the entire way, he couldn't help but feeling that something was wrong. He felt it in the air, in his gut. He'd looked back a few times as he'd run. There'd been nothing. No one. Yet his senses stood on full alert. He hated to break the spirit of the festivities that still permeated the atmosphere because of his joining, but whatever was coming, they'd better be ready for it. Anything less was unacceptable.

He'd have to have a conversation with his First Commanders immediately.

No sooner had the thought cleared his head, when suddenly Linc came riding up. To RuArk's surprise, the man was dressed in a one-piece jumpsuit done in the Draeman style, like Rhia's favorite workout garb. The lightweight looking garb was light gray and royal blue—the first color denoting his allegiance to RuArk's house and the second, his rank as First Commander.

"Wind Storm, we have a visitor."

RuArk slammed to a half and Linc swung down off his mount to walk beside him.

"Marth?"

"No, not yet. They are making their way down the River Dee. He said to expect his arrival any day now. Joan Rouillard, your mate's good friend, is well."

"Good, but don't tell Rhia. I'll do it." RuArk tilted his head to the side and observed his First

Commander.

"The Fire Storm is quite the handful, sir."

Linc was right, but RuArk knew this man as well as he knew himself. "But Rhia isn't what's bothering you, Linc."

"It is probably nothing." The man hesitated, then said, "But that Ricard person rode in while you were scouting on the other side of the wall."

"Ricard? Ricard Shae, the odd brother of my mate's companion, Brita, yes?"

"The very same."

"So what is the problem?"

"He said he came to bring Brita her things."

RuArk was losing patience. The longer he stood here, the more uneasy he became, yet there was no immediate threat. He sensed no ill presence or strange energy at all. What the blazes was going on here? "So what. Tell the story a little faster, Linc."

"Sir, he claims to have brought Brita's belongings, but Marth was the last of us to leave the High City and he had Brita's baggage sent before he left. It arrived two days ago."

"His sister is here. That is reason enough to visit. Why would he need to lie about coming to Province Springs?"

"I do not know," Linc said, "but I do know he is up to something. I can feel it."

With a nod of agreement, RuArk gave his orders. "Watch him, Linc. Closely."

"Yes, sir. Right now, he's getting settled in the barracks. Since he showed up unannounced, your cousin, Drefan, thought that was the best place for him rather than in your house."

"Good call. Where is Sharyn this morning?"

"On Rhia."

"Good. By the way, it was very well done of you to ask Sharyn to dine with you last evening."

"She did not accept my invitation, Wind Storm."

"That doesn't mean she does not accept *you*, my friend." With that, RuArk headed to the stables and Linc went to find 'the Ricard person'.

CHAPTER TWENTY-FIVE

Rhia closed her eyes and massaged her temples as she tried to get her brain to absorb all the information Sharyn soaked her with. Sigh. It was too early in the morning for anything that didn't fall into the coffee or physical training categories.

"Okay, tell me again how the Gifts were lost," Rhia said.

Sharyn settled her bow at her feet and relaxed on a firm, sturdy couch. A Houseman knocked discreetly on the door, then entered with a hot pot of rich Gaian chocolate. Sharyn picked up the small pot from the coffee table and poured them both a cup before answering Rhia's question.

"Rhia, I have only told the story of our history to you twice. Why do you expect to learn in a few days what takes many people cycle upon cycle?

"Because, this is important," she snapped a bit more sharply than she intended. She was starting to stress. Boy did she ever need a workout. "I'm sorry, Sharyn. Now, tell me again, thank you."

"After the Great Quakes, what you call the Breaking, the province of Draema managed to get their society back to some semblance of civilization, having sustained less damage than many of the others. People from lands that were completely destroyed traveled to Draema and it became home to many different peoples."

"Exactly. It's why Draeman skin, eyes and hair run the gamut, while Gaian are mostly golden brown with dark hair."

Sharyn nodded her head and took another long sip of hot chocolate. "The old Gaian Elders had no desire to abandon our customs, but knew it would be unwise to completely isolate ourselves. Through the treaty of Non-Aggression, we established a relationship with Draema, and the provinces farther to the East, like Maine and Varlmont. The treaty assured our Gaian forefathers that those provinces would respect our desires to keep to the old paths and they would not try to force themselves onto our lands."

"Okay, but what did the other provinces get out of the treaty?"

"The promise that Gaia would not annihilate her neighbors."

Rhia's eyebrows flew up.

Sharyn hadn't missed her expression. She smiled with pride, her dark eyes twinkling with just a hint of mischief. "Well, we are the most skilled and feared warriors in the world, as we have been for generations," Sharyn said with pride.

Rhia knew her friend wasn't simply boasting. There wasn't a single province that would dare go head to head with Gaia, not even Draema, advanced weaponry and all.

"What about the Gifts and all the spiritual woo-woo stuff? It's hard to believe I've never read anything about Gifts or this Source business in any of the histories."

"After the Quakes most, including the Draeman, still had the ability to touch their Source, but use of the Gifts quickly began to fade when they began to rely more on their inventions and achievements. They abandoned the traditions that linked them to the land and the Ancestors, from whom the Source is given. All people are born with the ability to touch their Source. Yet if a Gift is left dormant, over time it is eventually lost."

Rhia left the couch, and stretched out on the floor on her back. She pillowed her head in her hands and closed her eyes while Sharyn's soothing voice painted pictures in her head.

"In spite of what the Gaian considered to be Draema's abandonment of the Ancestors, we continued to trade with them. We have benefited from many of their accomplishments, but we choose what we wish to integrate into our society and what we wish to keep out."

"Like what," Rhia asked, sitting up long enough to take a large gulp of the hot and sweetly addicting cup of chocolate.

"For example, iozene gas is used in Gaia, as well as the famous white stone in some of our buildings. Some of the metal alloys are used in our weapons, though we have improved the recipes. However, we do not use the hover machines or eat the man-created food."

"What's wrong with hovers and synthetic food? It's a faster way to travel. And the food has everything in it the body needs to be healthy, though it tastes like wood. Okay, never mind."

"The Great Spirits did not intend for us to float

above the ground to travel. Nor did they intend for us to eat food that does not come from the earth."

Made sense to Rhia. She'd grown up on synthetic food, but lord, how she hated the stuff. Rhia couldn't think of anything blander than grain bread and pasty calmonut butter. Well, perhaps paint. She simply ate the stuff out of habit. Now she understood why RuArk had eliminated the serving of synthetic food in their new home. It was simply... unnatural. Besides, it didn't make sense to eat synth food imported from the central colonies when the natural stuff grew just fine way out here on the rim.

"So what's the deal with the flimsy little outfit you guys call clothes? And why wasn't I required to wear it when I first mated?"

"The sarand is an expression of our femininity. As you can see, I am a warrior like you, but I am still blessed by the Ancestors to be a woman. I see no reason why I cannot revel in my femininity and still be a carrier of the sword and the bow."

"I think I see what you mean. It's the same reason my uniform is cut differently than the male instructors'. I wanted something that screamed 'woman' loud and clear."

"You were not required to wear the sarand at your joining ceremony because you were not adopted into our family until the ceremony was completed. And as you saw, it continued for several days. Now the ceremony is over and you will be expected to dress appropriately."

Rhia blew the comment off. She knew the queen had left several sarands in various shades of gray, yet she was still dressed in her Draeman uniform. She just couldn't see herself in the skimpy thing. It was the worst garb in the world for a fight.

They weren't going to get anywhere on the subject of clothes, so Rhia was relieved when Sharyn moved on with the lesson. "We will practice touching our Source."

Rhia rolled her eyes, wondering if she'd ever get it. Sharyn had been trying to teach her to reach inside herself and feel her Source for the past few days, but she didn't seem to be able to do it. All she had to do was touch it, then maybe she would discover one of the Gifts waiting on the other side of that touching.

She closed her eyes, took in a deep centering breath and… Wait. There was a shimmer of subtle heat just out of reach. It felt like a gentle thrum of… something. When she reached for it, it danced away.

"You are learning quickly," Sharyn said gently. "You must learn to embrace the Source, not chase or fight it. Even reaching out to it rather than relaxing and letting it embrace you will have the same effect as fighting it. You will learn. It takes time. Do not be impatient."

Rhia threw her hands up. "It's frustrating being around a bunch of Gifted people. The little hairs on the back of my neck keep stirring all the time, and I know people are using the Gifts. It's a bit uncanny not being able to tell what they're doing."

"I understand. Are you ready?"

"Yes, let's do it again." Rhia stayed exactly where she was, laid out on the floor.

"Now, reach for your Source…"

It was early afternoon when she stood and declared herself done with her Gaian lessons for the day. Rhia was beyond restless. She hadn't had a good physical workout since she'd left the High City. Her mind raced furiously with questions for Sharyn, and her body buzzed with pent up energy. She needed, just had to do something.

Rhia rose, and moved toward the door.

"I'm going for a ride."

"You should change your clothes, Rhia."

"Why?"

"We've already been through this. You are expected to wear the sarand in the colors of the Wind Storm's house, which is the same color as your own house of Greysomne. You know this. You should not walk about dressed as you are, nor go without an escort."

"Well, I just can't see myself wearing that thing out of the house. What I can see, is it getting tangled around my legs while riding or fighting."

"But you are not to be fighting right now with anyone but myself or the Wind Storm. This is a time for learning."

"Aw, come on! This is fucking ridiculous."

"Just remember that the warriors and soldiers here are not yours to command. While we must all respect your station as First Heir and Blademaster, the Society of War has no standing in this township."

Yes, she remembered. This place had basically become an extension of RuArk's authority, an embassy of sorts. Sitting on Draeman land made no difference.

She sighed and backtracked a bit. "Look Sharyn, I've been walking around by myself in *my* province forever. I'll only be gone a little while. I'll go ride a bit and come right back."

"Not alone and *not* wearing that."

"Yes, *mom*."

"Sarcasm does not become you, Fire Storm."

Sharyn's words were stern, but the slightest tremble at the left corner of her mouth made it clear she was trying not to laugh.

"Of course it does."

This time Sharyn's lyrical laugh filled the space. Wanting to get outside more than she wanted to win the argument, Rhia finally said, "Fine. Meet me at the stables." She ducked out the door and Sharyn's quiet chuckles followed her.

Rhia waited as Moonlight was led out to the courtyard. She spotted Sharyn under one of the large trees just outside the stable doors. She wore a lightweight cloak over a blue sarand artfully arranged over black buckskin leggings. Her long black hair was pulled into a single fat braid, and her bow was slung across her back, as was her custom.

Sharyn's long blade was unsheathed, the tip angled down in the dirt. Her light gray mare grazed on the short grass as she leaned against the trunk of a wide oak, ankles crossed, and brows knit in confusion.

"Rhia, why are you dressed this way? I believed that when you left me that you were off to change your clothes. If RuArk sees you in aught but the sarand you will earn nothing but punishment."

She'd thought of nothing else since leaving her friend's apartment. She'd rebelled because she'd been angry, but now she just felt plain silly. Mounted quickly, she urged Sharyn to do the same.

After riding at a good clip out on the trails in the buffer zone, Sharyn slowed her mount to a walk.

"We agreed when we first became sisters that I would help you learn of our people, and most important, learn the Wind Storm. I do not recall recommending stubbornness. And regardless of whether you want to submit or not, you gave your word. Thirty days of total agreement, yes?"

She had indeed. Her word was so important to her that if RuArk asked her to strip naked, jump up on the tables during dinner and yodel, she would do it. So why wouldn't she wear what she was supposed to wear? With a sigh and a few blue expletives, Rhia relented.

"You're right. I did promise. I'm just having a hard time with being treated like a child."

"A warrior acts with the sole thought of protecting his family, his mate, whether she feels he needs to do so or not. Let him do his duty, Rhia. He will feel less than a man if he cannot do what he was born to do."

She hadn't thought of it that way. Did he really feel less than if he couldn't take care of her, make her happy? It was an amazing thing to hear, yet it made sense. She'd lived and breathed her responsibilities to the Society of War. Anytime she'd failed to keep her word or do what she'd promised, no matter who she'd made the promise to, she'd felt like crap. Who wanted to be known as a woman who didn't keep her word?

Another blasted mess you've gotten yourself into.

"You could have so much more from the Wind Storm if you bend but a little, Rhia. Bending branches do not break. If you give your mate what he wants by wearing the sarand and continue to learn the ways of the Gaian, what have you lost by doing so?"

Good question. Of course Rhia had no answer

for it.

"Or when he asks you to spend more time learning how your home is run, or to visit some of the women in the township to see how they fare? They may not be soldiers, but are they not worthy of your time?"

She felt her cheeks heat as Sharyn continued. Rhia remained silent and took her medicine like a woman. It was nasty stuff, but take it she did.

"There is a saying that you can gain more with sweet honey than with vinegar, yes? That applies to warriors, too. Give him what he wants, Rhia, and you will find you are able to do whatever you please, when you please because he will seek to give you all that you wish."

"You've got to teach me this stuff before I get in trouble, Sharyn," Rhia said, shaking her head at herself. "Let's get back before RuArk sees me dressed like this."

"Are you asking for my help in deceiving your mate, sister?" Sharyn asked, her expression one of pure innocence.

Rhia wasn't fooled. If there was one thing that Sharyn had learned about her since the day they met was that Rhia hated to ask for help.

"Sharyn Miwatani, you are exasperating." She flipped her palm up, slapped it over her forehead, and said in her most dramatic sigh, "Oh, please, please help me. I simply can't go on without your help, Sharyn! Oh, please help me...."

Sharyn waved her hands frantically, her expression one of horror. It was so out of character that Rhia burst out laughing as her friend said, "All right, all right! Anything if you will cease your wailing!"

They took the long way around the estate, and

slipped into the villa through one of the side entrances that led to the kitchens. There was a sally port between the cooking area and the great hall with small port-holes in the doors that allowed the housemen and kitchen staff to peek in and see how things progressed with the meals.

Standing just short of the doors, Rhia instinctively closed her eyes for a second and concentrated on her husband. The bond flared to life and she knew immediately that he was close by. With a quick glance, she spotted him on the other side of the great hall in front of the fireplace. His back was to her as he spoke with someone several inches shorter than himself. She couldn't make out who it was at this distance, and certainly wasn't going to take time worrying about it now.

She whispered to Sharyn, who had crept up behind her, "He's way over there by the fireplace. Ready?"

"I wonder how I, a warrior woman, have lowered myself to creeping," Sharyn hissed through her teeth, not missing the strange looks cast their way by the warriors and housemen filing in and out of the kitchens.

"Sssh! You're supposed to be helping me, remember? Not getting me caught."

Sharyn growled her response, and slipped her bow off of her back so it wouldn't be seen sticking up as they made their escape. They entered the great hall, whose exit doors were unfortunately right in front of the stairs that led to their apartments upstairs.

Running would bring more attention to them, so they walked briskly instead and cleared the room in seconds. On the way up the steps, both the women craned her neck to look quickly into the hall.

"Whew, he's still occupied."

With that, Rhia bolted silently up the stairway with a very annoyed Sharyn on her heels.

With Sharyn's help, Rhia donned a light gray silk sarand with gold threading woven throughout. Her hair was artfully piled atop her head with a few wisps left to dangle about her ears. She'd never been a big fan of jewelry, but her mother-in-law had given her several strands of the most precious black pearls. A single strand was clasped around her neck. Matching earrings finished off the ensemble.

To Rhia's surprise, the garment was light about her body and she could still move swiftly without the material floating up to expose her thighs to all. The slits in the harem styled pants allowed her to get to her mother's artfully etched dagger that was strapped to her thigh without having to sift through the layers of silk to find it. Perhaps it wouldn't be such a bad thing to wear after all?

Through the wide open great hall doors drifted conversation and the delicious smell of old fashioned, well-prepared food. Some chose to stick to the bland fare of their province, but many who served in the villa had quickly abandoned the tasteless stuff in exchange for Gaian food. She couldn't wait for Joan to see the place. Her friend would probably spend the majority of her time in the kitchen stealing recipes from the cook, who was really starting to get the hang of real cooking.

RuArk had just taken a sip out of a sturdy

looking cup when he looked up and caught her eye as she descended the same stairs she'd snuck up less than an hour before. The man stopped eating and went completely still, mid-chew.

She was surprised that his assessment made her tummy all wiggly inside. Sharyn had dressed her in a sarand that flowed about her body and gave the occasional glimpse here and there of silky caramel skin. Since the joining festivities had all been held in the clearing by day and the bonfires by night, this was technically their first meal in this room.

Rhia's back went ramrod straight when she realized that not only was RuArk watching her, but *everyone* watched her enter the hall. Her chest swelled with pride to see these people, *their* people, from different places and experiences mingling and learning one another. It wasn't anything she'd expected to experience in her lifetime. Yet, her father and RuArk had made this happen. Their motives didn't matter right then.

All of the men stood at once as Rhia made her way to RuArk at the head table. RuArk offered his hand, and slowly took in her curves before he seated her in the chair next to him. Linc, standing on RuArk's left, offered a seat to Sharyn. That particular First Commander only had eyes for Sharyn's dark beauty in a red sarand with gray trim. She smiled warmly, but declined his offer of a seat, and took up her usual post at RuArk's back. To RuArk's right was... Brita's brother?

"Ricard! It's so nice to see you. What are you doing here?"

He took one look at a granite-faced, fully-armed Sharyn. Gaze flared with recognition and he plopped down in his chair so fast it almost toppled over backwards. Quickly composing himself, he said, "I brought some of my sister's things. I hoped to visit with her a little while."

"How thoughtful of you," Rhia beamed, looking from Ricard to Brita. Brita's lips were pressed together in a tremulous line. She was clearly uncomfortable. Rhia subtly tipped her head in question, but Brita wouldn't look up at her. Strange. And when Rhia looked at RuArk, he now wore his civil granite face. He may have appeared polite to everyone else, but she was coming to know that look well. Whatever reason he looked so stoic, it wasn't good.

Ricard took a loud slurp from his wine glass, and broke the thick silence. "I know it's a bit soon to visit a newly married couple, but I hope you don't mind," he said hopefully. To RuArk he said, "I offer my congratulations on your joining."

Rhia watched RuArk chew slowly, methodically, and waited for him to answer their guest. But he didn't. Ricard began to shift his weight from one cheek to the other in his chair as a new, more tense silence began.

"Of course we don't mind." Rhia's voice was a bit too syrupy, even to her own ears as she tried to fill the awkwardness of the moment. She eyed her husband and Brita, and wished they would say something. Hell, *anything*. RuArk looked like he'd rather walk over Ricard than acknowledge the man's request to stay. The color had seeped from Brita's face all together. The woman looked pale as death as she twisted her napkin around her fingers. Rhia didn't think her companion had eaten a bite of the food she'd pushed around on her plate.

Finished eating, Rhia opened her mouth to ask

RuArk why he was behaving so strangely. Before she could form the words he stood, and took her gently by the elbow and pulled her into a sweet kiss.

When he eased back a bit, she stared up at him. The intensity that rolled off of him set her teeth on edge, but she could tell that she wasn't the issue.

Finally, he spoke. "I'll be near if you need me."

"RuArk, I'll be doing what I always do in the evenings. Bath, read, bed."

"Still, should you need me, just reach out. I'll come."

Her mind swung a dirty left.

"Careful, Rhia, or you won't make it out of here. Go on ahead. I'll catch up with you later. Brita, join her, please."

Rhia furrowed her brow. "But RuArk, we haven't had dessert yet. And we have a guest..."

"I am aware of what we have and have not done. Go, I will see you shortly. And no, Rhia, I am not angry with you," he said before leaning down to whisper for her ears alone. "Even though you did not wear the sarand today as you promised, you have more than made up for it by wearing it to please me this eve."

She gasped.

He winked.

Her mouth fell open and eyes went wide as dinner plates. Damn him, he knew! But, how? Quickly wiping the surprise off her face, she schooled her features, gave him a warm smile, and then turned and left the hall.

An hour later, RuArk walked into their bathing room, lifted her wet from the tub and took her straight to the bed.

The night was warm and the terrace doors were left open to let in some of the evening breeze. It did nothing whatsoever to cool her body. RuArk feasted on her breasts, and took the entire crown into his mouth until she arched up off the soft, silken bedcovers. He knew just how and where to touch, and his fingers, followed by his mouth, relished every inch of her body until the very hair on her head reached for the stars.

Breath whooshed from her chest in sharp pants. Body shuddered when his teeth came into play with playful nips here, there. Everywhere. Kisses rained from her neck, down her back and along the tingling globes of her cheeks. From her eyebrows to her toes, he played her like the finest instrument. He hovered at the juncture of her thighs, and blew over the damp skin.

Suddenly, her skin erupted with goosebumps as their bond flared to life. This time the potency of the connection they shared took her breath away. Suddenly, she felt what he felt, wanted what he wanted. Saw how her pleasure made him wild, and knew the more he gave her, the more he wanted to give. Her moans became wails, then raw, wild screams. She yelled his name, and begged him to surge inside her wet, willing body, and end the sumptuous torture. When his hard length stretched and filled her, she saw stars. Literally.

CHAPTER TWENTY-SIX

Before Rhia cracked open her eyes, she knew RuArk was gone. There was no alarm or worry, but rather a realization that in such a short time they were beginning to establish a routine around one another. Right now, he was working out with his men, or at the Society of Blacksmiths commissioning some wicked new weapon.

He did, after all, have excellent taste in gear.

She might still need work in the adjustment department regarding her new life, but at least there was progress. She smiled at the thought that her wonderful husband hadn't even slapped her with any "Yes, RuArk" challenge loss penalty days. Breaking her word meant forfeiture of the deal she'd made with RuArk at the creek that day, and her little foray out and about yesterday, minus her sarand, should have cost her two more weeks of service.

Out on the terrace, the edges of her robe flapped around her ankles as she soaked in a few minutes of early morning sun. The sky was crystal blue and the breeze crisp. It promised to be warm with a chance for some much needed rain later on. Dressed quickly, Rhia met her tutor in the great hall for a quick casual breakfast.

More bleary-eyed than usual, Sharyn nodded to the Houseman who'd delivered the largest mug of black coffee Rhia had ever seen. Loading up a plate with fresh fruit and protein she munched a bit, then turned to her tutor with a suggestion.

"So, since it's supposed to be crap weather later, how about we ride now, get back before the storm hits, then do lessons after?"

Sharyn took a huge gulp of coffee and nodded. "Excellent. Meet you at the stables?"

Another wordless nod.

"Soooo, what kept you up late last night?"

Sharyn glared.

Holy shit, was that a blush? Sharyn Miwatani, hard ass extraordinaire, was blushing... but not talking. There was obviously a story there, but as grumpy as the woman was right then, it was obvious she wasn't in a sharing mood.

"Fine. I've got to run upstairs and change. See you in ten."

Down at the stables, her excitement fell down around her ears as she neared her horse's stall. It was empty. Where the hell was Moonlight?

"I wondered when you would arrive. Moonlight was beginning to miss you."

She jumped at the deep voice behind her, surprised she hadn't felt or heard the approach of the man it belonged to.

Rhia jerked around to see RuArk leading her mount to a tie down post. Her heart burst at the sight of him while her mind momentarily flew off on its own, screaming, *'Come, touch me!'*

She shook herself and managed to remember

that she wanted to go out on the trails. If RuArk touched her, she would melt all over him, and riding would be out of the question. Besides, she was supposed to be annoyed at what had occurred once she'd gone back upstairs to put on a sarand over her riding pants.

Instead of snarling about it, she held her tongue since her agreed upon "Yes, RuArk" days were far from over.

She squared her shoulders and lifted her chin a few notches. Her body still tingled from the loving she received the night before. Images of her naked and writhing as she tried to impale herself on his long, wide cock danced before her eyes. She had to get control of herself.

Even after a deep breath and a step back, when she opened her mouth, her booted foot began to tap as she ground out her words.

"Linc showed up at our apartments just as I was headed out the door. He ordered, *ordered* me to take an escort even though he had no idea what I was going to be doing today. I understand needing someone at my back when I leave the grounds, but what the hell is going on RuArk? Having an escort at all times wasn't part of my "whatever you like for thirty days" agreement. Neither was having your First Commander order me around as if I'm subordinate to him or something."

A thick, dark brow winged upward as he replied with a simple, "And?"

"So, what's the deal then? Someone's going to come with me when I have to take a pee? Look, I know something is going on, RuArk. What?"

"I will tell you more when I have more, Rhia. For

now, you will accept my judgment in this," he said smoothly, not moved one whit by her rising temper.

Back ramrod straight, she looked RuArk in the face as best she could, given his amazing height, and then proceeded to deliver a thorough, though quietly controlled, tongue-lashing. Sharyn's words rang in her head. She should allow RuArk to protect her, but being constantly surrounded by a bunch of walking trees all the time was not what Rhia had in mind.

"I am a grown woman and a Blademaster. I will not be treated like a child. Regardless of what you might think, mister Protector of the Realm, I can bloody well watch out for my own blasted self, which I've done successfully for a whole lot of cycles before you came along. If you want to send Sharyn with me, fine. But I don't need a whole pack of giants at my back all the blasted time."

"Pack of giants?" he chuckled.

Rhia growled deep in her chest and nailed him with a glare. "Furthermore, I can take care of my own horse, thank you very much."

He stepped closer than was needed.

"In case you've forgotten, Rhia, I am lord here. If I so choose, I can be nice to my lifemate and brush down her horse anytime I please," he said before bending down to plant a loud smack on her lips. And now it was her turn to blush.

If she kept flashing back and forth between pissed off and flattered, she would soon be a summery shade of purple.

"I appreciate what you're trying to do here, but I'm just not used to having to give account to anyone of what I'm doing or where I'm going. Not even my father."

"I accept your apology," RuArk cooed, handing her Moonlight's reins.

"So does that mean I can forego the full escort?" she asked hopefully.

"There is new word of Joan."

Rhia froze, eyes wide with anticipation. Her lungs simply refused to work, but she could go without breathing for a while if Joan was really all right.

"One of my warriors is escorting her here, to Province Springs. They will arrive within the next night or two."

She screamed at the top of her lungs, jumped up to wrap her long legs around RuArk's waist, and held on for dear life. She hugged him and rained little kisses all over his face as she squealed between each loud, wet smack.

"Thank you! Thank you! Thank you!"

Moonlight danced about with all the commotion, and both warriors and soldiers alike appeared with weapons drawn. They took one look at Rhia plastered to the front of RuArk's body, shook their heads and exited the huge stables as quickly as they'd entered.

When she started to slip down his body, RuArk eased his strong hands under her ass, held her close against his body, and pressed into her. Her body responded instantly, swelling to press against his hot core. His lips lifted in a pained half smile when her thankful smacks became urgent, deep kisses and he met each one with equal fervor.

RuArk leaned back against the wall, cradled her in his hands, and rocked his hips, pressing his hard cock against the tightening bundle of nerves above her dewy mound. A glittering flame danced in her blood, the warmth flowed from the top of her head and made her scalp tingle before working its way down her body.

She knew he felt every tremor, every shudder. She wanted nothing more than for him to take her into the nearest stall and tumble her in the sweet grass.

He wore no shirt and his tight fitting leathers left nothing to the imagination. Instead, they revealed the flex of his huge thighs and the dimples of his firm buttocks. His chest boasted amazing strength, and each taut muscle formed a deeply indented shield over his upper body.

The smooth, clean skin was as smooth and firm as the golden apple she'd had for breakfast. And he was certainly just as sweet. She wanted to stroke him all over. Even with a bare chest, he had too many damn clothes on. Her fingers slipped up into his hair. She loved that it was longer than hers. It hung loose, blatantly inviting her hands to play in it. There was only one other place he had hair, and that's exactly where she felt him, hard and hungry.

"Do you see something you like, woman?" his deep voice floated over her sizzling nerve endings. The subtle circular movements of his fingers in the cleft of her bottom as he held her suspended against the wall set her senses ablaze. She looked up into his gray eyes and felt herself slip effortlessly into the depths of those beautiful, stormy pools. There couldn't possibly be another man like him in the entire world, so perfectly built, wonderfully handsome, and hers.

"Are you on fire, my Fire Storm?" he asked as she threw her head back on a moan, his tongue swirling at the sensitive spot at the base of her throat. He set her on her feet, but his fingers continued to draw lazy circles across her butt.

She shivered. *Good gracious! I'm supposed to be*

mad at him and I'm standing here rooted to the spot wanting him to take me in the sweet grass hay.'

"Rhia?"

'Aw, hell.'

Rhia eased away from RuArk and peered past his large frame. She sighed inwardly, shaking her head, only half glad at Sharyn and Brita's interruption. She'd been mad at RuArk only a few moments before because... What again?

Oh yes, his insistence of an escort at all times. His need to protect her was in his blood, in his very soul, and she knew it. Not to mention the whole reason she was here in this colony in Draema Neine was because they'd uncovered the plot of someone who wanted to "disappear" her. She just didn't want to *say* it. RuArk brought out the stubbornest bits of her sometimes.

'But he brings out the best when he's inside of you.'

No, she was mad at him for giving her such strict orders with no room for compromise.

'Liar. You're mad because you didn't get any cock just now.'

"Oh, shut up!"

"Excuse me?" RuArk asked wryly, a cheeky grin on his face.

"Not you, blast it." She turned and called "I'm here," to Sharyn and Brita, and tripped over Moonlight's hoofs in her haste to get to the doors. RuArk reached out a sinewy arm, and caught her falling frame. She pulled away and unhitched Moonlight from his tie down.

Sharyn was inside the stables now and readied her own gray mare. "Rhia, it is getting late."

"Yes, RuArk." He stood behind her, nuzzling the

back of her neck. "It's getting late."

Her mate planted a final loud and sloppy kiss on her cheek that had her slapping playfully at his hands.

He stepped back. "Go on," he said. "I will see you shortly." Then turned and walked away.

Rhia stood there, and watched his perfect backside disappear out the stable door and out of view.

Gah.

CHAPTER TWENTY-SEVEN

The thick clouds that had threatened all day finally unleashed the storm. In no time, any road that wasn't covered with cobblestone, brick, or blacktop was quickly rain-soaked and muddy.

With every passing moment, RuArk's apprehension grew until it was lodged in his throat, choking him. He touched his Source and called on his Gift of Vision, but all he saw was a smooth cinnamon face, amber eyes, and a dark mass of red streaked waves.

As the sun set, Brita and Sharyn guided their mounts inside the stables, where RuArk waited. He had just helped Brita dismount when someone shouted to him from the wide open door on the other side of the building.

"Wind Storm!" Linc called, bringing his mount to a skidding halt just short of RuArk's feet. "A scout has returned. There is trouble."

"Only one scout? Where are the others?"

"Dead. The one who returned is severely injured. The healers are with him now. They were ambushed while scouting the borders near the land bridge."

"By whom?"

"We do not know. The scout said they wore no sigil or crests, dressed in black and completely covered from head to toe. They were well armed, traveling this direction on foot."

"How many?"

"Too many."

Just then, Sharyn came to RuArk's side. "What is going on?" she demanded.

"Someone took out our scouts. Where is Rhia?"

"She was right behind me on the trail back. She must have stopped to wander a bit. We were so close to the inner gate, I did not give it any thought when she called out to me and said she'd be right along."

RuArk focused all thought on his wife. Their bond flared with such force it should have left a smoldering hole in his shirt just over his heart. But he couldn't tell where Rhia was, only that she was alive, near... and anxious.

Was she in danger? Was someone following her? Or was she concerned with something else? Damn it, he just couldn't tell. And he didn't have time to sit and ponder the matter.

Fuck!

Linc's horse danced beneath him, eager to get moving in the gods-awful storm. Hooves splashed in the puddles that quickly formed in the deluge.

"Sharyn, send someone to find Rhia. Now. Then take Brita to the healers to see if she can assist them in any way. Linc, tell our warriors to be prepared for an attack and be ready to close the inner gates on my command. And keep an eye out for my mate."

The First Commanders took off into the storm. The rest would be up to him and his men, Draeman and Gaian alike. The more he saw of this place the more he realized how much he hadn't considered before. This township had no public emergency system like in the central colonies closer to the High City. They'd have to spread word of the danger by mouth, meaning they were quite possibly, as Rhia would say, screwed.

Only a handful of soldiers were assigned from the Society of War. If not for the warriors he'd had reassigned here, they'd be fighting a losing battle.

In the harbor, there were no naval vessels protecting the waterways. No airships. No gunboats. Nothing.

He was already angry at the thought of his mate in danger. The realization that this place had less protection simply because it was on the edge of the province set RuArk off.

Minutes later, Drefan caught up with him. Riding bareback with no overcloak, his long dark hair was drenched and plastered down his back.

"Wind Storm, we have secured the outer gates. The province is locked tight against the Borderlands."

"The inner gates?"

"Still open so your woman can get inside. Once she's in, they'll close as well. That will keep anyone from the Borderlands or the other colonies of Draema from entering."

"And none of our enemies are getting out," RuArk growled.

"Understood," Drefan said.

The two men took off through the township and began calling all warriors and soldiers to arms. As the word spread, the townsfolk quickly took to their homes. Those who could fight remained, ready to defend their families.

Night fell so quickly it was as if the Ancestors had flipped off an iozene switch to the sky. The darkness was palpable, full of malice and evil intent. Rain continued to fall in sheets, and Rhia was nowhere to be seen.

What if she'd run into the attackers on her way home? He almost smiled because she would probably tell the bastards to come meet their end. Rhia was an excellent fighter, but if he could defeat her, others could as well. Now he wished he'd been more of a hard ass and forbidden her to ride out at all. But hells, that wasn't him, and it chafed against everything that was Rhia.

He'd have to worry about it later. Right now, he had a whole town to protect. Forcing himself not to invoke the bond with his mate, RuArk pushed his worry down to the base of his gut and readied his mind for violence.

Rage bubbled up in place of his worry. Anger at those who would dare attack what was his to protect. His thoughts turned to the innocents that inhabited this place, the many women, men and children, all the townsfolk who'd welcomed him and his people with a ready smile and extended hand.

The rage erupted.

He was the Protector of the Realm and that now extended to these people. There would be no mercy. No quarter.

RuArk pushed his horse hard through the town, yelling orders as he went. At the front steps of the villa he shared with his wife, he jumped off of Atsidi's back before the big, black mount had come to a stop. Up the stone steps, he flew passed a shocked Linus and headed straight for the weapons cache in the main hall.

He grabbed a set of long knives and metal alloy wrist guards out of a large display case, and then added a couple of daggers to the empty loops in his belt and an extra sword to the special double harness on his back. Weapons secured, he pulled his sword free and ran full speed for the front door. He met the first five attackers on the rise that led up to his home.

'Where in blazes did they come from?' RuArk wondered as he moved to engage the men. How the hell had they gotten this far into the township without someone sounding an alarm?

Sword in one hand and a long knife in the other, RuArk pushed every thought from his mind until even the remnant of the bond with Rhia winked out.

Quickly slicing his way through flesh and bone, he drove them back down the hill. More came out of nowhere, melted out of the night to join the fray until RuArk was pressed to keep up with the numbers. They fought like madmen, screaming and foaming at the mouth as they hacked at RuArk with their swords. They weren't very skilled, but skilled or not, enough numbers eventually overwhelmed any prey.

Behind him, the Draeman soldiers on duty in the house spilled out. Some fired laser pistols that left nice sized holes in several chests, others had razor sharp katanas a lot like the one Rhia preferred.

Linc, Dalmore and Osgar were there to sever the heads off their foes as they formed a tight circle, shoulder to shoulder, back to back. They guarded each other and dispatched one enemy after another until the pavement and grass around their feet were slick with blood. Unfortunately, some of that blood was their own.

"Wind Storm!" Linc called out urgently over the rush of the wind and rain. "Wind Storm, you are hurt! Withdraw!"

RuArk felt a slight sting over his left shoulder several minutes before, but hadn't paid it any attention. As he looked down at it now the realization of the full extent of the injury brought with it a pain that swooped in on him, fast and merciless. His leather tunic had been sliced clean open to show the muscle and bone beneath. The wound bled profusely even as the rain drove directly into the gaping wound with a force so intense his vision wavered. RuArk pushed away the agonizing pain, willed it to nothing until it was bearable enough to continue fighting.

"The battle is almost done, RuArk. Allow me to take you into the hall and see to your wounds," Sharyn insisted, pulling on his sword arm to get his attention.

"I will not withdraw until I know my woman is safe."

Together they hacked and slashed their way out of the courtyard and down to the villa's low front gates. RuArk pitched himself into the thick of it until he weaved on his feet, soaked to the bone, wet with his own blood.

"Wind Storm, you must withdraw," Linc yelled again. The noise of the battle was now accompanied by the boom of thunder. Lightening was off in the distance, not quite over them yet. He wondered at the intensity of the storm and realized his mind was wandering. Probably not a good thing.

"Find my lifemate, Sharyn."

"Rhia is well, RuArk. You must allow me to tend you." She pointed across the square toward the low gate that marked the entrance to their home and yanked on his clothing until he followed her frantic pointing. He squinted into the night and could just make out a shape in the distance. He recognized that shape, the way it moved, smooth and graceful, like a dancer with a blade.

Rhia.

She guarded the entrance to their home just on the other side of the gate, a blade in one hand and a laser cannon in the other. Her hair clung to her face and her leggings were glued to her body like a second skin. Cloak and sarand lay in a sodden pile on the ground behind her, shed to give her freedom of movement.

The woman had cut down at least a dozen of the masked intruders and was making quick work of several more. She gave no quarter, no ground and blew a smoking hole in the chest of one while slicing through the torso of another. The dim light of the iozene lamp posts glinted off her blade as it whirred in her hands. And when she brought her feet into play, the attackers didn't know what to make of her.

RuArk peeled his gaze away from his magnificent little warrior woman as another group of black clad insurgents approached. He shoved Sharyn away as he and Linc took up their positions. "Sharyn, Dalmore, guard Rhia's back."

Before they could reach her side, a victory cry echoed through the township. They'd won the battle. Rhia delivered the killing blow to her last opponent. When she turned and caught RuArk's gaze, her blade fell from her fingers as she bolted straight for him.

He raised his hand and gently caressed her cheek. "Are you unharmed? Are you well?"

"I'm fine." She smiled and pressed her wet face into his palm.

"You are late."

"I know, I'm sorry," she demurred as his large hand left her cheek and traveled down her shoulders and arms checking for wounds.

"RuArk, what happened?" she asked. "Drefan waved me through the inner gates and closed them behind me. I rode straight home, didn't even stop at the stables. But I didn't have a chance to find you before I was attacked. I joined in the fight to protect our home. I had to," she pleaded, needing him to understand.

He didn't answer and instead ran his hands over her body and nodded. Relief, deep and profound, flowed through his spirit, his soul. She was safe. He hadn't lost her.

The edges of his vision blurred to a dull gray. Gods, it was almost impossible to pull breath into his lungs. He was so tired. And the pain slammed into his brain until his skull throbbed from the inside out. But Rhia was safe. That was all that mattered.

RuArk promptly fell face down in the mud.

ALSO BY AUTHOR
T.J. MICHAELS

Carinian's Seeker, Vampire Council of Ethics One
Serati's Flame, Vampire Council of Ethics Two
Hatsept Heat, Vampire Council of Ethics Three
Seeker's Solace, Vampire Council of Ethics Four
Juicy, A Twilight Teahouse Story
Luscious, A Twilight Teahouse Story
Succulent, A Twilight Teahouse Story
Silk Road, Seals of Destiny
Spirit of the Pride, a Pryde Ranch Shifter Story
Niah's Pride, a Pryde Ranch Shifter Story
Pursuit of Pride and Pleasure, a Pryde Ranch Shifter
Story
Shiftin' Sassy: Derria Pryde, a Pryde Ranch Shifter
Story
Winter Blues, a Pryde Ranch Shifter Story
Gathering of the Storms ~ Wind and Fire
Gathering of the Storms ~ Reckoning
Just Peachy
Jaguar's Rule
Forever December
Egyptian Voyage
On the Prowl
Entwined Hearts
Elemental Heat
Caramel Kisses
Hide No More

ABOUT THE AUTHOR

USA Today and New York Times bestseller, T.J. Michaels, is also an award-winning author of several romance genres, including paranormal, fantasy, sci-fi and urban fantasy romance. Writing like a madman, T.J. hasn't lost steam. Her mind? Yep, that's gone, but steam there is a-plenty.

No matter the genre T.J. is penning, her favorite thing to do is build worlds. To take you somewhere extraordinary. To transport you to a place where you can close your eyes and slip into your fantasy...

Visit T.J. Michaels online at her Website
www.TJMichaels.com